THE STRANGE ADVENTURES OF TURQUOISE MOONWOLF

By Gerri R. Gray

A HellBound Books Publishing LLC Book
Austin TX

Gerri R Gray

A HellBound Books LLC
Publication

www.hellboundbookspublishing.com

Printed in the United States of America

Also by Gerri R. Gray:

The Amnesia Girl (HellBound Books, 2017)
Gray Skies of Dismal Dreams (HellBound Books, 2018)
The Graveyard Girls (HellBound Books, 2018)

Contributor to:

Ghost Hunting the Mohawk Valley (Black Cat Books, 2013)
Beautiful Tragedies (HellBound Books, 2017)
Demons, Devils & Denizens of Hell 2 (HellBound Books, 2017)
EconoClash Review (Thrill Hill Bottom Press, 2018)
Deadman's Tome Cthulhu Christmas Special (2018)
Hyper-tomb: Crypt of the Cyber-mummy (Horrified Press, 2018)
Trump Fiction (Thrill Hill Bottom Press, 2018)
and others.

CONTENTS

THE STRANGE ADVENTURES OF TURQUOISE MOONWOLF

TWISTED TEEPEE
Part One
The Squealing Squaw

Many moons ago, when the earth and the stars were not as old as they are now, a strange adventure, not unlike the fantastical tale your eyes are about to read, began…

The scream of a woman in peril rang out as the intense New Mexico sun mercilessly blazed down from a cloudless azure sky, its scorching rays baking the white, teepee-shaped, adult novelty shop that stood alongside a deserted stretch of highway in an unpalatable place called Chupacabra. Above the front door of the conical building, faded red letters spelled out: THE SQUEALING SQUAW TRADING POST.

A hot breeze, like an infernal fart sent straight from hell, cruelly ruffled the parched mesquite and creosote shrubs that dotted the bone-dry landscape around it. A rambling tumbleweed paused in front of the teepee for a few moments, as if contemplating the meaning of its existence, before continuing on its way toward the western horizon, where the soft silhouette of the Pechos Grandes mountains gave off a purple glow.

Another scream rang out, shattering the stillness of the dust-laden afternoon. The voice, discomposed, yet managing to retain the sweetness of a cactus flower in bloom, cried for help. It was a voice belonging to none other than Turquoise Moonwolf—a young Native American woman possessing eyes as blue as the semiprecious gemstone after which she was named. With her heart pumping wildly and her long, black braids undulating behind her head, she raced toward the teepee. Her moccasin-covered feet moved with all the swiftness of a wild gazelle.

In close pursuit was William Cyrus Ballschmieder—a grunting and profusely sweating man known to all the denizens of the small desert community of Chupacabra as "Billy Balls." His frequent and inappropriate sexual antics had earned him the unsavory, yet accurate, reputation as the local pervert. A ragged scrub of salt-and-pepper beard stubble covered his face. A black patch concealed his missing left eye.

The tantalizing sight of his lust object attired in cutoff jeans and a fringed, white halter-top that offset her dark skin to perfection set his hormones ablaze. With a hand dotted in brown age spots, he grabbed his flopping reproductive organ that was dangling from his unzipped pants, and shook it at Turquoise in a furious manner. "Here's a throbbing peace pipe for you to wrap your lips around, Toke-a-Hontas!" He began coughing from the small dust cloud she was creating up ahead of him. "Stop playing hard to get!" he shouted, breathlessly, trying his best to keep up with her.

Glancing over her shoulder, Turquoise let out a loud shriek. She began to run even faster, inadvertently kicking up a small pebble from the desert floor. It flew into the air, and with a tiny smacking noise, struck her perverted pursuer in the center of his sweat-drenched forehead, leaving a small, red indentation.

"I love it when you play rough!" Ballschmieder yelled, rubbing his stinging forehead with his free hand.

Turquoise yanked the screen door of the teepee open with such force that she nearly ripped it from its hinges. Making a mad dash into the shop, her shoulder accidentally brushed against an ill-positioned display of Mini Ha-Ha vibrating butt-plugs. The wire display rack wobbled to and fro, sending a dozen of the plastic anal devices to the bare wooden floor. Upon impact, they began to buzz like a swarm of angry bees and wriggle about.

From behind the checkout counter, the startled, leathery face of Turquoise's elderly grandmother, Loona, looked up from a day-old copy of *The Chupacabra Daily Times*. On the front page of the newspaper was a story about a local woman who claimed to have given birth to a rattlesnake.

"Turquoise Moonwolf! What in thundering buffalo balls is going on?"

Before Turquoise could explain, the over-stimulated pervert burst into the trading post, panting and wheezing, his fully erect member leading the way. Blinded by his impetuous lust for the lovely Turquoise, he inadvertently stepped onto the buzzing Mini Ha-Has and lost his footing. As if a rug had been pulled out from under his feet, his legs flew up into the air and he landed on his derriere with a loud thud, causing the teepee to tremble for an instant.

Grandmother Loona, who amazed people from near and far with her uncanny ability to remain in a state of perpetual perplexity, suddenly emitted a barbaric battle cry that was not at all unlike a yipping Chihuahua. Springing into action, she grabbed a nearby corn broom that was leaning against the wall and sped towards Ballschmieder. She then began swatting his crotch with the bristled end of her sweeping implement.

"Grubby, one-eyed maggot!" growled the old woman as she repeatedly swung the broom at her squirming target. "I told you before to keep away from my granddaughter, William Cyrus!"

Using his hands to shield his exposed genitals against the stinging blows from the corn fiber bristles, Ballschmieder grinned impishly and howled with laughter. His breath reeked of cheap whiskey. Grandmother Loona fumed and swatted him with even greater force.

From her hiding spot behind a display case of simulated human scalps complete with realistic dandruff for scalp fetishists, Turquoise sneaked a peek at the action and fought to hold back her laughter.

Ballschmieder began to moan ecstatically. His one eye rolled upwards. "I could really go for a broom-swattin' sexagenarian like you. Hit me harder, Looney Tunes! Harder! Oh, hell yeah!"

"Filthy degenerate!" roared Grandmother Loona. She violently swung her broom against the right side of the one-eyed man's quivering and profusely sweating head. His eye-patch flew off, revealing a squirm-inducing socket in his face that was unoccupied by an eyeball. "How'd you like to lose other eye?"

The roar of a flushing toilet heralded the emergence of Turquoise's cousin, Dolores Angry Cloud, from the teepee's restroom. With her bare, tattooed arms rippling with muscles and a bright yellow Mohawk hairdo adorning the top of her head, she bore an odd resemblance to a cockatoo on steroids. She craned her neck to see what was going on, and in a loud, gruff voice, queried, "What the hell is all this commotion about? I couldn't even hear myself shit."

From her hiding spot, Turquoise responded to her cousin. "It's Billy Balls. He's drunk as a skunk again."

The sound of Turquoise's voice prompted Ballschmieder's ears to perk up like those of an excited dog. He licked the drool from his salivating lips and turned his head, hoping to catch a glimpse of the object of his desires.

"Dolores! You old lez of the rez!" he called out. "Where's that blue-eyed cousin of yours hiding? I've got an inclination for some fornication."

"You're a nauseating parasite, Billy Balls!" howled Dolores Angry Cloud. "The tainted spawn of a syphilitic sewer rat… a urine-reeking, chromosome deficient pig!"

Ballschmieder snorted like a pig. "Hot damn! That kind of talk shifts my hormones into overdrive. How 'bout givin' ol' Billy some coitus with no interruptus?"

Dolores Angry Cloud spit on the floor. "I wouldn't touch a one-eyed teratoma like you with a ten-foot totem pole," she growled, a look of nausea twisting her face. "Not even if you were the last man on earth!"

"What's the matter, Dolores? Afraid a roll in the hay with a man-about-town like me might make you go straight?" He roared with obnoxious, drunken laughter, despite Grandmother Loona's repeated broom swatting.

"Straight… as an *arrow*?" Dolores Angry Cloud reached behind a counter and extracted a bow and a feather-adorned quiver of arrows. "Today is a good day for you to die, Billy Balls," she declared.

The sight of the weapon instantaneously brought Ballschmieder's laughter to a grinding halt. He scrambled to his feet and raced out of the teepee, stuffing his now-flaccid penis back into his pants. He ran into the dusty desert with Dolores Angry Cloud in close pursuit.

Turquoise popped her head up from behind the glass display case and breathed a sigh of relief. It wasn't the first time that William Cyrus Ballschmieder had chased her through the desert with indecent intentions on his mind, and Turquoise felt certain that it wouldn't be the last time either. He was as predictable as the howling of coyotes when the cool night sky was an inky blanket of twinkling stars. But as much as she found him physically repulsive and his sexual crudeness appalling, the occasional antics of the partially blind town pervert offered her a temporary diversion from the boredom of her daily work routine in her grandparents' roadside trading post. They also kept her leg muscles in tip-top shape.

Turquoise opened the screen door and peered outside. Thorny, brittle tumbleweeds, like withered childhood dreams, rolled across the desiccated ground. In the distance, a turkey vulture glided high above in search of a carcass. But there was no sign of the intoxicated masturbator. Turquoise envisioned him lying facedown somewhere in the desert with one of her cousin's arrows through his head. For some odd reason, the mental image of that made her chuckle. She then proceeded to gather up the fallen butt-plugs from the floor.

Grandmother Loona carefully placed her trusty corn broom back against the wall and returned to her place at the checkout counter where her newspaper was waiting. Beads of perspiration had sprung forth from her wrinkled forehead like droplets of rain and were now trickling down onto her face.

"I must say, this is the longest drought we've ever had here in Chupacabra," she declared, mopping up her perspiration with a crumpled handkerchief extracted from her fringed buckskin smock. "And the hottest one on top of it! I can't even remember the last time we had any rain in these parts."

"Neither can I," sighed Turquoise Moonwolf, as she meticulously arranged the Mini Ha-Has on their wire display rack. When she was finished, she returned to the screen door. Her mysterious turquoise-blue eyes, for which she was named, stared out at the tumbleweeds as she fanned her glistening face with a paperback copy of *Sitting Bull's Guide to Anal Sex*. "And I also can't remember the last time any tourists came into this twisted teepee and bought any of this ridiculous stuff!" she added.

"Hush, Turquoise!" snapped Grandmother Loona, as she looked up from her newspaper. "Do not *ever* let your Grandfather Fukowee hear you speak of the family business in such a disrespectful manner! The Squealing Squaw Trading Post has been in the Moonwolf clan for many moons. And some day, after your grandfather and I join your parents, Bald Beaver and Mad Cow, in the Happy Hunting Ground in the Sky, it will be passed down to you and your cousin, Dolores."

"Speaking of Grandfather Fukowee, where is he? I haven't seen him around today. I hope he didn't wander off and get himself lost again."

Grandmother Loona groaned. "That bumbling old man will be the death of me one of these days. You mark my words." Her eyes returned to the newspaper. "He went into town this morning to pick up a few supplies for the teepee. Hopefully he not screw it up."

She turned the newspaper to the next page and her eyes were instantly drawn to a large black and white photo of conjoined twins, each waving a small American flag. After reading the brief accompanying article, she let out a minute grunt. "Looks like the Gonzalez brothers are competing against each other in the Chupacabra mayoral race again. The paper says they're neck and neck."

Turquoise laughed. "That doesn't surprise me. After all, they *are* joined at the neck."

A puzzled expression came over Grandmother Loona's face. "I never understood why they're called 'Siamese twins.' They don't look at all like Siamese cats, unlike that toothless lot lizard, Boobs Callahan, who works at the Mother Trucker all-night truck stop out on Red Herring Highway." She paused for a few moments as a forgotten memory crept out of the haze that occupied her head. "Didn't you date them Gonzalez boys a few years ago?"

Turquoise's expression turned gloomy and she nodded her head. "I sure did, just before they went on tour with that traveling circus out of Albuquerque." She let out a sigh. "Sometimes I regret not going with them. Circus life would have been a hell of a lot more exciting than anything Chupacabra has to offer. I might have reaped the prestige of a career as a whip-toting lady lion-tamer, or maybe even a death-defying, castanet-playing trapeze artist. For the life of me, I'll never understand why those two decided to come back here of all places."

"They've always been very close," asserted Grandmother Loona.

"Inseparable," remarked Turquoise, as she lit one of her grandmother's Indian reservation-made cigarettes. She inhaled deeply, enjoying the rich sweet flavor of the tobacco, and then slowly exhaled the smoke through her nostrils. "They actually propositioned me for a perverted three-way in their inflatable swimming pool filled with guacamole. Naturally, I turned them down. I hate guacamole!"

"Filthy degenerates," Grandmother Loona declared with disgust. "They certainly have all the qualifications needed for politics."

Turquoise let out another sigh. "I'm so fed up with this unexciting life I lead in the middle of this barren wasteland of a desert," she groused. "It's about as thrilling as one of those dried-up, old tumbleweeds out there." She took another drag on the cigarette.

Grandmother Loona shook her head.

Turquoise toyed with one of her long, black braids. "I don't want to spend the rest of my life selling inflatable Cher dolls with vibrating orifices and running from Billy Balls every time he gets drunk and horny. I have a lot of dreams, Grandmother, but they'll never come true if I hang around this dusty dump of a town. Oh, I wish I were anywhere other than Chupacabra!"

Grandmother Loona lovingly placed her hand on Turquoise's shoulder and softly spoke words of ancient wisdom, "Old Moonwolf saying: Pluck the feathers for your dreamcatcher wisely, but never get finger stuck in ass of thunderbird. Or is it, pluck the feathers of a thunderbird wisely, but never get your dreamcatcher stuck in ass? Well, whatever old saying is, remember it always, Turquoise." She then waved her hand to shoo away a defiant buzzing fly that had found its way inside the teepee.

At that moment, a loud wailing, not unlike that of a sick cow, sliced through the silence of the desert. It was soon accompanied by the rhythmic sound of rattles and jingling bells.

A look of panic raced across Grandmother Loona's face and she let out a loud gasp. "Oh no! That sounds like your grandfather! I hope he isn't attempting to make it rain again! Like his father before him, he's a man of many good intentions—you might say a Chippewa off the old block—but his ceremonial rain dances always go wrong!" She rolled up her newspaper into a log and rushed out of the teepee.

From the screen door, Turquoise watched as her Grandfather Fukowee danced in the middle of the highway, while wailing out an ancient rain-invoking chant. His painted, half-naked body was garbed in a fox skin. Bells were strapped to his ankles and wrists, and covering his face was a multi-colored mask decorated with a fringe of horsehair at the bottom and several white feathers at the top. In his hands were painted rattles fashioned from dried and hollowed-out gourds that had been filled with tiny pebbles.

"Stop your dancing!" cried Grandmother Loona, flailing her arms in an unsuccessful attempt to catch the attention of her gyrating and nearly deaf husband. "Stop at once! You are performing the ceremony incorrectly! You will anger the gods again and bring great danger upon Chupacabra!" She commenced to smack him repeatedly with the rolled-up newspaper as though he were a disobedient dog.

"Get away from me, crazy squaw!" Grandfather Fukowee yelled as he vigorously stomped and twirled his body and shook his rattles at the sky. "Go back to the teepee!"

A tractor-trailer truck barreling down the highway at a high speed blared its horn and swerved to the right to avoid hitting the dancing Indian and his perturbed wife. As it sped by, the driver leaned his face out his open window and angrily shouted at them to get out of the road. Grandmother Loona immediately flipped the trucker her middle finger and retorted, "Blow it out your ass!"

To Turquoise's amazement, a battalion of puffy white cumulus clouds began to materialize in the sky. Within a matter of moments, they merged into one enormous and towering cumulonimbus. An eerie howling wind whipped up clouds of reddish dirt and blew helpless tumbleweeds across the highway. A myriad of zigzagging lightning lit up the tenebrous sky and thunder clapped with such intensity that it shook the ground beneath Turquoise's feet. The cloud then released a spectacular barrage of golf ball-sized hail, which transformed the highway and the desert floor into a blanket of white. From the base of the supercell there suddenly appeared a rotating funnel cloud, which wasted no time in dropping down and morphing itself into a dancing snake-like column of violently spinning winds.

Terrified, Turquoise watched as the swirling vortex corkscrewed down from the sky, made contact with the ground, and then, with a thunderous roaring not unlike an angry locomotive, headed straight for the Squealing Squaw Trading Post.

"Holy flying buffalo balls!" Turquoise screamed as she ran to take cover behind a large decorative stuffed buffalo. Her ears began to pop as the air pressure dropped, and a feeling of dread rushed into every nook and cranny of her being. Shutting her eyes tightly, she forced herself to gather up every ounce of courage that dwelled deep within her. She then braced herself for impact.

There was little else she could do.

The teepee trembled and creaked and then let out a frightful splintering sound as the voracious vacuum of the tornado savagely ripped it from the earth and sent it spiraling skyward. Higher and higher it rose, spinning faster and faster like a whirligig. Its screen door was torn away and disappeared up into the ravenous clouds.

Pummeled by a swirling barrage of strap-on bear claws, pink furry handcuffs, inflatable vamps, Naughty Nympho nipple clamps, and other products of pleasure, Turquoise ducked her head and clung to the stuffed buffalo for dear life. Whirling past her went battery-powered Custer thrusters, awe-inspiring pecker wreckers, glow-in-the-dark cooter rooters, and do-it-yourself medical kits for wannabe neuters. She could scarcely believe what was happening. A box of edible, gyrating anuses on a collision course with the side of Turquoise's head hurled through the air. It made impact, and everything went black.

* * *

As Turquoise came to, she groggily raised her eyelids. A shaft of hazy light trickled down from somewhere high above and slithered its way into her blurry eyes. She gazed up and saw that the source of the light was an odd rectangular opening in what appeared to be the ceiling; however, everything was looking off-kilter like the bits and pieces of a distorted dream. She had no idea how long she had been asleep, and for a few brief moment she was unable to recognize her surroundings or even recall what had happened to her. Then, as both her mind and her eyes came into focus, she remembered the tornado and realized that she was still inside the teepee-shaped trading post, which had taken flight from its foundation and was now lying on the ground on its side. It soon became apparent to her that the skyward-facing opening letting in the outside light was the teepee's doorway. Its screen door and tinkling shopkeeper's bell were gone—as were Turquoise's means of escaping the destroyed building. Talons of horror clawed at her as she came to the realization that she was trapped.

She called out to her grandparents, but received no reply. She then began to dig herself out from the small mountain of rubble under which her body was partially buried. Freeing herself, Turquoise was pleasantly surprised to find she had escaped her ordeal with nothing more than some minor scratches and a few bruises. She called out to her grandparents once more, this time in a louder, more frantic sounding voice.

Her call was answered only by an eerie silence.

A gamut of emotions swirled around in Turquoise's brain like the roaring winds of the tornado that had turned her world upside down. She was overjoyed to be alive and still in one piece; however, the grim thought that her grandparents might be badly injured or perhaps even dead shook her to the core with dread and sadness. She loaded up her lungs with a deep breath of air and then belted out a cry for help.

Still, there came no reply from outside of the teepee.

Turquoise staggered to her feet and was suddenly confronted by a dull, throbbing pain radiating from a small swelling on her left temple. She placed the palm of her hand against the side of her head and gingerly massaged the sore area, attempting to soothe the discomfort. Checking her hand for blood, she was relieved not to find any.

She looked up at the open doorway that beckoned from above. A sigh of desperation came forth from her mouth upon the realization that the opening was far too high for her to reach without an extremely tall ladder, which she didn't have. A sinking feeling invaded the pit of her stomach. An idea suddenly popped into her head like a rabbit out of its burrow: If she could pile up enough stuff, she might be able to climb up to the doorway and then, once outside, slide down the side of the teepee to freedom.

Energized by the hope of escaping the lopsided teepee, Turquoise began the task of gathering up pieces of the tornado-ravaged debris and stacking them into a pyramid-shaped heap. When she felt it was tall enough to enable her to reach the doorway, she began to slowly scale its slope, taking great care with each step. Excitement mounted steadily as she ascended higher and higher, and the doorway above grew closer and closer.

Turquoise had climbed more than halfway up when, all of a sudden, the unstable heap of junk crumbled beneath her feet, causing her to plummet, screaming, to the ground. With her ankle twisted and her hopes dashed, Turquoise sat down to nurse her injury and indulge in a good long cry. However, something hard and sharp poked at her right butt cheek, causing her great discomfort. Upon investigation, Turquoise discovered the object she was sitting on was Grandfather Fukowee's prized tomahawk; it had been passed down to him from his own grandfather, Crooked Canoe, who claimed it possessed magical powers.

An escape plan flashed through Turquoise's mind. *If I can't reach the door, I'll make a door!* With tomahawk in hand, she began chopping a hole in the wall. The minutes multiplied into an hour, and, at last, the hole was wide enough for Turquoise to squeeze through.

As she climbed through the portal leading to her freedom, her eyes encountered the startling sight of an unfamiliar desert landscape of shimmering emerald green sand dotted with odd-shaped cacti of poppy-red and purple. Overhead, a magnificent rainbow arched across a sky naked of clouds. A luminous flock of birds glided by without making a sound, the shapes and sizes of their bodies in a constant state of flux. One moment they were multi-colored eagles, and the next they were gigantic dragonflies, and then they were tiny pterodactyls. The highway where Grandfather Fukowee did his rain dance was gone, and in its place was a meandering road paved with red cobblestones.

Turquoise blinked her eyes in disbelief, expecting the dream-like environment that filled her vision to quickly evaporate into the ethers. However, this uncanny new world of psychedelic hues and strange creatures held steadfast.

An impish giggle suddenly darted through the air and Turquoise turned her head in the direction from which the sound arose. Her eyes widened in astonishment as they beheld the peculiar sight of a man and a woman sitting side by side atop a large multi-colored and strangely luminescent mushroom. Their skin was the color of alabaster and from out of their scalps grew cascading chalky-white manes into which were woven small wooden beads, peacock feathers, bright ribbons, and tiny bells. Their weird eyes of pink stared curiously at Turquoise as they simultaneously inhaled smoke from a jewel-encrusted double-hose hookah pipe that sparkled and glowed as the rays of the sun danced upon it.

"Where the hell did *you* come from?" Turquoise asked, perplexed by the sight of the two albinos. She shook her head as if to unravel the ball of confusion in her brain. "You weren't there just a second ago. That dildo must have hit my head harder than I thought!"

The white-haired woman giggled as she blew some smoke from between her pinkish lips. She turned her head to look at the man sitting next to her, who turned his head to look at her. A grin then appeared on their faces and they once again turned their gaze to Turquoise.

"My name is Gideon," the man spoke, his lips still curled into a smile, "and this is my sister, Euphoria. We're on a vision quest." He took another drag on the exotic water pipe and then asked Turquoise, "Are you a benevolent spirit, or a malevolent one?"

Turquoise was puzzled by Gideon's odd question. "I'm neither," she replied.

"Impossible!" Euphoria shouted. "All spirits must be one or the other. It's the law of the cosmos, and has been since the buds of time first bloomed. Everybody knows that."

"But I'm not a spirit," replied Turquoise. "I'm a mortal, just like you and…" She paused, suddenly unsure. "You *are* mortals… aren't you?"

Gideon and Euphoria looked at each other as if engaged in telepathic consultation. They then turned their faces back to Turquoise and simultaneously uttered the same words, "We saw you appear in the sky from out of nowhere. Mortals don't normally make entrances in such a fashion."

"But it's the truth! I'm not a spirit—either benevolent or malevolent. I don't possess any supernatural powers. My name is Turquoise Moonwolf and I'm just a girl from Chupacabra."

"Chupacabra?" asked Gideon, curiously.

"Where is that?" asked Euphoria.

"It's in New Mexico," Turquoise explained, "about an hour from Roswell. You know, the city with a McDonald's shaped like a flying saucer?"

"We've never heard of these places of which you speak and claim to be from," said Gideon as he shook his head from side to side. The bells in his hair gently jingled.

"You've never heard of New Mexico?" asked Turquoise with astonishment. "Where am I? What is this strange place?"

"This is the heart of the Los Sueños Desert," said Gideon. "Isn't it beautiful?"

"Yes, it's very lovely," answered Turquoise, her voice suddenly laced with sadness. "But this isn't where I belong. And I'm so worried about my grandmother and grandfather. And they must be equally as worried about me. All I want to do is go home, but I don't know how to get back. I don't know what to do." Turquoise's eyes began to well up with tears.

Euphoria flashed Turquoise an empathetic pout and held out her hookah hose to her. "Here," she said. "Take a few puffs. The smoke will answer your questions, and question your answers."

Turquoise thanked her and then wrapped her lips around the hookah's mouthpiece and inhaled deeply, filling her lungs with the sweet-tasting smoke. No sooner had she exhaled the smoke out through her nostrils, she began to feel lightheaded and giddy. The colors around her seemed even more vibrant than they did previously, and a curious swelling sensation overcame her head, leading her to believe that her skull was somehow expanding into freakish proportions like an inflating balloon. It wasn't until she placed both of her hands upon her head to determine its new dimensions that she realized no physical change in diameter or circumference had actually occurred. She was relieved to find it to be its normal size.

In response to this revelation, a tiny giggle that sounded eerily like one of Euphoria's flitted out of Turquoise's mouth, which was still sweet with the sapidity of the exhaled smoke.

To Turquoise's bemusement, the angular shape of Euphoria's face grew circular and distorted like a blob of molten paraffin in a lava lamp. Its ghostly whiteness rapidly darkened until it was light tan in color with a wrinkled leathery texture. Turquoise let out a gasp as the albino's facial features morphed into those of Grandmother Loona.

Euphoria tilted her head back, and from her mouth came Grandmother Loona's crackling voice, "Turquoise! Where are you?"

"Here I am, Grandmother!" Turquoise cried out excitedly, waving one of her hands in the air in an attempt to capture the old woman's attention. But much to her dismay, Euphoria/Grandmother Loona remained oblivious to her presence. She continued to stare up into depths of the orange sky, which was now kaleidoscopic with white swirling clouds resembling a melting Dreamsicle.

"Turquoise! Where are you?" The face of Grandmother Loona grew pale and frightfully distorted. "Come home." Within a matter of seconds, it morphed back into Euphoria. She presented Turquoise with a pixilated smile before proceeding to take a puff from the leather-wrapped hose attached to the sparkling hookah.

A tear escaped from Turquoise's eye and she wiped it away.

With his gaze fixed on Turquoise, Gideon embraced his sister and his tongue slithered into her ear. She cocked her head to the side and let out a girlish giggle. He then began licking her neck, working his way down to her shoulder, leaving a moist, glistening trail of saliva on her skin. She shut her eyes and emitted a tiny groan of pleasure. He placed his hand upon one of her breasts and fondled it, his eyes still focused on Turquoise.

"Join us in lovemaking," he said, much to Turquoise's astonishment. He gently twisted his twin's nipple from side to side like a radio dial tuning in a station. "Only the pleasures of the now are real. Everything else is but an illusion."

Euphoria opened her lids and gazed into Turquoise's eyes of blue. Her fingertips found their way over to Gideon's bent knee and gently danced their way up his thigh and into his excited crotch. "Join us, Turquoise. Feel us. Taste us. Become as one with us."

Stunned and embarrassed by the sexual invitation from the strange siblings, as well as by their open display of lust, Turquoise felt at a loss for words. "Uh, I, ummm, I appreciate the, uh, invitation, really, but, that's not, uh, not my thing. I just want to go home. But I don't know how."

"Maybe you should try a vision quest," Euphoria suggested. "Or maybe you're already on one and you don't even know it." Her words echoed inside Turquoise's ears.

Turquoise shook her head. "I think I've had enough visions for one day."

"The answers you seek are nowhere and everywhere." Gideon grinned, as if amused by the look of confusion he saw on Turquoise's face. "But don't despair. Quazi, the medicine man of the Thundermug Reservation, might be able to help you. He's said to be all knowing and possesses the greatest of supernatural powers. If anyone can show you the way, he can."

"A medicine man? I'm desperate enough to try anything. How do I find this Quazi?"

"Follow the twisted red road." Gideon pointed to the red cobblestones. "It will lead you out of the high desert, through the riffraff of Rabbletown, and eventually to the emerald gates of the reservation. But take great care, especially in the Fugacious Forest and in the Dunes of Devolvement. These places hold great danger."

"And beware of the demon named Ursa," Euphoria added. "She's a master of transformation, and a dealer of death and destruction. Ursa is older than the stars, and her powers are great. She can be anything, in any place, at any time. Her throne is forged from the bones of her enemies, and a relentless reign of terror is what she lives for."

Part Two
Forked Tongue

"When I was very young," Turquoise reminisced, "my grandmother used to tell me stories about shape-shifters—supernatural creatures that could change from humans into animals, and the other way around. How I envied them and wished I had the ability to do that."

A loud rattling sound commanded Turquoise's attention. She looked down to see a large, red-eyed viper upon the emerald sand, poised to strike. Its scaly body was coiled and its tail was shaking furiously. Paralyzed by fear, Turquoise dared not move a muscle, make a sound, or even so much as to take a breath. And then, to her ultimate horror, the snake bared its fangs snd suddenly whipped its head forward in her direction.

However, instead of sinking its fangs into her flesh, the snake transformed mid-strike into a gargantuan woman sporting long dreadlocks that were blacker than the blackest night. Her scale-covered skin of pale green, along with her large yellow eyes with tiny, black, diamond-shaped pupils, gave her a reptilian appearance. Her lips parted, revealing a mouth filled with jagged, razor-sharp teeth. From it, dripped a thick, yellowish fluid that appeared more like venom than saliva.

"Who dared to utter my name?" she growled in a ferocious voice.

Turquoise pinched herself to make sure she wasn't dreaming.

Ursa stared at Turquoise. Her eyes then shifted to the teepee. "What is this thing, and to whom does it belong?" she demanded. "Answer my question with haste, or all three of you will cease to exist!"

"It's the Squealing Squaw Trading Post, or rather what's left of it, and it sort of belongs to me," Turquoise replied, nervously. "Well, actually it belongs to my Grandfather Fukowee and Grandmother Loona. But, unfortunately, I am destined to someday inherit it."

"Silence!" Ursa thundered. Her eyes turned an angry shade of red and her nostrils began to flare. "The Los Sueños Desert belongs to me! I reign over these emerald sands and I have no tolerance whatsoever for squatters!"

"But..." Turquoise began. However, before she could spit out another word, Ursa roared again.

"Squatting on my land is a capital offense here, my braided beauty, and the penalty for this crime is death." She pointed a finger with a long black fingernail at Turquoise. "Prepare to die!"

While Turquoise pleaded for her life and frantically tried to convince Ursa that she wasn't a squatter, Gideon and Euphoria took drags on their hookah from atop their colossal fungus and watched eagerly. They appeared to be rather entertained by Turquoise's perilous predicament.

A smile materialized upon Ursa's face. However, it was not a smile of cordiality—far from it. It was a smile laced with the purest of evil. From her mouth there came a hissing sound and then a long black serpentine tongue that was forked at the end flicked in Turquoise's direction. She raised her arms to the sky, threw back her head, and belted out an incantation.

> "Teeth like sabers,
> Claws like fire,
> Rearrange to my desire!"

All at once, Ursa's flesh sprouted a short layer of shiny black fur and her body deformed—bending and twisting and elongating until her human features had completely vanished and she had assumed the form of a sleek panther.

The sudden transformation elicited a startled gasp from Turquoise's mouth, and her face went flushed with fear. The panther stared her in the eyes, bared its teeth, and emitted a loud and ominous growl. With a hair-raising roar, it lashed out with one of its paws in an attempt to claw Turquoise's mid-section. However, Turquoise's reflexes were swift and she managed to jump back in the nick of time to spare her flesh from a nasty slashing by the growling beast's dagger-like nails.

Being the quick-witted girl that she was, Turquoise sent a pile of emerald sand flying into the panther's face with a swift kick from her foot. It obscured the snarling animal's vision long enough to give her a head start on her dash back to the safety of the teepee.

The panther shook the sand from its face with a quick snap of its head, blasted out a loud sneeze that made the ground quiver, and then proceeded to give Turquoise chase. Its eyes, which were now bloodshot from the irritating grains of sand, flashed with red-hot anger and bloodlust.

As Turquoise neared the teepee, she spotted the tomahawk lying on the ground near the opening she had chopped in the wall. She grabbed hold of the weapon, turned, and with all of her might, flung it at the rapidly approaching panther just as it was about to make a lunge for her. The tomahawk spun through the air like a whirligig and then struck its target, its sharp blade slicing through the predatory beast's thick coat of black fur like a razor and imbedding itself in the flesh of its chest. A fountain of gore sprayed into the air from the gash, turning the green-colored sand around its forepaws a bright shade of red. The panther reacted with a thunderous wail of pain, stopped dead in its tracks, and vanished from sight.

With her heart beating a mile a minute, Turquoise scrambled to climb back into the teepee. Once inside, she immediately barricaded the opening with the large stuffed buffalo. Shaken to the core, she slumped down to the floor, out of breath from fear and running, and sat with her back against the taxidermied bison, feeling herself to be in danger of extinction as well.

As night began to fall, the desert grew bitterly cold. Turquoise wrapped herself in a warm blanket decorated with an image of the humpbacked, flute-playing fertility deity, Kokopelli. Her eyelids began to grow heavy and, despite her attempts to remain awake, she drifted off into a deep sleep. Little moans of pleasure intermingled with her gentle snoring as her brain, in its first stage of REM sleep, enjoyed an overwhelmingly perverted sex-dream involving Billy Jack, a can of creamed corn, and an armadillo.

* * *

Turquoise slowly awoke to the odd sound of songbirds singing backwards and the warm fingertips of dawn's light dancing upon her face as they brushed away the last deep purple hues of night from the tangerine-colored sky. Opening her eyes, Turquoise soon realized that she had been sleeping outside upon the desert sand. She sat up and brushed away the emerald sand clinging to her left cheek. The teepee and all of its contents had mysteriously vanished, as had the shape-shifter and the incestuous, hookah-smoking, albinos. Turquoise wondered if she had dreamed them; however, Grandfather Fukowee's bloodstained tomahawk, which lay on the sand just a few feet away, attested to their reality.

At that moment, Turquoise was startled to feel something creeping about underneath her blanket. She let out a gasp and yanked the blanket away from her body, revealing a frightful sight. Between her legs and attempting to burrow itself into her crotch was a most bizarre creature. Its long narrow body was in the shape of an erect penis. It crawled on eight hairy tarantula-like legs like a monstrous erotic spider, while a pair of furry drooping testicles dragged behind it.

Snugly encircling the base of its vascular shaft was a small collar encrusted with dozens of tiny iridescent jewels in an array of dazzling colors that were unfamiliar to Turquoise's eyes. They sparkled in the desert sunlight with an alluring—almost magical—beauty, which contrasted the monstrousness of the penile body they adorned.

Turquoise grabbed the creature by its shaft and tossed it out into the desert as far away from her as she could. It landed upside down on its back, but almost immediately flipped itself over and charged toward Turquoise, emitting a tiny grunting sound from the gaping slit at the tip of its pulsating head of purplish-red. When it got within striking range, Turquoise swatted it with the back of her hand. It flew through the air, once again landing on its back, and once again flipping itself over and charging. However, before it could lunge at her, Turquoise snatched up the nearby tomahawk and used the primitive weapon to deliver one swift and fatal blow to the phallic spider, which let out a high-pitched whimper before going completely limp. With its twitching body chopped in half by the sharp blade, the creature began to ooze from its wounds a white custard-like substance that gave off a pungent stench that turned Turquoise's stomach.

"I don't think you'll be giving anyone else the shaft today!" Turquoise declared as she removed the jeweled collar from the creature's lifeless body and slipped it onto her wrist like a bracelet. She then retrieved her tomahawk and started down the twisted road of red, unsure where its cobblestones would lead her to, or who and what strange things she might encounter along the way.

As the hours passed by, Turquoise's legs grew tired from the constant walking and her feet cried out for relief from the hot pavement beneath them. The unrelenting blazing sun of the Los Sueños Desert parched her thirsting throat, and her empty stomach rumbled with gnawing hunger pangs. But she kept her mind focused on the medicine man, whose great and mysterious powers were her only hope for returning to the somewhat-normal world she knew back in Chupacabra, and she persevered.

Something dome-shaped and Pepto-Bismol in color began to rise up in the distance, igniting Turquoise's curiosity. Her pace quickened as she headed in the direction of the pink peculiarity. It slowly grew larger as Turquoise drew nearer, and became a towering, mushroom-shaped, adobe structure; attached to it was a greenhouse of epic proportions and filled with thousands of terracotta pots, each containing a small, bluish-green, spineless cactus bearing a single pink flower. The spiked front gate, which was fashioned from white wrought iron, displayed a sign, which read: SKY-HIGH PEYOTE FARM.

A glimmer of hope danced in Turquoise's eyes. *A peyote farm! They must have some water around here*, she thought. She gazed upon the mushroom building through the scrollwork of the gate. *What a curious place. I wonder who, or what, I'll encounter here.*

Relieved to find the gate unlocked, Turquoise pushed it open and then followed a winding path of white stone chips, which lead her to a tall, studded, eight-panel door located at the center of the mushroom building's "stem." There was a bronze doorknocker in the middle of the door, in the shape of a wolf's head and holding a heavy, metal ring in its snarling mouth. Ignoring the ferocious wolfen eyes that glared at her, unwelcomingly, Turquoise reached for the ring to knock on the door.

The wolf's head suddenly took on the consistency of liquid metal, quivering and bubbling in a most mysterious fashion. With a startled gasp, Turquoise quickly withdrew her hand and stared at the doorknocker in a state of utter amazement. Its elongated snoot turned globular, and then became more humanistic in its appearance. Its brownish-gold patina rapidly converted to a sickly shade of green, and then, much to Turquoise's fright, its features transformed into a face that defined hideousness and reeked of evil. It was an all-too-familiar face that Turquoise hoped she would never see again. It was Ursa's face.

The doorknocker suddenly reverted to its previous shape as one of the panels on the door slid up, and a man's face peered out from the opening. He sported a head of glossy black hair that was slicked back. His hairline receded into a widow's peak, and a pencil-thin mustache outlined his upper lip. The irises of his wide set, almond-shaped eyes intrigued Turquoise with their strange, bluish-green color.

He looked her up and down, cleared his throat, and then, in a falsetto voice that reverberated with snobbery, asked, "Who, or what, are you supposed to be?"

"My name is Turquoise. Turquoise Moonwolf."

The man rolled his eyes. "That's the most preposterous thing I've heard in all my years as Official Minister of Peyotism! Turquoise

Moonwolf. What kind of name is that for a cactus plant?"

"I'm not a cactus plant!" Turquoise protested. "I'm a Native American, and my family is the Moonwolf Clan of Chupacabra, New Mexico."

The man displayed an unimpressed look. "How, very, interesting," he groaned in an underwhelmed voice inflected with boredom. "Do you have an appointment with Señorita Mescalito?"

Turquoise shook her head. "An appointment? Well, no, I don't. But…"

"Well, then you're out of luck," the man interrupted. "Señorita Mescalito sees no one without an appointment. You'll have to come back on another day when you have one." He then pulled the panel down, slamming it shut.

Turquoise was momentarily stunned by the man's rudeness. Her eyes wandered back to the doorknocker to ensure it had not undergone another transformation. With caution, she wrapped her fingers around its ring and banged it against the door several times.

A minute passed and then the panel once again slid up and the same mustachioed man peered out, a look of annoyance on his face. "Oh, it's you again," he grumbled. "As I informed you during your previous intrusion, you'll have to come back when you have an appointment. Are you sure you're not a cactus plant?"

"Yes, I'm quite sure," Turquoise answered, feeling the muscles in her face involuntarily forming her own look of annoyance in response to the repeated cactus question. "What the hell is wrong with you? Honestly, do I look like a cactus?"

The man stared at her, angrily. "That's irrelevant! However, since you asked for my honesty… yes, you do bear a striking resemblance to a saguaro, despite your color being somewhat off. I've encountered more than my fair share of cunning cacti, and you're obviously an imposter. But that, too, is irrelevant. You'll still need an appointment, whatever you are."

The panel slammed shut.

Anger surged through Turquoise and she envisioned herself scalping the man with Grandfather Fukowee's tomahawk. The thought brought her an odd feeling of satisfaction. A searing desert breeze swayed Turquoise's braided hair, reminding her of the dire situation she was in. If she went much longer without any water, she would surely perish from dehydration. She pounded on the door with her fist. "Hey!" she shouted. "You in there with the John Waters mustache! Come back!"

Minutes, which felt like hours, passed by, and Turquoise banged on the door again. Desperation was beginning to set in. And then the panel slid up and the mustachioed man peered out. His eyes flashed with incensement.

"Be gone, you pestilent thing!" he roared. "The Señorita hasn't the time for guttersnipes and urchins!"

"Don't be that way," said Turquoise. "All I need is a drink of water and perhaps a bit of food, if you please. This desert is pretty hot and I've been hoofing it all morning. I'm on my way to the Thundermug Reservation to see the medicine man."

"The medicine man? You mean the powerful and all-knowing Quazi?"

"Why, yes," replied Turquoise. "That's exactly who I mean. I must get to him. You see… he's the only person who might be able to help me find my way back to the faraway place that I come from."

The man peering through the open panel smiled like a grinning catfish and a twinkle lit up his eyes. "Well, why didn't you say so in the first place? Why, Quazi is my most valued customer! Thanks to him, my Sky-High Peyote Farm is the Thundermug's leading supplier of the Divine Messenger. It's a religious sacrament, you know." He pulled the panel down and then unlocked and opened the door.

Turquoise was caught off guard by the sight of the man appareled in a ruffled, black and red Flamenco dress embellished with rosettes. His large feet were crammed into a tiny pair of ill-fitting, ruby stiletto-heel shoes, and he fanned himself with a tasseled fan of black Spanish lace. He ushered Turquoise inside the strange, mushroom-shaped building with a wave of his hand. She resisted the overwhelming urge to burst into laughter.

"Come in, my braided beauty! Do come in! The desert wind will give you split ends. I'm Señorita Mescalito, in the flesh and at your service. I'll have my manservant bring you a peyote button at once."

"Thank you, Señorita Mescalito, but that really won't be necessary. However, some cold water and maybe something to eat would be most appreciated, if you please."

"As you wish. Follow me."

Turquoise followed Mescalito up a white spiral staircase that led to a circular labyrinth of passages and secret chambers. *This place is insanely weird and confusing*, she thought, as her sense of direction ceased to serve her. *It's like some kind of giant maze.*

They finally arrived in an oblong room that Mescalito called "the Red Room." It housed a transparent acrylic dining table and a set of equally transparent chairs. Everything else was a dazzling shade of red—the walls, the ceiling, the floor, and even the dangling chandelier crystals, which had the appearance of large, frozen drops of blood. Turquoise sat down on one of the see-through chairs, while Mescalito summoned his manservant on a wall-mounted intercom system.

"Marco, please bring my guest some water and a jackalope meat pie. And be quick about it!" He turned to Turquoise. "Marco makes the finest jackalope meat pies this side of Rabbletown. They're the bat's meow!"

"Jackalope?" Turquoise let out a laugh. "There's no such thing. Everybody knows jackalopes exist only in folklore. They're mythical creatures!"

Mescalito tossed his head back in a dramatic fashion. "On the contrary. Jackalopes are every bit un-mythical and quite plentiful, especially during lightning storms." He shook his head in disgust of Turquoise's ignorance. "Don't they teach you *anything* about the world, wherever it is you come from?"

"Yes, of course they do," Turquoise replied with a bit of a huff. "They teach us all about the world— the *normal* world, that is. Not this place, wherever…whatever it is."

"This *is* the normal world," Mescalito declared sternly. "*You* are the abnormality—a walking, talking anomaly that possesses neither rhyme nor reason. You only exist here because of a freak accident, which makes you nothing more than a freak of nature. *Que te folle un pez!*"

"Did you just tell me to get fucked by a fish?" Turquoise's blood started to boil and she clenched her pearly white teeth. She had to restrain herself from going on the warpath. *The nerve of that freak calling me a freak,* she told herself. *One more snotty remark out of that asinine drag queen and I'm gonna go Geronimo on his fuckin' ass!* All of a sudden, like a canyon wind singing in the night, Grandmother Loona's words of ancient wisdom echoed in the dark recesses of Turquoise's mind, melting her anger away like a snowball in a sweat lodge: *Curse not the eagle droppings that fall upon your head, for they fertilize the corn that drives away the hunger.*

The manservant named Marco arrived with a meat pie and a pitcher of water that had a strange, greenish tint to it. However, Turquoise's thirst was so great that she didn't concern herself with the odd color of the water. She eagerly gulped it down. It was cool and had an unusual bitterness to it, but was refreshing nonetheless. The meat pie, on the other hand, had a taste equivalent to air. Turquoise attributed that to the fact that jackalopes didn't actually exist; therefore, they couldn't possibly possess any flavor.

As she consumed her meal, she couldn't help but notice that the top half of Marco's hairless head was nearly triple the size of the lower half, giving him the appearance of a misshapen light bulb from the neck up. Protruding from his crown were several tumor-like bulges, each encircled by a meandering blue vein. His drooping left eye was, by Turquoise's guess, a good two inches lower than his right one, and it continuously stared at her while the other focused on Mescalito, as if awaiting the señorita's next command. Turquoise found herself unable to look away from the drooping eye, despite her best efforts to do so. The last thing she wanted was to appear rude. However, the ocular deformity was as mesmerizing as it was grotesque, and it held captive her gaze. It wasn't until Mescalito spoke that the strange spell of the left eye was broken.

"Don't be alarmed by Marco's physical appearance. Due to a rare genetic disorder, the upper half of his head has never stopped growing. Medical experts have assured him that, sooner or later, it'll reach such freakishly huge proportions that it'll detonate like a bomb! Oh yes, it's true. His skull will simply burst open and his brain matter— what little he has—will explode like a tomato in a microwave oven."

Marco grinned and nodded his colossal head, excitedly. A mad giggle escaped through his vibrating nostrils.

Turquoise wrinkled up her nose. "How horrible!"

"Yes," Mescalito agreed, nodding his head. "It's like having a ticking time bomb for a manservant. I will admit, though, I love a good cranial explosion just as much as the next girl; however, the clean-up afterwards is going to be murder on a manicure!"

Marco suddenly began leaping about the dining room, flailing his arms and howling like a gibbon. A ball of snot exited his bulbous nose and flew onto Turquoise's dinner plate. Her body jolted and she spit out what was left of her meat pie.

Outraged by his manservant's bestial behavior, Mescalito yanked up the left side of his ruffled dress and retrieved a small cat-o'-nine-tails whip that had been strapped to the outer thigh of his unshaven leg with a garter.

"Restrain yourself, insolent beast!" he screeched at Marco, while mercilessly inflicting welts upon the back and buttocks of his cowering, whimpering domestic with the whip. "Thirty-nine lashes should help remind you of your lowly station in life!"

A horrified expression swept across Turquoise's face as she watched the scene before her in disbelief. "Oh, my God! Stop it! Stop it! You're hurting him!"

The whipping came to an abrupt halt, and Mescalito turned his head in Turquoise's direction. He looked mortified. "Ah, *chinga tu madre!*" he blurted out. "Where are my manners? A good hostess always lets her dinner guests be the first ones to beat the servants. It's only proper etiquette." He handed the whip to Turquoise. "Here. You may flagellate him to your heart's content."

Turquoise handed the whip back to Mescalito. "I don't want your whip! Don't you understand? I have no desire whatsoever to flagellate him!"

Mescalito seemed perplexed by his guest's unwillingness to whip the deformed manservant.

He reattached the cat-o'-nine-tails to his thigh and lowered his dress. His eyes suddenly became luminous and his lips produced an ecstatic smile as if a realization had hit him.

"Ahh!" he exclaimed, zestfully. "I understand! You prefer to bury your hatchet in his gargantuan, dimwitted head! How magnificently primitive! Yes! Yes! By all means!"

"No!" Turquoise rose from her chair. "I don't want to do that either! That poor, unfortunate man hasn't committed any crime. You have no reason to punish him."

Mescalito tossed his head back and scowled. "Señorita Mescalito does not need a reason," he stated, indignantly. "Marco enjoys being punished. He *lives* for the pleasure of pain. How appallingly inconsiderate of you to deny this beast of burden a moment of happiness, you horrible creature." He then turned to the manservant and authoritatively clapped his hands three times. "You may leave us now, Marco, and return to your other duties. That will be all."

Marco grunted and lumbered out of the room.

With her thirst quenched and her hunger satiated, Turquoise decided that the time had come for her to be on her way. She had also had her fill of insulting remarks. She thanked Mescalito for his generosity, and shook his hand. The sparkling jewels of her bracelet mesmerized his eyes and he oohed at their breathtaking splendor.

"That bracelet on your wrist..." he began, his eyes transfixed on the precious stones. "Señorita Mescalito would not be averse to accepting it as a token of your appreciation."

Without hesitation, Turquoise slipped the bracelet from her wrist and handed it to her host. "It's yours," she declared.

Mescalito found the bracelet a rather tight squeeze, but with a grunt of determination, he forced it over his chubby hand and onto his wrist.

"It looks so much better on my wrist than on yours," he stated, admiring the bracelet. "Beautiful jewelry belongs on a beautiful woman. Oh, it's positively stunning! Look how it sparkles. Like magic! It's the bat's meow! Tell me… are these jewels real or fake? Wherever did you get this bracelet? Did you steal it? Oh, God, I hope so! Please tell me you stole it! Jewelry is more sexually arousing when it's stolen!" He began to breathe heavy and fast. "Shoplifting sprees! Kleptomania! Armed robbery! *Culo caliente!* Just thinking about crime arouses my *pito chiquito!*"

"Actually," Turquoise began, "I was attacked in the desert this morning by a bizarre creature. It was some kind of tarantula, I think, but it's body was shaped like a, you know, a cock. It was wearing those jewels around the base of its shaft, sort of like a cock-ring. I had never seen anything like it before in my life!"

"*Ay, caramba!*" Mescalito looked worried. "What did you do?"

"I put that eight-legged piss-weasel out of its misery," Turquoise replied, proudly holding up her grandfather's tomahawk. A look of triumph did a little victory dance upon her face, and she smiled, proud of her bravery and accomplishment in defeating the creature. "And then I took its cock-ring as sort of a trophy," she continued. "You might say those jewels on your wrist are the spoils of war."

Mescalito's mouth dropped open, and he gasped. A look of panic riddled his face, which had quickly acquired a ghostly pallor. His eyes bugged open, dread flickering wildly in the bluish-green of his irises, which Turquoise noticed had now taken on the appearance of tiny peyote buttons.

"You stupid fool!" the agitated transvestite barked. "Do you realize what you've done? That was Ursa's prized pet that you massacred! It was the only one of its species, and extremely valuable! When Ursa finds out, she'll be incandescent with anger! Heads will roll! Blood will spill! Oh, I knew I shouldn't have let you into my house!"

He desperately struggled to pull the jeweled bracelet from his wrist, but was unable to slip it over his trembling hand. "Don't just sit there like a slug on a shit-pile! Help me get this cursed thing off my wrist before…"

Before he could finish his sentence, there came a sound like rolling thunder, and the entire room started to tremble. The rumbling and shaking intensified, and the chandelier began to sway to and fro, its red crystals tinkling ominously. The dinner plate rattled and then slid from the table, exploding into a mosaic mess upon impact with the floor. A queasy feeling raced through Turquoise's stomach, and Mescalito grabbed onto the see-through table to keep from being thrown to the floor.

With a growl, Ursa materialized in the middle of the room, and a shrill scream rocketed from Mescalito's gaping mouth. The rumbling and shaking immediately came to a stop; however,

Turquoise's queasiness remained in full force. With her eyes glowing red, Ursa glared at Turquoise. Her gaze then shifted to the trembling drag queen.

"Who dared to utter my name?" she hissed, angrily, her black, snake-like tongue lashing the air. "Speak or I'll rip the tongue from your mouth!"

Discomposed and in fear for his life, Mescalito began to nervously stutter his words, and then raised his hand to his mouth in an attempt to stifle an impending scream. The multi-colored jewels encircling his wrist sparkled in the light of the still-swaying chandelier, drawing the shape-shifter's attention. She gazed upon them for a moment and then glared at Mescalito with murder in her eyes.

"Take off those ruby stilettos and give them to me," she ordered, pointing to his footwear.

"No, Ursa, please," Mescalito begged, taking a step back. "Not my ruby stilettos. Please, have mercy!"

"Remove them at once," the shape-shifter thundered, "or I'll make them burst into flames… with your feet still in them!"

Mescalito gasped and immediately kicked the high-heeled shoes from his feet. He then collected them from the floor and obediently presented them to Ursa, along with a feeble smile formed by his trembling lips.

She took one of the shoes and tenderly caressed it. "Mmmm. Pretty." Her voice was like a demented purr. Her lips stretched into a sardonic smile as she observed a trickle of perspiration make its way from Mescalito's temple to his jawbone, and then trail down his neck. With great force and without a word, she suddenly swung her arm at Mescalito, stabbing him in the eye with the stiletto heel of his ruby-red shoe. A green, custard-like substance spurted out, fouling the upper front of his Spanish dancer dress. He let out a blood-curdling scream and fell to the floor, his body writhing.

Ursa then turned to Turquoise. "And you, my braided beauty," she hissed. "You're more trouble than you're worth! I wonder if you're as tasty as you look. Let's find out, shall we?" She then proceeded to growl out a nefarious incantation:

"A pair of wings to carry my claws
Into the flesh of troublesome squaws!"

Before Turquoise's disbelieving eyes, Ursa instantaneously transformed into a great, airborne vulture with glowing red eyes and razor-sharp claws poised to slice and dice. Turquoise grabbed the tomahawk, and with precise aim, flung it at the swooping bird, striking its breast. It let out a raspy hissing sound and plummeted to the floor with a crash landing.

Not wishing to wait around for Ursa to transform into something else, Turquoise bolted from the dining room. She soon found herself lost in the labyrinth of passageways, unsure how to find her way back to the spiral staircase. A grunt caught her attention. Turning her head to look, her eyes beheld the sight of the colossal-headed manservant. He was pointing to the open door of a large, antique wardrobe, while beckoning with his other hand.

It seemed a suitable hiding spot from the bloodthirsty shape-shifter, so Turquoise darted inside the cabinet. Marco immediately shut the door behind her and latched it. She was instantly consumed by darkness, but felt a slight sense of relief, nonetheless. Relying solely on her sense of touch, she navigated her way through a hanging hoard of ladies' garments to the rear of the wardrobe… and then suddenly found herself standing in the middle of a dense forest, ankle-deep in white, fluffy snow, which blanketed the ground. The wardrobe and its contents had mysteriously vanished, along with the entire peyote farm. An overwhelming silence engulfed her, and she wondered if she had stepped into a dream. Her mind reeled with confusion. She blinked her eyes in disbelief. "How the hell did I get *here*?"

Part Three
Wounded Knee

Surrounding her for as far as her eyes could see was woodland filled with massive conifers and towering deciduous trees, their branches white with clumps of glistening snow that appeared to be newly fallen. Tiny snowflakes danced gracefully in the air, which, to Turquoise's surprise, did not possess the slightest trace of coldness. Oddly, even the flurries that came to rest upon the exposed skin of her face and hands produced no icy sensation whatsoever.

"This is crazier than a fish with titties!" she exclaimed out loud to herself.

Nearby was a small wrought-iron lamppost, standing no more than three feet high. It had an old-fashioned look about it—*Victorian*, Turquoise reasoned—and had been painted white, making it nearly indistinguishable from the wintry whiteness around it.

Turquoise felt puzzled as to why anyone would choose to put a lamppost in the middle of a forest, as it seemed a rather odd spot to come upon one.

But then, there was certainly no shortage of oddness to be found in this post-tornado world, which fascinated Turquoise almost as much as it basted her with fear, and from which she yearned to escape. Unlike the familiar desert of New Mexico in which she was born and raised, this place and all of its inhabitants seemed not to conform to any known laws of science—at least not the science of the world that she, through no will of her own, left behind.

Looking down, Turquoise noticed a trail of tiny footprints in the snow. Despite their miniscule size, they appeared to be human in their shape, and not unlike those belonging to a toddler. Turquoise made up her mind to follow them, curious as to where they might lead her. The sounds produced by her gentle, rhythmic breathing and the crunching of the snow beneath her feet as she tramped through the woods supplanted the deep stillness that clung to the densely wooded area like the fearful calm that slumbers in the portentous pause of a storm.

Deeper and deeper into the wintry wilderness she ventured, unsure of her direction or destination, and wondering if this was the Fugacious Forest that Gideon and Euphoria had warned her about.

The trail of miniscule footprints came to an abrupt end, leaving Turquoise perplexed. *How could they just stop like that?* she asked herself, looking around for some sort of clue. *It's like whoever made them just disappeared into thin air!*

Suddenly, a large, heavy net dropped onto Turquoise from the tree branches high above, trapping her like a fly in the web of a spider. Expletives flew from her mouth like angry hornets. While she struggled to free herself from the entanglement of the net, a drooling dwarf descended from a nearby tree. Licking his salivating chops, he dashed toward his captured prey, howling with exhilaration. In his hand was a crudely crafted hunting knife.

A searing pain surged through Turquoise's leg as the little tree-dwelling man sunk his tiny teeth into her knee. She let out a scream and delivered a swift kick to the balls of the manikin, dislodging the knife from his hand and sending him airborne. She snatched up the cutting instrument and began to saw through the knotted ropes of the net, as dozens of other cannibal dwarfs descended from the trees, armed with forks and knives.

Free at last, Turquoise took off running, in spite of the agonizing pain produced by her blood-dripping wounded knee. The tribe of flesh-eating dwarfs immediately gave chase, yipping and yowling like a pack of wild animals on a hunt.

The crunching white snow beneath Turquoise's feet suddenly turned into emerald-green sand, and she found herself back in the anomalous desert. The wintry woods, along with the carnivorous dwarfs, had mysteriously vanished without a trace. Shifting sand dunes surrounded Turquoise for as far as her eyes could see. Gideon's voice reverberated inside her head, *The Dunes of Devolvement*. A warm, gritty wind stung her eyes and burned her knee, which had swelled to alarming proportions and felt like the recipient of a red-hot branding iron. But, still, she persevered.

Scaling the windward slope of one of the dunes, Turquoise thought she heard the voice of her grandmother calling to her. She wrote it off as merely a trick of the bone-dry wind, and continued climbing until she reached the top of the dune. Gazing down the other side, something dark and shimmering caught her eye. It was a small spring of midnight blue, surrounded by palm and fig trees, and lush vegetation. Turquoise climbed down the leeward side of the dune and stumbled toward the serene oasis, blinking her eyes several times to make sure it wasn't a mirage.

Turquoise waded into the spring until the water reached the middle of her thighs. It felt cool and refreshing, and extinguished the fire raging in her knee. The dancing ripples on the surface slowly formed into the image of her grandmother's smiling face. *Come home, Turquoise. Come home*, it whispered, dreamily, inside her head. Turquoise was transfixed. "Grandmother Loona?" she asked, her hand slowly reaching out to touch the water.

All at once, the image morphed into the frightful face of Ursa, and a scaly green hand with long black fingernails burst out of the water, grabbed Turquoise by the wrist, and yanked the stunned girl into the dark depths of the spring. A scream bubbled forth from Turquoise's open mouth, muffled by the density of the water. Thrashing about like a trout with its snout caught on a fishing hook, she struggled to free herself from Ursa's powerful grip, but was unable to compete with the super-human strength of the shape-shifter. Water began to rush into her burning lungs. Her vision began to swirl. Intense iciness gripped her like the fingers of death, and she felt her spirit begin to slip away from her body.

* * *

Turquoise opened her eyes. A blur of unrecognizable shapes and colors surrounded her. "Am I dead?" she asked.

A male voice rose up from out of the sea of blurriness and spoke softly. "Death, like life, is but an illusion. We all exist in a constant state of transformation. But if you mean, is your heart beating, are your lungs breathing, then the answer is unequivocally affirmative."

Instinctively, Turquoise turned her head in the direction of the unfamiliar voice. Her vision gradually cleared and her eyes focused on a man with fur-covered, elongated facial features resembling those of a ferret. His colorful attire was reminiscent of a medieval court jester. Startled by this strange and unexpected sight, Turquoise blinked her eyes and then inquired, "If I'm not dead, then am I dreaming?"

"Dreams are due to the arousal of particular brain patterns," the man stated, his nose twitching in a manner that was rather queer. "Do your particular brain patterns feel aroused?"

Turquoise shook her head no.

"Allow me to introduce myself. I'm Oddball Paul."

Turquoise sat up and poked her arms out of the blanket that was wrapped snugly around her. She introduced herself while looking around at her surroundings. It was a long and narrow room that reminded her of a boxcar. There was a doorway at one end, and a small window covered by a curtain fashioned from strands of multi-colored beads. Directly across from the ornate loveseat upon which Turquoise sat, stood a bunk bed and a rack of costumes that were fascinating and strangely beautiful in their grotesquery. From the center of the arched ceiling, dangled a light fixture with a scalloped dome shade of green and purple paisleys with yellow beaded fringe. The walls of the room were plastered with posters and photographs of sideshow performers: Dante the Human Cockroach, One Millimeter Peter, Nugget the Dancing Torso, Miss Carriage the Nine-Nippled Wonder, Ramrod the Mutated Member, and others.

Turquoise surmised that she was in a circus caravan. She turned back to the ferret-faced man. "Where am I?" she asked him. "How did I get here?"

"Ramrod and I had gone down to the spring in the hopes of catching some hermaphroditic piranhas for dinner. We heard splashing and saw you floundering in the water. Ramrod lassoed you with his penis and pulled you out of the spring before you drowned. Well, needless to say, we carried you back home to our showman's wagon to nurse you back to health. That was three days ago."

"His penis?" Turquoise blinked in befuddlement. "I've been asleep for three days?"

Oddball Paul nodded his head. "And the entire time mumbling something about a twisted teepee. I couldn't make any sense of it. And neither could Ramrod."

"Ramrod… the 'mutated member' guy?" Turquoise pointed to the poster on the wall.

Oddball Paul once again nodded.

The loud tramp of heavy footsteps suddenly resounded, and the floor of the showman's wagon vibrated in response. "Did I hear someone mention my name?" a gruff male voice inquired from outside Turquoise's field of vision.

Turquoise turned her head to see who was speaking, and was instantly flabbergasted to the point of discombobulation by a sight even stranger than the ferret-faced gent: Standing in the doorway was a muscle-bound man sporting a thick handlebar mustache. He was garbed in an old-fashioned circus strongman costume consisting of a skin-tight, red and white striped singlet with one shoulder strap. Black leather wrist bracers hugged his forearms, and a pair of leather gladiator-style sandals covered his feet. From a vertical, oval-shaped opening in the crotch of his shorts protruded a freakishly elongated penis that coiled itself around his waist several times like a snakelike sash.

"That's my brother, Ramrod," Oddball Paul revealed to Turquoise.

Rendered slack-jawed by the sight of the strongman's interminable trouser snake, Turquoise stared in amazement at his famed mutated member. She felt it necessary to introduce herself and to thank him for saving her life, but was momentarily incapable of formulating words.

"I see our houseguest has finally risen." Ramrod smiled. "We should celebrate with a cocktail."

Turquoise felt herself going faint.

"Are you feeling all right?" Oddball Paul asked Turquoise. "You've gone all flushed and sweaty on me."

"I'm… I'm okay," Turquoise replied as the shock of the penis slowly wore off. "I just wasn't prepared for the lengthiness of Ramrod's… uh…"

"Of my mischief-maker?"

"Well, yes. I suppose you could call it that. I don't mean to appear rude, but I've never seen one so… so long! You'll have to forgive me for staring at it like that, but it was rather… shocking."

Ramrod beamed with pride.

"Well," Oddball Paul began, "if you thought *that* was shocking, just wait until you feast your eyes upon *this*!" Without hesitation, he pulled the blanket away from Turquoise's body like a magician yanking a tablecloth out from under a table setting.

Turquoise looked down at her leg and was instantly gripped by horror from what she saw. Protruding from the wound made by the flesh-eating dwarf was a hideous amorphous mass of tissue from which sprouted clumps of stringy black hair, crooked teeth, and a single bulging eye resembling that of a tree frog. Turquoise stared at it in a state of shock; she was too overcome by the odiousness of the thing to even muster a scream. And then the deformed face spoke to her, telepathically, informing her that its name was Tito, and it intended to be her constant companion, feeding off her blood supply, until the day she died.

Turquoise's daze suddenly wore off and she shrieked. "Oh my God! What the fuck is that thing on my leg!"

"It's your parasitic twin," Oddball Paul explained, casually. "It grew out of that little circle of teeth marks that was on your knee. You must have been bitten by a crotchgoblin in the Fugacious Forest. There's no telling what kind of weird diseases those things carry."

"Get it off of me! Get it off of me!" Turquoise cried, pounding her fists on the bizarre growth. It jiggled like a blob of gelatin, but its eye remained unblinking. "It's absolutely monstrous! Oh my God! I've turned into a freak of nature!"

"Isn't it wonderful?" Oddball Paul asked. His voice rang out with mirth. "You've just been elevated to freak status! There's nothing more aristocratic than that, my little peacock!"

"One of us! One of us!" cheered Ramrod. "We accept you!"

"But I don't want to be a freak," Turquoise sobbed. "No offense to either one of you. I just want to return home to Chupacabra, to my semi-normal life with Grandmother Loona and Grandfather Fukowee. Oh, how can I go back now with this atrocious thing sticking out of me? People will stare at me; they'll whisper things behind my back."

"If it's any solace, you could always run away and join the circus like we did," Oddball Paul suggested. "I'm sure circus life would be more exciting for you than anything Chupacabra has to offer."

Those familiar words were haunting to Turquoise, tugging at her memory. An odd sense of déjà vu prickled the tiny hairs on the back of her neck. "If circus life is so wonderful, then what are the two of you doing here in this godforsaken desert?"

Oddball Paul let out a sad-sounding sigh. "We were quite happy as sideshow attractions with the Mandrake Brothers' Circus of Repulsion. Sure, the spectators could be cruel at times, but the pay was decent and our fellow freaks were some of the nicest and most talented individuals that I've ever had the pleasure of working alongside. We traveled the world over and saw the most amazing sights—places and things that some people can only dream about. Circus life *was* wonderful. Until that rather unfortunate… incident." His gaze shifted to Ramrod.

"What incident?" Turquoise asked, her curiosity rising like a charmed cobra from a wicker basket.

"It was accidental," Ramrod chimed in, hanging his head as if in shame.

"It happened many years ago at a birthday celebration for Mary Christmas Neuter the Juggling Jezebel," Oddball Paul explained. "As usual, she had too much wine to drink and proceeded to make a complete spectacle of herself in front of the entire circus. She grabbed Ramrod's manhood, wrapped it around her neck like a feather boa, and then attempted to juggle his gonads. To everybody's horror—especially hers—he sported an erection and it snapped her neck. She died instantly."

Turquoise let out a gasp.

"Needless to say," Oddball Paul went on, "it was a bigger scandal than the time Weirdo Willy the Feline Freak-a-Zoid accidentally devoured

Lisa the Tuna Woman during a heated moment of cunnilingus."

Ramrod buried his face in the palms of his hands and began to weep.

Oddball Paul patted the muscleman's arm in an effort to comfort him, and then continued with his gut-wrenching tale. "Mary's ill-tempered boyfriend, Rico the Swordfish Swallower, vowed revenge against poor Ramrod, and organized a lynch mob. However, before they could execute their circus justice on my brother, we 'borrowed' Rico's wagon and his horse with no name and fled into the desert. To make a long story even longer, the horse rudely ran off one night while we were fast asleep, stranding us right here on this very spot. We've been living in this wagon as fugitive freaks ever since."

"How dreadful!" Turquoise exclaimed, empathetically. "You poor guys." At that moment, she felt something warm and wet oozing down the front of her leg. Upon inspection, she was startled to observe Tito, her newly acquired parasitic twin, crying.

Turquoise, herself, was suddenly overcome by an outpouring of emotions, and joined Oddball Paul and Ramrod in a group hug. The feelings of Ramrod's mighty phallus pressing against her belly and his sibling's furry, ferret-like face tickling her cheek set off a strange and unexpected tingling within Turquoise's loins. Fingers began to roam and explore new territories, and lips began to pucker and kiss. Tongues began tonguing, and juices began flowing. Turquoise had never before felt so aroused, and surrendered herself to the flames of lust burning deep within her lady parts.

Soon, what had started out as an innocent group hug metamorphosed into a bizarre and electrifying ménage à trois, complete with copious amounts of deep thrusting, impassioned grunting, and euphoric moaning. Ramrod tickled Turquoise's fancy with a handlebar mustache ride, while Oddball Paul, with his odd number of balls, teabagged her into delirium. Like a she-wolf baying at the moon, Turquoise howled with delight. Not even in her most perverted Billy Jack fantasies involving creamed corn and armadillos could she imagine such ecstasy! It was truly intense. Fornication with circus freaks went beyond the mere pleasures of the flesh. For Turquoise, it was an epiphany. She felt, at any moment, she might begin speaking in tongues.

The unrestrained sexual three-way rocked and rolled for hours like an erotic earthquake before exploding into multiple mind-blowing climaxes, leaving Turquoise and her bizarre duo of lovers drenched from head to toe in the aftermath of lovemaking, and happily exhausted.

The urge to light up a cigarette gnawed away at Turquoise, and she cursed her luck for not having any. How delicious one of her grandmother's reservation smokes would taste right now. The thought of it reeled her mind back to Chupacabra, rendering her homesick once again. Tears welled up in her eyes as she collected her clothes from the floor and proceeded to get dressed.

"What's the matter, Turquoise?" Ramrod asked, noticing the girl's glum expression and teary eyes. "I didn't accidentally cock-knock you, did I?"

Turquoise shook her head no. "I was just thinking about the place I come from, so very far away. I should have never made that wish to leave Chupacabra! I guess I was too stupid to appreciate what I had."

"Stupidity is a virtue!" Oddball Paul declared.

"A virtue?" Turquoise asked, looking puzzled. "I'm afraid I don't understand."

Oddball Paul rolled his eyes. "You see? That's precisely my point. I tend to articulate statements that most people are incapable of comprehending because my mind is always busy analyzing worthless data, forming trenchant theories, and solving useless equations. Believe me, Turquoise; an intellectual mind is more of a curse than a blessing. Oh, how I've always envied people with a low intelligence quotient. They're shielded from life's ugly truths by the grace of their ignorance, and too dimwitted to worry about anything of any great import. Haven't you ever noticed that the less brain cells one possesses, the happier they tend to be? To speak in the vernacular of the peasantry, I'd give anything to trade in my overabundance of irritating intelligence for some simpleminded stupidity."

"I'd give anything for a proportional sex organ," said Ramrod, gazing down at his penis, which was once again coiled around his waist.

Turquoise sighed. "And I'd give anything to be back in Chupacabra, but it's impossible to go back the way I came. That's why it's imperative that I get to the Thundermug Reservation and see the medicine man there. He has great, mysterious powers, so I've been told, and is the only one who can help me get home. I was on my way there when that shape-shifting creature attacked me and tried to drown me in the spring."

A look of worry crept across the face of Oddball Paul. "Oh dear. You'll have to go through Rabbletown to get to that reservation; there are no alternative routes. Rabbletown is the filthiest, most deranged place in the world. And it's also, without a doubt, the most treacherous one you'll ever have the displeasure of visiting. Trust me, Turquoise; it would be neither wise nor safe for a pretty, young thing such as you to travel through that malignant metropolis all by herself. There are a million and one dangers waiting there to devour you."

Ramrod did a double bicep flex. "The Oddball is right. It's far too perilous for you to go there all by yourself. To ensure your safety, we'd be more than willing to accompany you on your journey. Provided, of course, that you wouldn't feel degraded being seen in the company of a couple sideshow misfits."

"Of course I wouldn't!" Turquoise protested. "There are no sideshow misfits I'd rather be seen in the company of than you guys! In fact, I would be honored, as well as delighted, to have you as my chaperones." She turned to Ramrod. "And, if the medicine man can help me find my way back home, perhaps he can give you a non-lethal penis." She then turned to Oddball Paul, who was blushing through his furry cheeks. "And he might even give you the stupidity you've always craved."

Ramrod stopped flexing and smiled. "Then it's all settled. We'll see that you get safely to the medicine man, whether he helps us or not!"

"We're off to see the medicine man!" Oddball Paul proclaimed, joyously.

The trio engaged in another group hug, and then disembarked from the circus wagon and took off, arm-in-arm, down the twisted red road.

Part Four
Rabbletown Rejects

As Turquoise, Ramrod and Oddball Paul neared the outer fringes of Rabbletown, there arose an acrid odor of decaying garbage, diesel exhaust, and depravity. The sparkling emerald sand turned a shade of dirty gray, and apocalyptic smog began to obscure the rainbow sky. From the jutting branch of a dead tree hung a large, rotting carcass of undetermined species, swaying ominously in the foul breeze. Decrepit buildings and factories belching forth black smoke sprung up like cancerous growths on the landscape. The nauseating stench grew stronger as a battered wooden sign came into view. It read:

RABBLETOWN CITY LIMITS
* Enter at Your Own Risk *

"Now that's what I call hospitality," Turquoise declared, indulging in a much-needed moment of sarcasm. "It's almost as welcoming as that stomach-turning odor assaulting my nostrils."

"What you're smelling is the perineum of misery," Oddball Paul explained. "It's a cesspool into which some people descend, never to be seen or heard from again."

As the twisted red road led Turquoise and her two companions deeper into the bowels of Rabbletown, the sights and sounds grew increasingly bizarre and repulsive. They passed a bald-headed woman pushing a coffin-shaped baby carriage with a black wire canopy fashioned to resemble a spider web. Peeking into the carriage, Turquoise was aghast to discover it contained not a baby, but the decapitated head of a horse, partially wrapped in a pink, crocheted baby blanket. The bald woman grinned and let out a deranged cackle before disappearing into a dark alley where some drunken woman was shouting, "Hey! Where the fuck are all the registered sex offenders in this shit-hole of a town? I need some action!"

Noxious piles of maggot-infested garbage, along with grubby, sleeping drunks and overdosing drug addicts, occupied the gutters. Dumpster-slugs, pickpocketing waifs, and all manner of undesirables and mental deficients roamed about; some drooling and some mumbling incoherently to themselves. On one side of the street, two chancre-covered men were engaged in a knife fight; on the other side, a man clad only in a black leather jockstrap and rubber hip waders was hawking human body parts from an umbrella-covered vending cart. The fetor was overwhelmingly vile.

Walking through the rancid heart of the business district, Turquoise found herself simultaneously stunned, amused, and disgusted by the surreal environment surrounding her. Next door to a serial killers union hall was the Snuff in the Buff film production company. Directly across the street from them was a bustling restaurant specializing in aborted fetuses and other vomit-inducing cuisine. Farther down the block was the Sin-o-Rama playhouse, featuring live suicide performances; Professor Morbus Gallicus' Museum of Living Oddities; and The Tree Stump—a run-down nightclub for lesbian amputees and their admirers.

She could scarcely believe her eyes when she observed a squatting man in clerical attire unabashedly defecating on the sidewalk in front of the Church of Divine Filth. He then scooped up his excrement with one hand and ate it while a small band of heckling guttersnipes pelted him with pebbles.

"Holy shit!" she exclaimed.

Entering the underbelly of the city's red light district, Turquoise and her friends were greeted by a bare-breasted, old hag standing on a garbage-strewn street corner. Her hair was a matted disaster from years of bleaching, and copious amounts of smeared, black mascara lent her eyes the appearance of a rabid raccoon. She held up a handmade sign upon which were printed the instructions: "Degrade me! Humiliate me!" Across her sagging boobs, in Old English font, someone had tattooed the words: "Twist my dirty bags."

In the grimy windows of the seedy brothels, male and female prostitutes alike exposed their disease-harboring genitalia; some were busy inserting automotive accessories and other objects into their stretched-out orifices, while others put on debauched sex shows involving vacuum cleaner attachments, potted plants, and even aquatic mammals.

"Lowly virtue is the jest of fools," Oddball Paul whispered into Turquoise's ear.

From graffiti-defaced doorways, whores and hustlers shouted lewd propositions as Turquoise and the two sideshow freaks passed by them, avoiding eye contact. A hefty woman in a gold lame mini-dress yelled, "I'll vomit on you for ten dollars! Or you can vomit on me for twenty!" She scowled as the trio kept on walking, ignoring her offer. She then flipped them the bird and exploded with rage, "Highfalutin genital warts!"

In another doorway stood a shivering, profusely perspiring man with a hypodermic needle sticking out of his tattooed arm. Next to him, slumped against the door and attracting flying insects, was the discolored corpse of a young woman with a grotesquely made-up face. "Hey, man! I'll let you fuck my dead girlfriend in exchange for some heroin!" the pimp-junkie proposed, his voice filled with desperation. "She's still kind of warm!"

At the end of the block, a sign informing travelers that they were now leaving Rabbletown's city limits conjured jubilation within Turquoise. Her joy, however, proved to be short-lived upon seeing the road leading out of the city barricaded up ahead by a gate to which was attached a crude wooden sign. Its running red letters, like dripping blood, spelled out: "ROAD CLOSED." To the side of the gate stood a less-than-friendly looking uniformed guard. He was armed with a semi-automatic rifle, which he aimed in the direction of Turquoise and her companions as they approached. They stopped dead in their tracks and instinctively raised their hands.

"Don't shoot!" cried Turquoise.

A small wet spot suddenly appeared on the front of Oddball Paul's pants. "My bladder would overflow with gratitude if you would kindly point that thing somewhere else."

"And just where do the three of you think you're going?" the gun-toting man inquired, angrily. "Can't you weirdos read the sign? It says the road is closed. Now beat it!"

Desperation, like an electric current, surged through Turquoise's body, from the tips of her braids to the toes of her feet. "But I just *have* to get to the Thundermug Reservation! I've traveled such a long way. Oh, please, let us through."

"No can do," replied the guard, his face seemingly frozen in a perma-scowl. His gun remained pointed threateningly at the three travelers. "I have my orders to not allow anyone to cross this barricade, and that includes you and your friends there. You'll just have to turn around and go back to wherever it is you came from."

"But this is an emergency," Turquoise pleaded. "A matter of life and death! I realize you have your orders, but couldn't you find it in your heart to make an exception for us, just this one time? Oh, please? I promise we won't tell anyone."

The guard stubbornly shook his head no, unmoved by the glistening tears welling up within Turquoise's eyes.

"Why *is* the road closed?" Ramrod asked with curiosity, attempting to peek over the barricade. "There doesn't seem to be anything wrong with it."

"It looks fine to me too," Oddball Paul added, his voice tinged with suspicion.

"The road is closed, and that's all you need to know," snapped the guard. "No one is permitted to leave or enter the city until further notice. And anyone who tries it, will be shot on sight!"

"This is just terrible," Turquoise bemoaned to the sideshow freaks, a sinking feeling swiftly forming in the pit of her stomach. "We've come all this way for nothing. I'll never get to go home now! Oh, what am I going to do?"

"Don't you fret, Turquoise," Ramrod spoke in a gruff, yet consoling, voice. "There's got to be some other way to get you to that reservation. We'll figure something out; don't you worry."

"Let's go home," said Oddball Paul, glumly. "The sooner we get out of Rabbletown, the safer we'll all sleep."

He and Ramrod each put an arm around Turquoise to comfort her. Dejected, the three of them started away from the roadblock in the direction of the squalid city when all of a sudden a cargo van pulled up alongside of them. A rattling, rumbling leftover from the 1940s, it was a drab army-green in color and appeared to be made more of rust than of metal. The name, Fish & Squish Taxicab Company, was sloppily spray-painted in white on the side. The driver, a thirtysomething man sporting a blond buzz cut stuck his head out the window. His square jaw was accentuated by a hint of yellow stubble, and his eyes were hidden behind a pair of dark steampunk goggles.

"Say! Don't I know you two guys from somewhere?" he asked, giving Ramrod and Oddball Paul the once-over. "You look awfully familiar to me. Didn't you used to be sideshow performers with that traveling circus of freaks… what was their name?" He paused for a moment to recollect. "Uh… oh yeah… the Mandrake Brothers! That's it!"

The two brothers turned their heads and faced each other, as if reading the other one's thoughts. They then turned their gaze back to the driver and shook their heads no. Turquoise could sense their mistrust of him, and kept herself tight-lipped.

"How utterly preposterous!" Oddball Paul declared with a false air of indignity. "Whatever would give you the insane notion that we were sideshow performers with a circus? You're quite wrong."

"Yeah. You must have us confused with someone else," Ramrod propounded. "A lot of people have look-alikes these days. It's the in thing."

The driver stared in amazement at the 'mischief-maker" coiled around Ramrod's waist. "Hey man, I'm not queer or anything, but I couldn't help but notice that mile-long tube steak you're slinging there. It sure is one hell of an impressive pecker! Damn! I bet you could kill someone with that thing!"

Ramrod's chest puffed out like a peacock. "I appreciate the compliment."

"That's it!" the driver exclaimed, excitedly. "Now I know why you look so familiar. You're that super-hung, fugitive circus freak who broke that woman's neck with your deadly erection!" He smiled like a Cheshire cat. "Wow! This has got to be my lucky day! It's a great honor to meet you in person, sir. I'm a huge fan of the sideshows, plus I've a few broken necks under my belt as well!" He let out a boastful laugh. "So what brings you and your fine friends here to our fair city, besides the scenic views?"

"We were on our way to the Thundermug Reservation," Ramrod replied. "Our lady friend here, Miss Turquoise, urgently needs to see the medicine man. You see… she has a quite serious problem, and he's the only one who can fix it."

The driver shifted his gaze to the parasitic twin staring at him from Turquoise's knee. The smile disappeared from his face. "Yeah, I can see that."

Oddball Paul pointed to the barricade. "But, for some reason not explained to us, the road leading to the reservation has been closed. And that brusque knuckle-dragger there at the gate had the unmitigated audacity to threaten us with gunfire."

The smile returned to the driver's face. "Hey guys, there's no need for you to despair! It just so happens that I know of another way to get you to where you need to go. It's a back road through no man's land that few people know about."

His words renewed Turquoise's hope, and the sparkle returned to her eyes of blue.

"The only thing is," he continued, "it's a complicated route to travel, and if you don't know your way around, well, you're likely to get yourselves hopelessly lost. I'll tell you what… why don't the three of you hop into the back of this here taxicab, and I'll drive you there. The fare's on me; I'm a huge fan of the sideshows!"

"A free taxicab ride?" Ramrod looked surprised. "You wouldn't be dicking us around, would you?" His choice of words momentarily attracted everyone's attention to his freakish penis.

The driver shook his head no. "Absolutely not! My word is good."

Oddball Paul seemed a trifle bit on the apprehensive side. "A man's word is only as good as the keeping or the breaking of his last promise."

"I think we should let Turquoise decide," Ramrod proposed.

"If you ask me, I'd say this man is a godsend," Turquoise declared with glee. "With the road closed and guarded by that gorilla with the gun, the taxi driver is our only hope of getting to that reservation."

"Hmmm. I wonder." Oddball Paul raised his eyebrows and shrugged his shoulders. "My ferret intuition is making my nose twitch, and that's never a good sign."

"You and that bloody ferret intuition of yours!" Ramrod derided. "When has it ever been right?"

"Make up your minds!" the driver impatiently shouted from the window. "I can't sit here all day, waiting for you to decide. Do you want a ride or not?"

"Yes!" Turquoise proclaimed loudly. "And thank you!"

The Cheshire cat smile returned to the driver's face. He climbed out of the van, and opened the back doors. Ushering Turquoise inside the windowless compartment, he gave her a smile. "In you go, little lady. Make yourself comfortable. It's nothing fancy, mind you, but it'll take you to where you need to go before you can say, tits in a panini press."

"Hang on there!" shouted Ramrod, as he climbed into the back of the van, followed by his ferret-faced sibling. "We're coming along too!"

"Fasten your seatbelts. It's going to be a bumpy ride." The driver then shut the doors and bolted them from the outside. The sound of the lock echoed ominously through the rear of the makeshift taxicab.

Oddball Paul took a seat next to Turquoise. "I want you to know, my little peacock, that the only reason I'm accepting this ride is because I want to see that you get to that reservation safely. I firmly remain wary of the kindness of strangers."

"I'm sure once the medicine man gives you some stupidity, you'll be much more trusting of strangers," Turquoise reassured.

"Do you really think so, Turquoise?"

She nodded her head, and her braids bounced gently on her shoulders.

"Oh, I do hope you're right. I'm so tired of being too smart for my own good," the oddball lamented. "It just sucks all the joy out of life."

"I can practically smell the sagebrush of Chupacabra now," Turquoise purred, dreamily.

Oddball Paul's nose began to twitch. "All I can smell is rotten eggs." He stared at Ramrod, accusingly.

"It wasn't me!" Ramrod stated, defensively.

At that moment, there came a strange hissing noise from above. Gazing up, Turquoise was gripped by horror to see a green gaseous vapor emitting from a canister mounted to the ceiling. It rapidly filled the back of the van with its foul-smelling noxiousness. With panic sweeping through her every nook and cranny, Turquoise pointed to the canister and cried out, "Oh my God! Look! We're in a gas chamber on wheels!"

She and the sideshow freaks sprung from their seats and rushed to the locked doors at the back of the van. Frantically pounding on them with their fists, they coughed and cried, "Help! Help! Let us out!" The gas was beginning to sting their noses and eyes, and make breathing difficult.

"Brother! Unleash your battering ram!" Oddball Paul shouted.

Ramrod shook his head, woefully. He fought to restrain his coughing long enough to reply. "I can't! The smell... of that gas... it's stopping me from getting hard!" His penis, like a lifeless python, suddenly uncoiled from around his waist, falling limp onto the floor with a thud. Within a matter of seconds, the rest of his body followed. Turquoise let out a scream.

Alternating between gasping for air and coughing violently, Oddball Paul scurried about the van, pounding and kicking the walls in a fruitless effort to escape. His eyes rolled up into his head. His tongue flopped from his mouth.

And then his body, too, went limp, and he joined his brother on the floor.

Turquoise's mind reeled. A cold sweat beaded up on her forehead. Expanding waves of nausea and a throbbing pain within her cranium began to overwhelm her. She drew enough air into her lungs for one final scream before the gas robbed her of her consciousness. She then dropped to the floor, her body sprawled out on top of the two freaks, like a deflated Cher blow-up doll.

* * *

"Rise and shine, lassie!" a booming voice rang out, jolting Turquoise from her dreamless slumber. "We open in less than an hour and the tourists prefer gawking at exhibits that aren't sleeping! They don't pay admission to be bored!"

Turquoise's eyelids flew open. Her mind spun in confusion. She felt something poking at her belly. The sleep quickly retreated from her eyes, and she found herself lying upon a bed of straw, her body curled up into a fetal position. In front of her face sat two stainless steel bowls: one filled with fetid water, and the other with bloody scraps of raw meat, some of which had strands of hair growing out of them. A monocle-wearing man in a tartan-patterned kilt with a matching tam upon his head was prodding her with the tip of his cane. Turquoise sprung up into a sitting position and realized that she was locked inside of a large cage like an animal in a zoo. She tried to make sense of it all, but her mind felt like a swirling mess, unable to latch onto anything solid.

"Where am I?" Turquoise asked. "What is this place?"

"Welcome to my Museum of Living Oddities," said the man with the prodding cane and the booming voice. "My name is Professor Morbus Gallicus, and I am the curator and mastermind of this menagerie of misfits. I guarantee you won't find a finer one in all the land. I've assembled the foremost *lusus naturae* from all corners of the world."

Looking around, Turquoise observed rows of heavy steel cages of varying shapes and sizes, each one containing a person or beast possessing a startling anatomical peculiarity of one sort of another. Animals having more legs or tails than normal nervously paced back and forth, while others stared at Turquoise from between the bars that held them a prisoner. A three-headed piglet of pale pink oinked in triplicate. A lovely yellow canary sitting upon a swinging perch opened its beak to sing, and shot out a tongue of fire.

Inside of one cage, a creature that was half-dog and half-cat ran endlessly in a circle. Turquoise was unsure if the dog half was chasing the cat half, or if it were the other way around. Inside a neighboring cage, sitting upon a log, was an elderly man with bulging eyes and a pair of discolored ivory tusks growing from his upper jaw like a walrus. Preoccupied with producing strange clicking noises with his mouth, he seemed oblivious to everything around him.

A naked midget with fleshy flippers in place of arms occupied another cage. He ran inside a circular steel contraption that looked like a gigantic hamster exercise wheel. His body was tattooed from head to toe, and dangling from his septum, like a door knocker, was a metal ring. From his hindmost part, there wiggled a tail nub. Turquoise could scarcely believe what she was seeing; it all seemed like some sort of bad dream. Across from the midget, a half-ton woman with a third eye staring from the center of her forehead sat on the floor of her cage, gobbling up a bucketful of wriggling, sugar-frosted maggots with gusto. Turquoise responded with a dry heave. She suddenly heard two familiar voices calling out her name.

Turning her head to look, she spotted Ramrod and Oddball Paul, together in a cage, waving their hands at her. The sight of her friends imprisoned and on display filled her with despair, but at the same time she breathed a sigh of relief at finding them still alive.

"Ramrod! Oddball Paul!" she called out. "Are you guys all right?"

"We're fine, I think," Ramrod replied. "But if that monocled madman's harmed one hair on your head, I swear I'll…"

"Calm your monstrous chromosomes!" Professor Gallicus ordered, while banging the tip of has cane against the floor. "I can assure you that the wee lassie here is in tip-top physical shape. She, like you and the other exhibits, received a thorough examination when she was brought in, and passed with flying colors. I have no intentions of harming her, or anyone else for that matter. My living oddities are far more valuable to me alive and well than dead."

"But the taxicab… the poison gas…" Turquoise began.

"Soporagen, lassie," Professor Gallicus blurted out before his braided captive could finish her sentence. "A non-lethal, yet nonetheless potent, sleeping gas. Its effects are temporary and quite harmless, I assure you. And how do I know this? The answer to that is quite simple: I'm the one who created it."

"This is all starting to add up." Oddball Paul bared his pointed teeth. "The roadblock… the taxicab driver… That was all just an elaborate setup to capture us so you could put us on display in this sordid museum of yours and exploit us for monetary gain."

Professor Gallicus smiled. "I must say, you're rather astute for being a shockingly repulsive product of your parents' exchange of genetic material," he complimented.

"You tricked us, you paleface son of a bitch!" Turquoise cried, angrily kicking over her stainless steel bowl of water.

"Aye, lassie."

Ramrod let out an acrimonious growl. "I should have realized that taxi driver's generous offer to take us to the reservation was nothing but a cock and bull story!"

Once again, the strongman's choice of words momentarily drew everyone's attention to his phallus of incredibly abnormal length.

"This madness has gone far enough! Release us from these cages at once, you repugnant conglomeration of intellectual constipation!" Oddball Paul demanded, shaking his clenched fist. "We aren't zoo animals. We demand our freedom!"

"Be quiet, you degenerate, all-defiling aberration of nature!" The professor yelled. "You'll be released *if* and when I see fit to do so!"

A burst of insane laughter resounded from a bandaged and severed head sitting in a fluid-filled enamel pan on a nearby laboratory table. Its face appeared to be female, and attached to its neck and temples were a variety of tubes and wires. The very sight of it filled Turquoise with a macabre mixture of horror and curiosity.

"Don't fall for his lies!" the head spoke in a gurgling voice. "The truth is, he'll never set you any of you free! He'll keep you on display in this nightmare museum for the rest of your lives, just like he does me."

"Oh my God!" Turquoise shrieked, her baby blues transfixed on the horrendous decapitated noggin. "What is that thing?"

"That *thing* is my wife, Jayne," Professor Gallicus explained with sadness taking up residence in his words, "or rather what's left of the poor dear. She was decapitated in a tragic hairdressing accident. Her body was unsalvageable, except for a couple anatomical parts that I keep next to the bed for, uh, special occasions." He winked at Turquoise with his non-monocled eye. "But with the scientific sophistication I possess, I've found a way to keep her head alive, as you can see. Out of all the grotesque visual experiences offered by my Museum of Living Oddities, Jayne has quite understandably risen to the level of star attraction!"

"Star attraction!" Jayne's head hissed, mockingly. Her words seethed with an acridness that only a scorned head without a body could produce. "I'm nothing but a horror that no normal mind could ever imagine! You should have let me die, you enema-addicted bastard! Death would have been preferable to this! I won't allow you to carry out your twisted plan to transplant my head onto the body of that young woman there with the braids. I'll stop you somehow!"

Turquoise let out a loud gasp as the words from the horrible head rang inside her ears like the bells of doom.

"That will be enough out of you for one day, my decapitated dearest," the professor declared as he tossed a white sheet over his wife's head to muffle her.

Determined to break out of confinement and save Turquoise from the professor's evil clutches, Ramrod wrapped his mighty fists around two of the steel bars of the cage, and with a loud, guttural groan, attempted to bend them apart. Oddball Paul also sprang into action, his sharp, ferret-like teeth gnawing on the lock of the cage door. Professor Gallicus watched with amusement. However, despite the brothers' best muscle straining, teeth-grinding efforts, the sturdy bars proved to be unyielding, and the two men begrudgingly gave in to exhaustion and defeat.

"These cages were constructed to be circus-proof," boasted the professor with a grin. "You may try to your heart's content, but you'll never escape." He looked down at his wristwatch. "Half an hour until opening time! We have a large tour group scheduled for this morning, and I expect all of you oddities to give them their money's worth."

Just then, Turquoise's attention was diverted to a grunt-filled commotion making its way along the rows of cages. "Marco!" she cried out, recognizing the colossal head of Señorita Mescalito's grunting manservant. Handcuffed and shackled in leg irons, he was being led to an unoccupied cage by two men, whom Turquoise instantly recognized as the driver of the gas van and the armed roadblock guard. From the other side of the museum, some wisenheimer answered back with a cry of, "Polo!"

"We've got another oddity for you, professor!" the taxicab driver announced, breathlessly, as he and his partner pushed and pulled the resistant manservant closer to the waiting cage. "We captured this one as it walked out of a pawn shop."

"And it put up a good fight," the man in the guard uniform added, equally breathless.

Professor Gallicus immediately began to examine Marco's head. "Most extraordinary! Just take a look at that hyperostosis of the cranial bone… the vascularity of the tumors! Why, this has got to be, by far, the finest living example of macrocephaly I've ever encountered! An extraordinary specimen to be sure! You've outdone yourselves this time, Mister Fish and Mister Squish. Rest assured, there'll be a generous bonus attached to your usual finder's fee."

The museum curator then skillfully placed his left hand upon Marco's tumorous crown, prompting the spooked manservant to grunt with displeasure and jerk his head away. "Yes, yes! The tourists will thrill to this one!" As Gallicus continued the visual examination, Marco's head suddenly began to pulsate and exhibit signs of expansion. From her enamel pan underneath the sheet, Jayne's decapitated head erupted in mad laughter. Gallicus withdrew his hand and used it to fish a ring of jangling keys from the horsehair sporran that he wore on a chain, positioned in front of his groin. As if embarking on a mission, he excitedly began searching through the keys to locate the one that unlocked the cage intended for his new living oddity.

As the rate of expansion accelerated, a look of anguish appeared in Marco's rapidly dilating eyes, and a forceful grunt came from his gaping mouth. Suddenly, and with a thunderous boom, his head exploded like an over-inflated balloon of gruesomeness. Pieces of his detonated skull, along with blood and globs of spongy brain matter flew in all directions.

Standing at ground zero, Professor Gallicus and his pair of reprehensible henchman received the brunt of the cranial eruption. Flying fragments of skull struck the heads of Fish and Squish, knocking them to the floor in a state of unconsciousness. A large and rather sharp piece of Marco's cranium smashed through the professor's monocle like a guided missile, blasting through his eye, and exiting the back of his head. His hand instantly released its grip on the ring of keys. With blood spraying from his eye socket like a garden hose, his lifeless frame crashed to the floor, which was slick with copious amounts of splattered gray and white matter and pungent gore.

The color departed from Turquoise's cheeks. She could feel the gorge rising in her throat like magma working its way up the conduit of a volcano. Her nose wrinkled up with disgust, and she announced, "I think I'm going to throw up!"

"Don't waste your vomit!" shouted the obese third-eye woman from the repellent confines of her cage. Her voice sounded fraught with anxiety. "Save your upchuck for me!"

Surveying the grisly aftermath of the exploding head incident, Oddball Paul spotted the professor's ring of keys lying on the floor next to his dead body. Crouching down, he slid one of his arms through the bars of his cage in an attempt to retrieve them. Highly descriptive words of obscenity poured from his mouth upon realization that the keys to freedom were more than an arm's length away.

Ramrod began to unwrap his penis from around his waist. "There's never a rose without a prick. But never fear; Ramrod is here! I'll reel in those keys with my problem-beater peter!"

"You seem pretty cocksure of yourself," Oddball Paul observed.

Ramrod propelled his penis through the bars like a fisherman casting a fishing line. He missed his mark on the first try; however, on his second attempt, the head of his member seized the ring of keys, and, as promised, he reeled them into the cage. In less than a minute's time, he had the door to the cage unlocked and open, and he and his oddball brother made a beeline for Turquoise's cage and provided her with the sweet taste of freedom.

"Let's scurry out of here before Fish and Squish over there come to." Oddball Paul suggested with a tone of urgency in his voice. "I have no desire to re-encounter that petulant pair any time in the near or distant future."

A look of alarm swept across Turquoise's face. "We can't just leave here without freeing all those poor oddities! It wouldn't be right!"

Ramrod nodded his head in agreement and then turned to Oddball Paul. "I agree with Turquoise. Come on, help me get those two creeps into a cage while they're still out like a light."

With Fish and Squish safely locked behind bars, Turquoise and the two former circus freaks darted through the museum, unlocking all of the cages. Stunned, they watched as the newly liberated oddities ran amuck, overturning cages and smashing every smashable thing in sight. In ecstatic celebration of their newfound freedom, they stampeded through the building, trampling the curator's body until it was but an unrecognizable bloody pulp.

In the midst of the chaos, the laboratory table, upon which sat Jayne's decapitated head, was knocked over. The flammable fluid from her enamel pan spontaneously combusted, quickly turning the museum into a raging inferno.

"I'll see you in hell, Morbus!" Jayne gurgled. "You should have let me die!" She then burst into spine-chilling, maniacal laughter as her flesh sizzled and blackened in the ravenous flames that consumed her.

Followed closely by Ramrod and Oddball Paul, Turquoise bolted from the burning museum. Pausing to cough the smoke out of their lungs, the trio watched from across the street as an array of uncaged exhibits spilled out of the building and scattered in different directions. Soon, flames of orange and red were licking at the roof, sending billows of ebony smoke high into the sky. They intermingled with the canopy of smog that hung over the rancid city, obscuring the rays of morning sun. Ash particles, like dirty snowflakes falling from a bad dream, danced aimlessly in the air before making their way to the ground with a burnt odor.

A robust man garbed in a black and yellow Rabbletown Fire Department uniform quickly arrived on the scene. He stood next to Turquoise, facing the burning building. His eyes were transfixed on the blaze. "Just look at that fire. She's a real beauty!" he remarked. His eyes sparkled. His bushy walrus mustache joggled as he let out a loud wolf whistle that nearly pierced Turquoise's eardrums.

"Aren't you going to put it out?" Turquoise questioned, a tone of urgency gripping her voice. She thought it odd for a fireman to stand idly by while a building burned down in front of him.

"Put it out? Why, it's just getting started!" He pointed to the fire. "Watch how those sensuous flames consume the materials fuelling them. Listen to that sexy crackling sound. It's like music to my ears! Feel the heat as it caresses your flesh like tantalizing fingers of taboo." With a delirious grin, he turned his face to Turquoise. His eyes were wide and wild. "Did you know that an average house fire can elevate the internal temperature to over eleven hundred degrees?"

Turquoise stared at the fireman. The bewildered expression on her face clearly revealed that she was in doubt of his sanity. "Uh, no. I wasn't aware of that. Thank you for telling me."

The fireman shifted his gaze back to the fire. He looked to be entranced. "It's like watching a pornographic movie. I tell you, there's nothing more erotic than watching a structure engulfed by flames… except, of course, for committing an act of arson! Did you and your friends torch this building?"

"Certainly not!" Turquoise replied, defensively. "We would never do such a thing!"

"You don't know what you're missing then," the pyrophiliac fireman declared. "The sexual thrill is incredible! Forget Viagra. Forget Spanish fly. The best aphrodisiac in the world is a can of gasoline and a book of matches. Erection guaranteed!"

Beads of cold perspiration started to form on his forehead. Excitedly, he began rubbing his bulging crotch through his pants while panting like an overheated dog. "Hot damn! My fire hose is harder than a rock! I need to touch my private parts! Oh, yeah, come on, baby. Light my fire. Mmmm, that's it! Burn, baby, burn!" His words gave way to animalistic grunts as he worked himself into a masturbatory frenzy.

"You're one sick puppy," Turquoise observed, shaking her head in disgust.

"Come on, Turquoise. Let's go," Oddball Paul suggested. "The twisted red road is calling!"

Turquoise had taken no more than a few steps down the sidewalk when her attention was seized by a familiar-looking object on display in the window of the Swindleton Pawn Shop. Her heart began to thump with excitement as she peered at it through the glass.

"Grandfather Fukowee's tomahawk!" she exclaimed. "Marco must have pawned it! That would explain what he was doing here in Rabbletown!"

Ramrod and Oddball Paul looked puzzled.

Turquoise let out a little laugh. "It's a long, weird story. I'll fill you guys in later. But first, I need to get that tomahawk back. It's been in the Moonwolf Clan for generations and my grandfather would have a conniption fit if I returned to Chupacabra without it!"

She rang the bell on the front door of the pawnshop and then waited with anticipation growing within her. Half a minute passed and then a man's voice crackled from an intercom speaker mounted above the entrance.

"Can I help you?"

"Yes!" Turquoise shouted up at the intercom. "That tomahawk that you have in the window…"

Before Turquoise could continue, the man interrupted her in mid-sentence. "I only allow one customer in the shop at a time. It's our security policy. Cuts down on the shoplifting. I'll buzz you in, but your companions will have to stay outside."

Observing the unease on Turquoise's face, Ramrod reassured her. "It's all right, Turquoise. We'll be right outside. Don't worry."

The door buzzed open and Turquoise stepped into a grimy vestibule. A pungent mustiness instantly rushed into her nostrils like a diesel locomotive plunging head-on into a tunnel. A steel security gate resembling the door of a prison cell slid open and Turquoise was greeted by Mr. Swindleton himself. He was a balding, gelatinous man, possessing, as they say, more chins than a

Chinese telephone directory. Reeking of jellied eels and stale cigars, he ushered Turquoise into his dingy, junk-filled shop.

Pausing in front of a large shadowbox containing a pinwheel of safety pins, nails, thimbles and buttons, he announced, "This authentic, faux-wood display case houses an amazing mosaic made up of thirteen hundred seventy-five non-edible objects, all of which were removed from the stomach of a female mental patient suffering from a compulsive swallowing disorder. I can let you have this stunning art piece for sixty-nine bucks. At that price, you can't go wrong, little lady!"

Turquoise stared at the shadowbox on the wall, a look of disgust on her face. "It's, uh, very artsy, but the tomahawk is what I've come about."

"It's obvious you have a keen eye for one-of-a-kind antiques," the pawnbroker complimented as he retrieved the tomahawk from the window. The two circus freaks smiled and waved at him from the opposite side of the glass. "I acquired this handsome relic just this morning, as a matter of fact!"

He presented the tomahawk to Turquoise for her inspection. "It's undoubtedly the most interesting piece of primitive weaponry I've come across in all my years as a pawnbroker." he pitched, eager to make a sale. "The workmanship, the quality of the patina, the extraordinary fine state of preservation… you'll never find another one quite like it! And the dried blood only adds to its appeal and value! I can let you have this museum-quality artifact for the mere sum of… two hundred and fifty dollars."

At that moment, Tito wailed like a banshee. Swindleton focused his eyes upon the hideous, blob-like growth on Turquoise's knee. An expression of revulsion distorted his sebaceous face, precipitating the flapping of his jowls. "Ugh! What *is* that thing?" he asked.

"It's my parasitic twin," Turquoise replied with nonchalance. "Now, getting back to the tomahawk… the man who sold it to you had no right to do so. It wasn't his to sell. You see, this tomahawk belongs to my Grandfather Fukowee! It's been in my family for generations and I need to bring it back with me when the medicine man sends me home!"

"You don't say? I had no idea that it was a priceless family heirloom of yours. In that case, you can have it for… five hundred dollars."

"Five-hundred dollars?" Turquoise cried with outrage, scowling at the unscrupulous pawnbroker. "You just told me, less than twenty seconds ago, it was two hundred and fifty, which happens to be two hundred and fifty more than I have! You can't just go and double the price like that! Don't you have any business ethics?"

"I am the proprietor of this shop and I can do whatever I deem appropriate in regard to merchandise and pricing," Swindleton replied, his nose in the air with a gesture of superiority. "If you don't approve of my prices—which are more than fair, I might add—or the way I conduct business, there's the door. Good day."

A sinking feeling filled the pit of Turquoise's stomach as she watched the corpulent moneylender return her grandfather's prized tomahawk to the window. "I need that tomahawk, Mr. Swindleton! But I'm afraid I don't have any money. How on earth am I supposed to raise half a grand?"

"There are plenty of ways to make money in Rabbletown: Rent out your armpits to an underarm hair fetishist, or sell one of your kidneys to the butcher shop across the street," Swindleton suggested. "I hear they pay top dollar for those. Or, you could try the Church of Divine Filth down the block. They might be willing to buy your soul… if it's filthy enough."

"Rent out my armpits? Sell a kidney? Sell my soul? Are you serious, or just seriously insane? What kind of ludicrous advice is that?"

"It's the kind of ludicrous advice that will cost you seventy five dollars," Swindleton replied, pointing to a sign on the wall, which read:

SOLICITED ADVICE: $75.00 ~

UNSOLICITED ADVICE: $100.00.

"You can choose to either follow it, or cram it up your shit-hole. Makes no difference to me. However, as the sign up there says, I don't dispense free advice. I'm a businessman and my time is money. So that'll be seventy five dollars, please." He held out his right hand, palm up. "Cash," he added. "Payable immediately."

Turquoise gasped in disbelief. "Do you really expect to be paid for those crackpot suggestions?" The absurdity of the idea made her laugh. "You've got to be joking! I wouldn't give you a pissed-on penny for them! Besides, I couldn't pay your fee, even if I thought your advice was helpful, which it isn't. Like I already told you: I don't have any money. Not a single dime."

Swindleton nodded toward the window. "What about your circus troupe out there? Freaks usually have hefty amounts of cash."

Turquoise shook her head from side to side. "They don't have any money either. They're retired from the circus and as broke as I am."

Eyeing Turquoise's cleavage, the pawnbroker inched his way closer to her. She reacted by backing away from him. "I believe I have a payment option that'll solve this little dilemma you've created. You might not have any money, but you *do* possess something of minimal value that can be used as a down payment." He made a V with his middle and index fingers and slithered his tongue between them.

The sight of the obscene gesture imbued Turquoise's face with a look of revulsion. "In your dreams and up your ass," she snarled.

"You're a feisty little shrew, aren't you?" Swindleton licked his chops. "Mmmm. I like 'em feisty. I really do. It's more fun that way." His lips began to glisten with the drool of his arousal. "Now prepare your ass to be maimed and tamed!"

"Fuck you!"

"That's precisely what I had in mind," Swindleton oinked, as his hands lunged for her breasts. "I want you to call me 'Daddy' when I bite off your nipples with my dentures!"

Flinching, Turquoise yelped as the man's putrid paws gripped her like a vice, sending waves of searing pain through her bazooms. Wasting no time, she directed her mutated knee up into his groin with head-spinning swiftness and fury. Upon impact, Tito released a caustic spray of acid, which immediately burned through the crotch of the pawnbroker's trousers and boxer shorts, and began eating away at his stubby, moldy-smelling penis and pimple-dotted balls. His flesh sizzled like a slab of bacon in a frying pan and bubbled with pinkish froth like a blood-tinged Valentine latte. Roaring with excruciating pain, he released his grip on Turquoise, dropped to the floor like a defecated turd, and thrashed about, thundering with threats of murder and mutilation.

"I'll get you—and your little parasitic twin too!"

Horror-stricken and with her mouth involuntarily agape, Turquoise watched as Swindleton, like some great imperiled beast, exerted tremendous effort to drag his blubbery frame across the floor, leaving behind an atrocious snail trail of effervescing sludge. Grabbing onto a vintage prison electric chair, he slowly pulled himself up from the floor with a grunt and then stumbled over to his desk. He slid open a drawer and retrieved a loaded revolver, which he began firing in Turquoise's direction.

Turquoise snatched up her grandfather's tomahawk and made a beeline to the exit, only to find the steel security door locked. She was trapped. Another bullet flew past her head, striking the door with a loud ping. Keeping her head low, she rushed to the front window and smashed the glass with the tomahawk, triggering the ear battering ringing of an alarm bell. Ramrod and Oddball Paul gasped and leapt out of the way to avoid the flying pieces of glass. As more shots rang out, Turquoise knocked over a taxidermy warthog and an eye-catching display of rectal dilators and jumped from the window, landing feet-first like a cat on the sidewalk.

Across the street, the museum was completely engulfed by flames, and the fire had spread to the adjoining buildings. By now, the entire Rabbletown Fire Department had assembled on the sidewalk, watching the blaze and masturbating.

Running as fast as they could, Turquoise, Ramrod and Oddball Paul followed the twisted red road out of Rabbletown. As a rainbow-colored sky greeted them up ahead, the black smoke floating above the city behind them formed an ominous message in the sky: *Turquoise must die!* But, at last, they were off to see the medicine man—the wonderful shaman of Thundermug.

Part Five
Having Reservations

A breezy field of poppies beckoned Turquoise and her two travel companions, an ocean of vivid reds and greens emblazoning the landscape like a Van Gogh painting come to life. The air was sweet with the melody of songbirds. In dreamy rays of golden sunlight, Monarch butterflies dipped among the red blossoms, their wings like flickering flames of orange and black.

Turquoise slowed her pace as a wave of drowsiness suddenly swept over her. Her knees began to weaken. Her energy began to fade. The only thoughts her mind could entertain were those of curling up into a ball and surrendering herself to the lure of sleep. She stopped in her tracks and yawned. "I'm suddenly so tired. I don't think I can make it any farther. I need…" she yawned again, "…a nap."

"Don't fall asleep now, Turquoise," Ramrod cautioned. "I can see the emerald gates of the Thundermug Reservation from here!"

"We're almost there," Oddball Paul added, his nose twitching. "We need to keep moving. Who knows what danger this poppy field might hold!"

A strange rumbling resounded in the distance and the ground trembled. The songbirds went silent and the butterflies quickly departed.

Turquoise let out another yawn and her head began to droop. "But I'm… I'm so… so drowsy." Her eyelids were growing heavier by the second and she was finding it difficult to keep them open. Her legs felt like lead. Unable to resist the onslaught of sleep any longer, her body went limp like a rag doll and she plummeted to the ground, a soft bed of opium-producing flowers cushioning her fall. The field of poppies and the voices of her friends frantically urging her to wake up faded away as she drifted like a cloud on a breeze into a dream…

The faint sound of calliope music seeped into Turquoise's ears as she walked alone along an unfamiliar shoreline shrouded in mist. Above a sea the color of onyx, a waning moon peered down from the lampblack sky. The ghostly fog parted and an abandoned seaside carnival came into view. Turquoise began to run toward it. As she drew closer, the music became louder. The colored light bulbs on all the amusement rides suddenly lit up. The Ferris wheel began to turn and the brightly painted horses of a carousel broke into a gallop as the circular platform beneath them rotated. But there wasn't a single person anywhere to be seen.

A man's voice whispering Turquoise's name drew her, as though in a trance, to a dilapidated house of mirrors attraction. Stepping inside, she quickly became lost in a maze of grotesque distortions. Hideous faces, winged demons, and skulls laughed at her in the reflections. And then she came upon a mirror that showed her normal image. The calliope music grew louder, and again the disembodied voice whispered her name. Turquoise gazed at her reflection; something about it didn't seem right. It suddenly beckoned her to follow, before turning and walking away into the depths of the mirror. Startled, yet curious, Turquoise stepped through the glass and the calliope music came to an abrupt stop.

She was now inside the mirror, trapped in a strange dimension of shadows, and wearing an ivory wedding gown of satin and lace with a flowing train in the back. Candlelight suddenly illuminated an open casket, around which stood half a dozen mourners, their faces concealed behind black veils. Again the voice whispered Turquoise's name. It was then joined by another whispering voice, and then another, until dozens of voices were chanting her name in unison. Slowly, she approached the casket, her curiosity compelling her to peer inside.

The unexpected sight of a ventriloquist dummy lying in repose took her aback. But even more startling was the human skin that covered the contours of its face. Its black-lined eyes flew open and it sat up in the casket, twisting its head in Turquoise's direction. Its blood-red lips parted and it spoke. Its words filled Turquoise with horror.

"I've been waiting for you, my pretty," it said, its mouth making a clicking sound as it moved.

"Come to me, Turquoise, and we'll be together… until death do us part."

Turquoise stepped back from the casket, and the sound of the calliope music once again filled her ears. She attempted to run but found herself frozen to the spot in which she stood, her feet refusing to budge. The mourners lifted their veils, revealing their ventriloquist dummy faces. Erupting into macabre laughter, they rushed toward Turquoise, their bony hands transformed into hideous black claws.

Turquoise let out a scream and the distorted mirrors, like the nightmare itself, shattered…

"Wake up, Turquoise!" Ramrod was yelling. "We have to get out of here!"

Turquoise opened her eyes. She was back in the field of poppies with the two circus freaks, a look of fear impressed upon their faces. The distant rumbling noise was now louder than before and the ground was squirming like some creature come to life. Something monstrous and gray was moving through the field at a rapid speed and heading toward Turquoise and her frightened friends.

Springing to her feet, Turquoise cried out, "What is that thing?"

Oddball Paul shook his head. "I don't know, but I don't want to wait around here and find out!"

"To the reservation, as fast as lightning!" Ramrod boomed.

Running as though their lives depended on it (and none had any doubts that their lives did), the trio followed the twisted red road until it terminated at the emerald gates of the Thundermug Reservation. The rumbling noise was intensifying as the unknown gray terror drew closer, slithering through the poppies like a gigantic snake.

Horrified to find the gates locked, Turquoise and her companions began pounding on them with their fists and hollering to be let in. Within moments, the gates were unlocked and swung open. An old Indian bearing a peculiar resemblance to Grandfather Fukowee stood at the entrance of the reservation, bewilderment clouding his eyes. His face was creased with lines and reminded Turquoise of the weathered stone hoodoos back in New Mexico.

The rumbling noise suddenly ceased, prompting Turquoise to look over her shoulder. To her relief, all she saw was a field of red poppies gently rippling in the breeze. The singing of the songbirds had resumed and even the butterflies had returned. Whatever had been chasing her and the others had vanished without a trace.

Breathless, and with her heart still pumping wildly, Turquoise turned back to the old Indian and introduced herself. "My name is Turquoise Moonwolf, and my friends and I have traveled a long way to get here. We need to see the medicine man—all three of us! Please, it's very urgent!"

"What so urgent, Blue Eyes? Quazi has day off."

Turquoise's jaw dropped. "The day off?"

"Yes. It Lima Bean Respect Day. Come back tomorrow."

"Oh, please don't send us away," pleaded Turquoise. "This is probably going to sound unbelievable to you, but my grandfather accidentally conjured a tornado with his rain dance, and it carried me off into the sky and I somehow ended up in your world. I don't know how it happened, but I'm stranded here with no way of returning home and I seem to have made enemies with a shape-shifter who wants me dead. I was told that Quazi, with all his wondrous and mystical powers, would be able to send me back to where I come from. Is that true? Is he a clever enough medicine man to manage it?"

The old man stared into Turquoise's eyes as though examining her soul. "The prophecy!" he gasped.

"The prophecy?" Turquoise asked. "What are you talking about?"

"According to ancient prophecy, the end of the shape-shifting demon's evil reign is presaged by the descent of a blue-eyed Indian maiden from the heavens—that's you. Your arrival here, and your very existence, is a threat to Ursa's power and that is why she seeks to destroy you. Quazi will know what to do!" He gestured with his hand for Turquoise and the others to enter.

Stepping through the gates, Turquoise was astonished to find herself in a sprawling subdivision of teepee-lined cul-de-sacs. On manicured lawns there sat smiling women of all ages, some with a papoose in a cradleboard strapped upon their backs, weaving baskets and grinding maize into meal with their stone rolling pins. Little girls in fringed buckskin dresses and little boys in loincloths ran about and played in the streets with raucous laughter. Erected on a hillside, white capital letters, which Turquoise guessed to be at least forty feet tall, overlooked the reservation and spelled out: THUNDERMUG.

"This place is amazing!" Turquoise remarked, feeling as though she had stepped back into the past. "I've never seen a reservation like this before! It isn't at all what I was expecting."

"Oh? And what were you expecting?"

"Poverty, squalor, human misery," Turquoise replied.

A tear trickled from the left eye of the old Indian. "Follow me," he instructed. "I will take you and your friends to Quazi."

Acting as their guide, he led them through the sacred lands of the reservation, across a sacred river, past sacred burial grounds, a sacred smoke shop, and a sacred casino. Finally, they arrived at the sacred medicine lodge of the medicine man. It was a conical structure, resembling a huge teepee. It was composed of long, wooden poles leaned against a tall center pole, upon which sat the sun-bleached skull of a buffalo. Cattail mats covered its sides, and it was roofed with rolls of birch bark.

"You wait here, Blue Eyes," the old Indian instructed before disappearing into the medicine lodge.

Ramrod grinned. "I can almost feel my meat monster shrinking!"

Oddball Paul beamed. "And I can almost feel my I.Q. decreasing. Goodbye brain cells!"

"And I'm as good as on my way home!" Turquoise's face was aglow with happiness. "Oh, it'll be so good to see Grandmother Loona and Grandfather Fukowee again, as well as my crazy cousin, Dolores… and even Billy Balls, as much as I can't stand him. He's a mangy, one-eyed pervert who's always chasing after me trying to get him some action, if you know what I mean. Grandmother always said he jumped into the gene pool when the lifeguard wasn't watching."

"I caught a case of the strange mange once," Oddball Paul confessed. "Half the fur on my face fell out, and it took six months to clear up!"

At that moment, Quazi emerged from the medicine lodge, looking suspiciously like the old Indian who had gone into it. He wore a tan, buckskin medicine shirt, to which were attached rows of feathers and shells. Upon his head of cascading gray hair sat a buffalo horn headdress, adorned with shaggy buffalo fur, eagle feathers, coyote tails and colorful beadwork. Under his dark, mystery-filled eyes were two horizontal lines of white paint. His left hand clutched a long wooden staff surmounted by a crystal skull; in his right hand was a large leather drawstring pouch, ornamented with feathers and beads.

"I am the great and powerful Quazi," the medicine man stated in a voice that sounded suspiciously like the old Indian's. "Quazi knows why the three of you have come to Thundermug. Step forward, Ramrod! You disturbing display of perverted penile peculiarity! You dare come to me for a reproductive organ of normal proportions, do you?"

Ramrod took a step forward and nodded his head. "Yes sir! I do."

Quazi put down his staff and reached into his leather pouch. He fished around for a few seconds and then extracted a plumber's tube cutter. He gave the red handles a squeeze. "This magical device will grant your wish."

Clutching his penis, Ramrod stared at the cutting tool in utter horror. "Uh, thank you, but on second thought I'll just cancel that wish and keep old Long Dong Silver."

"You heap big sissy." Quazi returned the tube cutter to his leather pouch and then pulled out a silver hammer and a long-handled surgical instrument resembling an ice pick. "And you, Oddball Paul. Step forward! You have the unmitigated gall to ask me for stupidity, you asinine archetype of unnatural ugsomeness?"

Oddball Paul stepped forward and flinched. "That wouldn't happen to be an orbitoclast for performing transorbital lobotomies, would it?"

Quazi smiled and nodded, his buffalo horns nearly sliding off his head. "I place magic pick behind your eye socket, and with one swing of magic hammer, you magically change into blabbering idiot with I.Q. of a moccasin. This some powerful medicine here!"

Oddball Paul stared at the lobotomy instruments in horror. "If you don't mind, Mister Quazi, I think I'll withdraw that silly request for stupidity."

Exasperated, the medicine man shook his head and returned the hammer and orbitoclast to his leather pouch. "Suit yourself, Ferret Face. You already stupid if you ask me."

A look of dismay overcame Turquoise's face. "I don't think there's anything in that medicine bag for me," she speculated, glumly.

Quazi sighed. "Don't be so pessimistic, Blue Eyes." He once again reached inside his leather pouch, this time pulling out a painted gourd rattle that looked exactly like the one Grandfather Fukowee used during his ill-fated rain dance ceremony. He shook it at Turquoise and began chanting.

"Hoo-ga-cha-ka! Hoo-ga hoo-ga!
Hoo-ga-cha-ka! Hoo-ga hoo-ga!"

All at once, there came a mighty rumble and then a plume of soil and rocks shot upward like a geyser as an enormous worm-like creature erupted out of the ground. Its head, consisting of a massive, black armored beak with hooked mandibles, unfolded like a grotesque flower. From out of its throat rose a trio of hissing, writhing, serpentine tentacles, each terminating in a venom-dripping, fang-filled mouth.

As a scream rushed out of Turquoise's mouth, the medicine man shook his rattle at the creature, Ramrod assumed a basic boxing stance, and Oddball Paul—ever the embodiment of bravery—wet his pants.

With a thunderous roar, the creature lunged at Turquoise, entwining its tentacles around her body like a vine strangling a tree. It lifted her from the ground and began carrying her toward its gaping beak.

Having no desire to be lunch for an oversized earthworm, Turquoise struggled with all her might to break free. She soon found the grip in which the creature imprisoned her was too tremendous a match for her human strength to conquer. She then remembered the tomahawk in her hand and began swinging it at her monstrous assailant, the sharp blade chopping into the creature's gray, rubber-like flesh until it hacked off one of the tentacles. From the severed appendage, a yellow, pus-like substance shot into the air and then rained down upon the ground. The behemoth worm ejected a terrifying screeching noise from its open beak, and promptly released Turquoise, dropping her onto the ground. She quickly sprung to her feet and took off running toward a Joshua tree, which she took cover behind.

With its remaining tentacles, the monstrous worm then snatched Quazi from where he stood and pulled him down its hungry gullet, swallowing him whole. Still ravenous, it let out a hair-raising screech and made another lunge toward Turquoise. But before it could ensnare her in its tentacles, Ramrod sprang into action, locking the creature in a stranglehold with his freakishly elongated penis. With its air supply cut off, the creature bucked like a bronco and thrashed about for several terror-filled minutes like a bedlamite before going limp and hurtling to the ground with a loud thud.

Before the dust could settle, the creature began to undergo a metamorphosis. Its worm-like body contracted, its gray and rubbery skin turned green and scaly, and its man-eating tentacles changed into dreadlocked hair. When the transformation was complete, Ursa lay on the ground, motionless.

With her adrenaline pumping, Turquoise grabbed the shape-shifter by her dreads, and using her other hand, swung the tomahawk with all her might, contenting herself by scalping Ursa with a single blow. A thick and foul-smelling substance resembling green diarrhea flowed from the top of the butchered head. Turquoise placed her right foot on Ursa's chest and held up the severed scalp like a trophy.

Ramrod and Oddball Paul cheered and then burst into song:

"Ding dong, the bitch is dead!
Without a hitch! Without a glitch!
Ding dong, she'll need more than one stitch!"

"You defeated the shape-shifter!" Ramrod announced with glee.

"With the help of that formidable shlong of yours!" Turquoise added.

Oddball Paul suddenly exhibited a sad expression. "It's a shame about old Quazi, though. He seemed like a rather nice guy, before he got devoured."

Realization struck Turquoise like a bolt of lightning. "Oh shit! The medicine man was the only one who knew how to send me back! Now that he's dead, I'll never get home!" Tears welled up in her eyes and began running down her cheeks. "I'll never see Grandmother Loona or Grandfather Fukowee again."

Turquoise felt something warm and wet running down the front of her leg. Looking down, she found her parasitic twin crying. "Even Tito feels my sadness."

Ramrod gave Turquoise a hug. "Don't cry, Turquoise. Stay with Oddball Paul and me. We could start our own traveling circus; just the three of us."

Oddball Paul smiled and nodded his head in agreement.

Turquoise wiped away the tears streaming from her eyes. "That's very sweet of you, but I don't belong in your world. It could never be like Chupacabra."

A slight motion out of the corner of Turquoise's eye caught her attention. Jerking with muscle spasms, Ursa's body twitched like a hound running in its sleep. And then, with a sound similar to the rubbing of an inflated balloon, her belly began to swell, steadily growing larger until it reached startling proportions.

"What's happening?" Ramrod asked, mystified. "I thought she was dead!"

Turquoise shook her head, anxiety swimming in the blue pools of her eyes. "I thought she was dead, too! Maybe it's impossible to kill her; she just shape-shifts into something else?"

"Let's make a run for it while we still have a chance!" a frantic-sounding Oddball Paul suggested, readying his body for a sprint.

Just then, two sharp horns poked through Ursa's belly. There came a loud ripping sound as her gut split apart, and then Quazi emerged. He was covered in a green, jelly-like goop, but alive and seemingly unharmed. The sight filled Turquoise with disgust and elation.

"The prophecy of the ancient ones has been fulfilled!" the medicine man declared, wiping the muck from his face. "The demon Ursa is dead!" He then showered Turquoise and Ramrod with thanks and words of praise for slaying the shape-shifter. "Come, Blue Eyes," he said to Turquoise. "It is time for your departure."

With tears glistening their eyes, Ramrod and Oddball Paul hugged Turquoise and bade her farewell. She kissed both of them, and then, with jubilance, followed Quazi to the rear of the medicine lodge, where he showed her a mysterious circle composed of several hundred stones. It was roughly eighty feet in diameter, and arranged in the shape of a wheel with twenty-eight "spokes" radiating from a central cairn to half a dozen smaller ones around the rim.

"Take your place in the center of the sacred medicine wheel," Quazi told Turquoise. "And then begin clicking the heels of your moccasins together while chanting these powerful words: *Medicine wheel start a-turning, carry me home to Moonwolf Clan. Sweet home Chupacabra, here I come as fast as I can!*"

Turquoise followed Quazi's instructions, and with a low rumble and a loud crunching sound, the circle of stones began to rotate in a clockwise direction. Turquoise waved goodbye to Quazi and the two circus freaks—all of whom she knew would forever occupy a special place deep within her heart. She continued clicking and chanting. Faster and faster the medicine wheel turned until it was spinning at a dizzying rate of speed. Turquoise shut her eyes as tightly as she could and repeated the mystical, magical chant. Images of Chupacabra began to rapidly flash within her mind's eye like an out-of-control slide projector. An electrifying tingling sensation shot through her body and goosebumps sprang up on her arms. Ever her braids tingled.

A glowing white beam of light suddenly lowered from the sky to the center of the stone circle, and

Turquoise felt the odd and unsettling sensation of her feet lifting off the ground. Her body floated in the beam, ascending slowly at first, and then rapidly zooming upward at the speed of light.

Within the blink of an eye, she materialized aboard a huge, rotating spaceship. A wild-eyed, brunette woman wearing a shimmering spacesuit of silver greeted her. Something about the woman's face looked strangely familiar to Turquoise. She had seen it before somewhere, but was unable to place it. And then recognition dawned. The woman in silver was none other than the infamous homicidal hooker, Aileen Wuornos!

Turquoise let out a gasp of surprise. "Aileen Wuornos! I thought the state of Florida executed you!"

Aileen Wuornos grinned and then chuckled. "Yeah. Society railroaded my ass, but I told 'em I'd be back on Independence Day with Jesus in a big ol' mothership!"

"Jesus is on board?" Turquoise asked, her eyes scanning the interior of the spaceship for the Son of God.

Aileen Wuornos lit up a cigarette and shook her head. "Nah. He changed his mind at the last minute. Ain't that just like a fuckin' man? They all deserve to be shot like those seven raping bastards I robbed and put out of their misery. And I'd do it again! Want a cigarette?"

Turquoise nodded her head. "I haven't had a cigarette in ages. Oh, the nicotine withdrawals! I could kill for a good smoke!"

Aileen Wuornos beamed upon hearing Turquoise's killing remark. She handed her a cigarette and then lit it for her.

"Thanks, Aileen." Turquoise inhaled on the cigarette and slowly exhaled the smoke through her nose like a dragon. "Wow! This is all so incredible! I have so many questions, beginning with: who's flying this spaceship and where are we going?"

The grinning serial killer took a drag on her cigarette and then popped open a can of beer. "It's on auto-pilot and should be arriving at Roswell, New Mexico, any minute. I'll beam ya down when we pass over Chupacabra, which should be right about… now!"

Once again Turquoise found herself in the beam of light. Her skin tingled and her braids danced wildly as she descended to Earth at a rapid speed, and then…

William Cyrus Ballschmieder raised his eyelid and realized he was on the floor of the Squealing Squaw Trading Post. The side of his head throbbed with a dull pain, and through his one bleary, bloodshot eye, he could make out Turquoise, her grandmother Loona, and her cousin Dolores Angry Cloud standing over him and staring.

"Are you all right, Billy Balls?" Turquoise asked.

"Yeah," Ballschmieder replied, rubbing his sore head with his hand. "I think so. But I've got one humdinger of a headache."

"Grandmother Loona swatted you so hard with her broom, she knocked you unconscious!" Turquoise explained.

"And I will do it again if you mess with my granddaughter!" Grandmother Loona added, shaking the bristles of her broom in front of Ballschmieder's face as a warning.

"You were out cold for a while," Dolores Angry Cloud chuckled. "We all thought you were dead. Oh well. Hopefully next time."

Ballschmieder staggered to his feet, still rubbing his head. "Man, I had one hell of a weird dream. I dreamed I was Turquoise, and a tornado conjured up by Fukowee's crazy rain dance blew this teepee, with me in it, off to some bizarre world. There were incestuous, hookah-smoking albinos, tree-dwelling cannibal dwarfs, circus freaks, a man with an exploding head, and all kinds of other weirdos! Oh, and there was this ugly, green shape-shifter with dreadlocks that kept trying to kill me… I mean, Turquoise."

Grandmother Loona shook her head and rolled her eyes, while Turquoise and her cousin laughed until tears rolled down their cheeks.

Ballschmieder pulled up his pants leg and examined his knee; he was relieved not to find a parasitic twin named Tito growing out of it. "What a long, strange trip it's been," he concluded. "But, damn, it sure is good to be back; there's no place like Chupacabra!"

"I'll get you an ice cold beer to celebrate your return," Turquoise offered, despite a disapproving look from her grandmother. She could feel Billy Balls' one-eyed gaze zeroing in on her derriere as soon as she turned her back to him. As she headed for the cooler on the other side of the teepee, the spiked heels of her ruby stilettos clicked along the wooden floor like the castanets of a death-defying trapeze artist.

THE END

WIGWAM, THANK YOU MA'AM
Part One
Strange Smoke Signals

It was the third of June, another sleepy, dusty Chupacabra day. The sun, like a testicular hydrocele blazing in the morning sky, beamed down upon the teepee-shaped Squealing Squaw Trading Post as Turquoise Moonwolf helped her grandmother get ready to open the shop.

The familiar sound of a sputtering mail truck engine popped the cherry of the desert's silence, and grew louder until it stopped in front of the teepee. Grandmother Loona took a peek out the screen door. An elderly woman with hair styled in a Marcel wave like a Roaring Twenties flapper was ever so slowly climbing out of the mail truck with a package in her hand.

"That Matilda Carriage is slower than a constipated bear!" Grandmother Loona blurted out, her eyes focused on the slowly approaching mail carrier. "I've seen copulating turtles move faster than her."

"Well, she *is* ninety-seven," Turquoise replied as she feather dusted a shelf of Braille sex manuals for blind fornicators. "And before becoming a carrier of the U.S. mail, she *was* a carrier of rare infectious diseases."

"She should have been put out to pasture years ago," Grandmother Loona groused. "At the rate of speed she's going, that package won't get here until sundown tomorrow. She better not drop it in a gopher hole like last time!"

"Is it those Abyss of Bliss rubber rectums you ordered for the shop?"

Grandmother Loona shook her head. "No. Package too small for those. But too big for electric shock doormat I ordered to keep Billy Balls out of teepee. Must be the Dirty Deeds anal beads from Nagasaki." Her eyes grew doleful and she let out a dispirited sigh. "It so sad, granddaughter. Nothing made in America anymore," she lamented. "Rubber rectums all imported from China. And all the anal beads we made by hand are nowadays made in Japan."

Turquoise nodded her head in agreement.

The sluggish mail carrier arrived at the door of the teepee. "Good morning," she chirped. "It sure is cold out today."

"Good morning, Miss Carriage," Turquoise answered back. "It's eighty-five degrees in the shade."

"Brrrr!" the mail carrier shivered. "If I had known it was going to be this cold today, I would have worn *two pairs* of thermal underwear instead of just one. I have a package for you, Miss Turquoise. I'll need you to sign for it."

A look of surprise registered on Turquoise's face. "A package for me?" She signed for the package and then looked it over with curiosity. It was postmarked, "Coyote Gulch, N.M." but bore no return address. "I wonder what it is and who sent it?"

"Must be important, whatever it is," the mail carrier stated, her yellow teeth chattering. "They sent it postage due. That'll be a dollar twenty-five, dearie."

"Highway robbery!" yelled Grandmother Loona as she angrily retrieved the money from the drawer of the cash register.

Turquoise gently shook the package. "It's so light; it feels like an empty box."

The mail carrier stuffed the money into her pocket. "Well, ladies, I'd better get back to my mail truck and crank up the heater before I freeze to death. Have a nice day, and try to stay warm!" She shivered again and then shuffled out of the shop at a snail's pace.

"That Miss Carriage sure is an odd one," Turquoise remarked, still shaking the mysterious package and wondering about its contents.

Grandmother Loona grunted in agreement. She then added, "Her postage stamp is missing the glue, if you know what I mean. Well, don't just stand there playing with your box. Open it up!"

At that moment, one-eyed William Cyrus Ballschmieder drunkenly staggered into the trading post, his breath reeking of whiskey. "If you need someone to open up your box, I'm your man," he slurred. "I never met a box I didn't like. Except maybe for Boobs Callahan's at the Mother Trucker all-night truck stop. Don't tell *me* she didn't have a fish head hiding up in there!"

"You want a box?" Grandmother Loona asked. "I'll give you a box! It has six sides and is called a coffin! And you'll be buried in it if you lay one of your mangy fingers on my granddaughter!"

Ballschmieder chuckled. "You got nothin' to worry 'bout, old lady. I always use all nine and a half of my mangy fingers for that!"

Grandmother Loona responded with a growl. "Old lady? Just wait until I fetch my corn broom! I'll show you old lady!"

Turquoise began to rip open the brown paper that covered the box. "Billy Balls; don't upset grandmother. Or did you forget what happened the last time? Hmmm. What on earth could be inside this package?" She pulled off a strip of transparent tape that sealed the end flap, and the box popped open. Thick white smoke immediately began pouring out of it and Turquoise instinctively flung the parcel onto the floor.

Ballschmieder's one bloodshot eye bugged open in terror and he began to hyperventilate. "It's a bomb! Run for your life!" He turned, pushed Grandmother Loona out of his way, and barreled out the door, shouting, "Ocular prosthesis wearers first!" Within seconds, he disappeared into the desert.

Laughing like an unhinged hyena, Grandmother Loona retrieved the smoking parcel from the floor and carried it outside, where she calmly set it upon a large rock in front of the trading post. She then stepped back and observed the smoke.

"It not bomb," she explained. "It is box of smoke signals—old Indian way of long distance communicating."

Fascinated, Turquoise watched as the smoke rose high into the air, taking on strange shapes. "What does it say?"

Grandmother Loona put on her reading glasses. "Smoke signals say, Great Aunt Uvula has gone to happy hunting ground in sky… wake and reading of will held tomorrow at Chateau Catatonia in Coyote Gulch… two o'clock in afternoon… your attendance is requested… signed, Rudy Pannowahoo, Esquire."

"Great Aunt Uvula?" Turquoise asked. "Wasn't she the wealthy cat-lady accused of hacking her best friend over one hundred times with a meat cleaver, disemboweling him, putting his dismembered body parts through a meat grinder, and then serving him as pâté to her feline guests at the bed and breakfast?"

Grandmother Loona nodded her head. "With friends like that, who needs enemas?"

The smoke signals came to a stop, and what had risen up into the sky quickly dissipated as a warm breeze dismantled them. Turquoise picked up the box from which they had emerged, and looked inside. It was empty.

"I thought she was on Death Row at the Weasel County Correctional Facility for Women."

Removing her reading glasses, Grandmother Loona shook her head. "Nope. She was acquitted after the court ruled her friend's death an accident. It was heap big news, and the Bald Eagles even wrote a song about it. I used to sing you to sleep with it when you were a little girl." She cleared her throat and began to croon, off-key:

Welcome to the Chateau Catatonia
Human pate, any time of day
They're grinding them up at the Chateau Catatonia
The cats are well fed
They get breakfast in bed
Plenty of room at the Chateau Catatonia
You can scream, you can shout
But you'll never check out.

* * *

"Next stop, Coyote Gulch!" the conductor barked into his hand-held megaphone, even though Turquoise was sitting only a few feet away from him and was the only passenger on board. "Coyote Gulch, next stop!" He then turned and departed, moments later barking out the same announcement in the adjoining car, which was empty.

Gazing out the grimy window as the train rattled past a sphincter-shaped meteorite crater, the wreckage of a 1950's station wagon plastered with Bible verses, and other scenic delights offered up by New Mexico's jewel of the desert—Coyote Gulch, Turquoise lost herself in thought. *Finally, I'm on my way to some place where they're expecting me. I'm on my way. I'm actually on my way. One of these days, I'll have a wigwam of my own with a pair of stone lions guarding the front gate. I wonder what Great*

Aunt Uvula was like. I wonder who else will be at the reading of the will. I wonder what Chateau Catatonia is like. I wonder why I'm asking myself all these questions.

The blaring of the train whistle jolted Turquoise from her musings. Turning her face away from the window, she was startled to discover a man with a white cane and a tin cup filled with pencils standing just several feet away from her. Looking up, she could see that his eyes were hidden behind a pair of darkly tinted glasses, and upon his head he wore a red fez with a long, black tassel. He raised his cane and poked Turquoise's right breast with its rubber tip.

"Hey!" Turquoise snapped, aghast at the man's lack of etiquette. "Watch what you're doing with that damn thing!" Hit by the sudden realization that the man was without sight, Turquoise cringed with embarrassment and regretted her inappropriate choice of words. She quickly attempted to rephrase her directive. "Sorry, I meant to say, look before you... uh, never mind."

The man thrust his tin cup in front of Turquoise's face and gave it a few vigorous shakes. The pencils within it made a rattling noise like a skeleton in a closet.

"Excuse me, Miss. I spent all my money on this white cane and tin cup full of number two pencils stamped in gold with an authentic facsimile signature of the pope. If you can find it within your heart to help me, I would happily repay your kindness with one of these fine pencils with an attached eraser. I accept cash, traveler's checks, and all major credit cards."

Feeling sorry for the blind beggar, Turquoise opened her fringed leather purse and extracted a crisp five-dollar bill, which she folded into thirds and tucked into the tin cup.

"Five dollars?" the man roared, his voice laced with derision. "Five stinking dollars? I have Lexus payments to make, lady. Five frigging dollars. Are you sure you can afford to be so generous?"

"Hey, wait a minute," Turquoise snarled, realizing she had just been swindled out of her money. "If you're unable to see, how did you know the denomination of the money I just gave you? You aren't blind at all! You're nothing but a scam artist, and you should be ashamed of yourself! Now, give me my money back!"

"Oh, so you're an Indian giver as well as a cheapskate. No, you may not have your money back. What kind of panhandler would I be if I gave refunds? Besides, I never told you I was blind; therefore, I'm not responsible for your incorrect assumptions."

Turquoise felt her blood beginning to boil. She clenched her teeth, fighting to resist the urge to grab the white cane and brutally introduce it into the arrogant man's rectum. Her attention was suddenly drawn to the sight of a heavyset woman entering the passenger car, her corpulence threatening to burst forth from her stretched-to-the-limit yoga pants like an alien popping out of Sigourney Weaver's stomach. She plodded her way over to Turquoise, who, by now, had given up her verbal sparring with the non-visually impaired pencil hustler.

"Excuse me, could you good folks spare any money for a worthy cause?" the rotund woman asked, her double chin glistening with perspiration like a greased pelican. "The thing is, I need to raise enough cash for a helicopter to break Gary Goretti out of prison. He's my boyfriend."

"You don't mean Gary 'Gory' Goretti, the infamous wood-chipper murderer, do you?" the man with the white cane asked. He sounded impressed.

The woman smiled and nodded her head. "Yes, the one and only! You see, we met through a prison pen pal website, and it was truly lust at first sight." She let out a sigh. "There's just something about serial killers that makes me moist."

"I'm always happy to contribute to a worthwhile cause," the man stated as he rested his white cane against the side of Turquoise's seat. He then plucked the five-dollar bill from his tin cup and handed it to the crime groupie, who smiled with delight. "Here you go, little lady. And please help yourself to a couple of these fine pencils, too—one for you and one for Gary. They're stamped in gold with an authentic facsimile signature of the pope!"

The yoga pants woman beamed. "Ooh! Bless you, dearie."

Incensed, Turquoise rose from her seat. "Excuse me, but that's *my* five-dollar bill you have there."

"Oh, well in that case, bless *you*, dearie!" the woman responded to Turquoise as she slid her pudgy hand down the front of her sports bra and tucked the money away into the dark depths of her clammy cleavage.

Before Turquoise could verbalize an objection, a longhaired man garbed in tattered jeans and a tie-dyed shirt entered the car, accompanied by a heavily perfumed woman wearing a melon-colored tweed skirt suit. Wasting no time, they zeroed in on Turquoise as if on a mission to escalate her exasperation.

"When I was a child," the woman in tweed began, "I was abducted by blond-haired extraterrestrial beings who resembled the Christ the Redeemer statue in Rio de Janeiro. They implanted a small device in my left nostril that transmits signals into outer space. I'm a Republican now and running for Congress. Would you care to make a contribution to my political campaign?"

Turquoise shook her head. "I don't think so. I never vote Republican."

The man in the psychedelic shirt took a bow before Turquoise and then made a strange hand gesture, bringing the tips of his fingers together. "Greetings and salutations," he said. His vocal intonation, like his cocoa-colored eyes, was somber. "I'm a desperate man in need of money. I suffer from a rare condition known as onism. My frustrating awareness of how little of the world I'll actually get to experience being trapped in just one body, inhabiting only one place at a time, sometimes leads me to commit unspeakable acts."

To Turquoise's delight, the train conductor returned to the car and angrily ordered the congregation of panhandlers to leave at once. Aggrieved, they marched to the exit like a collective unit, and within a matter of seconds they were gone. Turquoise breathed a sigh of relief and thanked the conductor for chasing them away.

"My pleasure, ma'am," he replied, tipping his dark blue cap. "Incidentally, I'm collecting money for the Railroad Conductors' Anorectal Anomalies Fund. Our motto is: Don't be a pain in the ass; give until it hurts."

At that moment, the train puffed and wheezed to a halt alongside the platform of the Coyote Gulch railway station. Turquoise hurriedly retrieved her overnight satchel from the overhead luggage rack and ran from the train.

Dark clouds were beginning to gather above, and a gust of vagrant wind sent a puff of dust sailing down the deserted main street, which bore a quaint resemblance to a ghost town. Signs hanging from large metal bars outside closed-down shops with boarded-up windows creaked out an ominous melody. A distant rumble of thunder heralded an approaching storm.

Turquoise looked down at her wristwatch and wondered where the taxicab she had prearranged was. Her attention was suddenly diverted to the strange pricking of her thumbs. *Something wicked this way comes*, she quoted Shakespeare within her head. Growing impatient, she began to pace the platform like a tigress in a cage, her gaze periodically alternating between her wristwatch and the approaching inclement weather.

At last, a yellow taxicab arrived at the train station. Pumped full of relief, Turquoise grabbed her satchel from off the ground, hurried to her waiting ride, and climbed into the backseat.

The taxi driver, a middle-aged Caucasian man clad in a drab green army jacket, asked, "Where to?"

Turquoise noticed his head was shaved bald, except for a narrow strip of short hair that originated at the top of his forehead and terminated at the nape of his neck like a black skid mark. Next to him, on the front seat, sat an amassment of handguns and several hundred rounds of ammunition.

"Chateau Catatonia," Turquoise answered, somewhat unnerved by the sight of the weapons.

The taxi driver hit the gas. "Looks like some bad weather's heading this way." As he spoke, his voice began to grow manic. "One of these days, a real storm is going to come and blow away all the scumbags from these streets. Space cadets, fudge packers, bean queens, bums, dope pushers, toe jam gobblers, B-girls, stiff sniffers, dental floss fetishists. Sick puppies!"

Turquoise responded with silence.

The taxi driver's voice returned to normalcy. "Chateau Catatonia—that's that old cat hotel on Hershey Highway. I thought they shut that place down after the meat grinder murder back in eighty-four. You know, some people around these parts are convinced that the place is haunted. Some even believe it's jinxed... has some sort of curse on it." He let out a little man-giggle. "That's what some of the crazy local yokels think. But not me; I'm a rational thinking, levelheaded guy." He broke into a fit of sardonic laughter.

They say laughter is the best medicine, Turquoise thought while listening to the hyena-like sounds emanating from the guffawing man at the steering wheel. *Unless, of course, you're laughing out loud for no reason... Then you need to be on some meds!*

The taxi driver suddenly slammed on the brakes, turned and pointed a gun at Turquoise's startled face. His eyes glistened with unhinged fervor. "You talkin' to me? You talkin' to me?" His voice grew maniacal as he screamed out his spittle-laden words. "You talkin' to me?"

"I didn't say a word," Turquoise replied, her eyes staring down the barrel of the gun.

"Oh." With a dazed look, the taxi driver returned his gun to the front seat and the cab proceeded forward. In a now calmer voice, he asked, "Are you sure you weren't talkin' to me?"

"Quite sure," Turquoise replied, checking her wristwatch for the time.

A fine drizzle of rain was falling like a ghostly mist when the taxi driver pulled up outside the tall front gates of the Chateau Catatonia, a sagging Second Empire monstrosity perched high atop a scrub-covered hill. The mansion overlooked an old, abandoned chemical plant and the adjoining Timothy Leary Memorial Institute of Psychedelic Consciousness, which had, over the years, metamorphosed into a nudist colony for geriatric hippies. A dilapidated remnant of Victorian era splendor, the chateau had stood for well over a century, but in its present state of disrepair, it seemed doubtful it would remain standing for another.

"It's not too late to change your mind." The taxi driver made eye contact with Turquoise via his rearview mirror. "I could turn this cab around and drive you far away from here. And no one would blame you one bit."

"Don't be ridiculous!" Turquoise quipped, her voice not quite as steady as she would have preferred. "I'm not going to let silly stories of hauntings and curses scare me away from my inheritance. And besides, I *am* expected in the house."

"Suit yourself."

Turquoise handed the driver the fare, and he sped off without bothering to count it.

Crazy bastard.

She paused to peek through the iron gates at the old mansion, which stood at the end of a flagstone path like a silhouette of impending doom. She looked up, half expecting to see the skeletal remains of Norman Bates' mother staring down at her from the attic window. Something about the house, a weird vibe if you will, made the tiny hairs on the back of her neck bristle. It was almost as if the house were alive… watching… waiting.

Pushing open the creaking iron gates, she was met by hordes of feral cats prowling the grounds; at least a dozen cats sat on the rickety front porch, swishing their tales and eyeing Turquoise's every move as she made her way up the flagstone path leading to the house.

Before she could ring the bell, the ornately carved front door of the mansion opened, its rusty hinges announcing her arrival with a somewhat interminable squeak. In the doorway stood the sour-faced, Nigerian housekeeper, Jambalaya Jetson, her licorice-colored hair pulled back into a bun tight enough to produce oxygen depletion in most living organisms. Around her thick neck hung a black thong necklace strung with a three-inch-long crocodile tooth intricately carved with mysterious squiggly sigils. She motioned for Turquoise to enter, and then led her into the dismal bowels of Chateau Catatonia.

Following Jambalaya Jetson down a seemingly endless white corridor carpeted in a vertigo-inducing hexagonal pattern of orange, brown and red, Turquoise noticed that every black paneled door that they passed displayed a small wooden plaque, each bearing a woman's name. Among them were: Lizzie Borden, Belle Gunness, Aileen Wuornos, Judy Buenoano, and Madame LaLaurie.

"Why are all the guest rooms named after female serial killers?" Turquoise asked. Like the readers of trashy supermarket tabloids, her enquiring mind wanted to know.

"Your Great Aunt Uvula—Baron Samedi rest her soul—was an admirer of women who left their mark on history," the housekeeper replied. "You might say the chatelaine was a connoisseur of crime… a devotee of the complexities of the femme fatale." She stopped outside a door with a plaque engraved with the name, Nannie Doss, and fished a ring of keys from her pocket. As she unlocked the door, she continued, "This is your bedchamber, the Nannie Doss room."

Maintaining her inquisitiveness, Turquoise asked who Nannie Doss was. The name did not ring any bells for her.

Jambalaya Jetson opened the black paneled door and ushered Turquoise into the musty-smelling bedroom. She pointed to a large portrait above the fireplace depicting a heavyset, grandmotherly woman in her late fifties, curly-haired and bespectacled by a pair of horn-rimmed glasses.

"Nannie Doss, who was affectionately nicknamed the 'Giggling Granny' by the press, confessed to murdering four of her five husbands, two of her children, her two sisters, her mother, her grandmother, and one of her mothers-in-law."

"That's quite an impressive track record," Turquoise remarked, gazing up at the oil painting in its baroque frame. "How did she do them in?"

"Stewed prunes spiked with rat poison was her specialty," the housekeeper replied. "She was quite the culinarian. The autopsy of her fifth husband revealed he had enough arsenic in his system to kill twenty men."

Turquoise's face betrayed only a slight hint of astonishment with the widening of her eyes. She placed her overnight satchel on the squeaky bed and observed a diminutive puff of dust rise up from the moth-eaten comforter. "So, why did they call her the Giggling Granny?"

"Nannie couldn't control her giggling when the police arrested her. She giggled when they interrogated her, and she giggled when they shipped her off to prison."

Turquoise's eyes returned to the painting of the murderess. "Well, they *do* say a good sense of humor contributes to one's psychological well-being."

"The reading of the will is at two o'clock. It'll be in the drawing room, where Miss Uvula's body is laid out," Jambalaya Jetson announced as she departed from the Nannie Doss room. Before shutting the door behind her, she paused to stroke her crocodile tooth and then flashed Turquoise a mocking grin of pearly teeth that were startling white, contrasted against her ebony face.

Turquoise headed to the en suite to freshen herself up; however, no sooner had she stepped foot inside the bathroom, it suddenly dawned on her that she forgot to ask the housekeeper for directions to the drawing room. In a place as sprawling as the Chateau Catatonia, one could easily wander about for hours, lost, if unfamiliar with the layout of the house.

Turquoise rushed over to the door and opened it, hoping to catch Jambalaya Jetson before she disappeared to wherever it was that sardonic housekeepers disappeared to after showing guests to their malodorous and killer-commemorating accommodations. However, the Nigerian domestic and her crocodile tooth were nowhere in sight, only the south end of a northbound Siamese cat scampering down the corridor.

Turquoise shut the door.

Haunted by the unsettling sensation of being watched, she looked around the room and then gazed up at the portrait of Nannie Doss. The eyes in the painting seemed to be following her. Turquoise shook her head. *It was just my imagination running away with me,* she told herself. She suddenly heard her Grandfather Fukowee's voice inside her head, telling her, "There you go again, *imaginating* things."

Turquoise was all of twelve years old when she first heard those all-too-familiar words uttered from her grandfather's lips…

"But it's true, Grandfather," young Turquoise insisted. "I really did see the sacred White Buffalo

Woman coming out of Lewinsky's Dress Shop on Main Street. She was wearing a shining white buckskin dress, decorated with rainbow-colored porcupine quills. She was carrying a bundle on her back, and in her hand was a fan of fragrant sage leaves. She had the most beautiful face I had ever seen, and when she smiled at me, her eyes glowed. She then walked off into the fiery ball of the setting sun and turned into a white buffalo. And then she disappeared."

Grandfather Fukowee shook his head. "You *imaginating* things, Granddaughter."

"No I'm not! And the correct word is imagining."

"Correct word is *imaginating*. They not teach you anything at that Rattlesnake Road Elementary School?"

Lightning flashed outside the window of the Nannie Doss room. It was followed, moments later, by a crash of thunder that rattled the panes. As if in response to Mother Nature's fury, the unexpected sound of a woman giggling crept into Turquoise's ears.

"I know I'm not *imaginating* anything this time!" Turquoise said out loud.

All at once, a weird and inexplicable urge to chop wood and check on the boathouse (despite the chateau not having one) came over Turquoise. Ignoring it, and turning a deaf ear to the irritating sound of the incessant giggling, she returned to the en suite to freshen up. Switching on the light, her eyes beheld a bubbling black goo of undetermined origin overflowing from the toilet bowl, green slime oozing from the walls like mucous from a draining nose, and the salmon-colored face of a voyeuristic, spectral pig peering in at her from outside the bathroom window.

Thoroughly disgusted, Turquoise turned to exit the en suite.

Without warning, a plague of houseflies materialized from out of nowhere and descended upon Turquoise, the buzzing of their wings commingling with the giggling that continued to emanate from some unknown source within the bedroom, creating a two-part harmony of cacophony most inharmonious.

Thrashing her arms about in an effort to keep the swarming flies at bay, Turquoise bolted from the Nannie Doss room, slamming the door behind her.

"I'd hate to see this place's *TripAdvisor* reviews," she mumbled to herself.

Taking Turquoise by surprise, a young boy, appearing to be around six years of age, pedaled past her on a Big Wheel tricycle at a prodigious rate of speed, his shaggy pageboy hairdo dancing wildly in the slipstream behind him. He rudely wiggled one of his index fingers at her as the left rear fat-wheel ran over the toes of her right foot.

"Owww!" Turquoise howled with pain as she grabbed her foot to massage it. "Watch where you're going, you little shit!"

Without stopping or slowing down, the juvenile speed demon continued racing down the corridor, disappearing around the corner.

Turquoise hobbled her way down the dizzying passageway, past the profusion of black paneled doors with their plaques of deadly damsels, and down the creaking stairs to the foyer, where she spotted a rather elegantly dressed man with a handsome pallor.

"Excuse me, sir!" Turquoise called out to the dapper stranger. "Could you tell me how to get to the drawing room?"

Without speaking a single word, the man motioned with his hand for Turquoise to follow him, which she did. He led her down a dimly lit hallway, blighted by the same wall-to-wall tawdriness as the one upstairs, past the chateau's kitchen, formal dining room and its adjoining vomitorium, until they came upon a pair of intricately carved pocket doors where the hallway terminated. Remaining silent as a catacomb, he pointed to the doors and gave Turquoise a slow and single nod with his head.

Turquoise slid the doors open to reveal a massive paneled room with high ceilings, towering mahogany shelves crammed with moldering books, and a wrought iron spiral staircase winding its way upward to a door, presumably leading to the attic. She turned to thank the man, but to her surprise, there was no trace of him, only the pungent aroma of cat food. It was as if he had simply vanished into thin air.

Part Two
Ten Little Indians

A cold chill did a little tap dance routine along her spine. Turquoise shrugged it off and then proceeded into the drawing room, which was loaded with a number of relatives, many of whom Turquoise had not seen since she was a child. She glanced around to see who all had come.

There was neurotic cousin Wenonah Winnebago, a lazy-eyed spinster afflicted with unceasingly trembling hands and an unnatural and debilitating fear of falling space junk. She sat on one of the many folding chairs that had been set up throughout the room, nervously glancing up at the ceiling and periodically breathing into a paper bag as a curative measure against anxiety-induced hyperventilation.

Seated next to Wenonah, and casually flipping through the pages of *Totems and Scrotums Magazine*, was gangly cousin Silent Wind from Santa Fe. Like his father, Breaking Wind, who had recently passed, he was a man of very few words and prided himself on his reputation for being silent, but deadly. Glancing up from his informative reading material, his eyes met Turquoise's and he nodded his head to acknowledge her.

Cousin Chappaquiddick, the idiot savant of the Moonwolf Clan, wandered aimlessly about, smoking the wrong end of an unlit cigarette and showing off his prized collection of yellow gallstones in a glass mayonnaise jar to anyone who would feign interest. At the age of seven, during a canoe trip along the Pecos River, he had acquired an unusual affinity for cryptozoology after a particularly strenuous evacuation of his bowels severed an artery on his frontal and temporal lobes.

Sashaying across the room, with a silver fright wig sitting on his head and a camcorder clutched in his bony hands, was cousin, Randy Warpath—Chupacabra's very own eccentric and deeply superficial pop artist, revered by dozens for his semi-pornographic, underground art films, complete with plotless plots, themeless themes, and non-acting actors.

"Oh. Hi, Turquoise," he said, impassively, a look of boredom on his unsmiling face. "Wouldn't it be glamorous to be reincarnated as a big diamond ring on Elizabeth Taylor's finger? You really should let me film you some time." Before Turquoise could reply, Randy Warpath sashayed away.

Glaring at him from across the room was Uncle Squatting Dog, a no-nonsense former Marine Corps officer from Comanche County, Oklahoma, with bulging biceps and a buzz cut. His right forearm bore a tattoo of a rabid bulldog foaming at the mouth, and his passions included binge-watching reruns of *Gomer Pyle, U.S.M.C.*, stockpiling M1 carbines, and biting off the heads of live snakes and chickens.

Sitting next to Squatting Dog was his androgynous, half-breed wife, Sioux-Ellen Ocala. An amateur blood-splatter expert with a face resembling her husband's bulldog tattoo, she possessed an antisocial personality disorder, which she claimed aided her in the pursuit of her hobby.

In the far corner of the room, next to a white floral wreath on a metal stand, was a partially open, black steel casket containing the body of Uvula Mae Moonwolf. It rested upon a wooden casket bier with intricately carved posts and four swivel casters, and atop the closed half of its lid, a semi-cross-eyed Siamese cat called Mister Nips sat, keeping a silent vigil.

The only feline of the mansion distinguished by a name, he wore around his neck a rhinestone-encrusted collar of purple leather from which hung a carved crocodile tooth, identical to the one worn by Jambalaya Jetson, but on a smaller scale. His tail swished from side to side.

Turquoise felt the stare of her relatives' eyes upon her while she made her way over to the casket to pay her respects to her dearly departed aunt. It made her rather uncomfortable, yet she managed to ignore it. Peering down at the face in the casket, she was stunned to find its flesh to be void of any noticeable wrinkles or other signs of aging. As she studied the face of the elderly woman, who curiously didn't look to be much older than Turquoise herself, she wondered if her aunt's secret to ageless beauty was massive injections of industrial-strength Botox or merely a pound or two of postmortem makeup. *Hmmm. Does she or doesn't she?* Turquoise pondered. *I guess only her mortuary cosmetologist knows for sure.* Her great aunt's evil deed suddenly popped into her head. Mental images of human body parts chopped into little pieces and extruded through a meat grinder to make cat food materialized in the periphery of her mind, saturating her with a mélange of morbid fascination and queasiness. *It must have been a gruesome sight to see.* She couldn't help but to wonder if insanity ran in her family.

Just then, something moving behind the casket caught Turquoise's attention. Craning her neck to get a better look, she was caught off guard by the lurid sight of hypersexual Uncle Hawk Nose and his promiscuous collector of social diseases, Auntie Rosebud, rolling around on the floor, making out like teenagers in heat. Turquoise wrinkled up her nose upon observing the old man's dental bridge fall out of his mouth as he and his wife grunted, gyrated and entwined their flicking tongues. This was the first time Turquoise had seen the elderly couple since their relocation to a swingers' retirement community in the Florida Keys, and their exhibition of carnal tomfoolery was something she quickly tried to erase from her memory.

Turquoise heard a familiar voice calling out her name. It was her cousin Dolores Angry Cloud. She was dressed in a studded, black leather punk outfit, and her multi-colored spiked Mohawk was comparable in appearance to a stegosaurus on an LSD trip. She motioned for Turquoise to sit next to her.

"Doesn't it strike you rather odd that ten of us were invited to the reading of this will?" Dolores Angry Cloud whispered into Turquoise's ear. "Think about it, Turquoise. This could turn out being like that Agatha Christie novel where ten assholes get murdered, one by one, in all kinds of weird ways." Her eyes sparkled. "Wouldn't that be sweet?"

Turquoise took a quick head count of everyone in the room, with the exception of Great Aunt Uvula, of course. There was, indeed, an assembly of ten. But before Turquoise could respond to her cousin, an antique clock on the fireplace mantel chimed two o'clock. Uncle Hawk Nose and Auntie Rosebud emerged from behind the casket, and Mister Pannowahoo, the estate lawyer, entered the room, wearing a pinstriped zoot suit. His face was unsmiling with primitive features like those of an ancient Olmec sculpture. His eyes scanned the room as he took his own head count to ensure that everyone was present.

"Before I commence with the reading of the will of the late Miss Uvula Moonwolf, would any of the relative care to say anything?"

As he spoke, the juxtaposition of his upper teeth, which sparkled like pearly-white mosaics, and his misaligned lower ones, which were brown and not unlike miniature facsimiles of tombstones in a haunted graveyard, became alarmingly apparent to all who were present.

Cousin Chappaquiddick eagerly raised his hand like a child in a classroom. "Ooh! Ooh! Yes, I would like to say a word. And that word is…

helminthophilia. It means, of course, an unnatural attraction to being infested with worms."

The room went as quiet as a stone, and all eyes, including Turquoise's baby blues, stared in wonder at cousin Chappaquiddick. A large vein jutted out from the forehead of Uncle Squatting Dog and began to throb as he clenched his teeth. A muffled giggle floated out of the mouth of Dolores Angry Cloud. Uncle Hawk Nose shook his head in disgust.

The lawyer cleared his throat. "Yes, well, uh… does anyone have anything else to add before I proceed with the business at hand?"

Dolores Angry Cloud rose from her seat. "I don't know about the rest of you guys, but I think the old broad in the box deserves more respect than just a lousy word about worms. After all, she was a great lady. She truly was. And what made Great Aunt Uvula so great was the fact that she single-handedly converted a fully-grown man into one hundred and eighty pounds of cat food, *and* got away with it! If only we all could aspire to such greatness!"

The room shook with thunderous applause, and Dolores Angry Cloud smiled and took a bow like an actress on the stage. Turquoise fought to hold back her laughter with every ounce of strength she possessed.

"That was a lovely eulogy, dear," Auntie Rosebud sniffled, dabbing away her tears with a tissue. "I only hope that when my time comes to meet the Great Spirit in the sky, someone will eulogize me in as touching a manner."

Ever the provocateur, Dolores Angry Cloud chortled. "I'm glad you liked it, auntie. Here's a little something touching you can have chiseled on your gravestone as an epitaph: Here lies Rosebud, cold and dead. Amazingly, her legs aren't spread!"

Turquoise's eyes bugged out in disbelief upon hearing her cousin's words. "Dolores!"

Auntie Rosebud let out a gasp as she threw her head back. "Well! I never!"

"Oh, give us a break," Dolores Angry Cloud sassed as she casually inspected her long, black fingernails with the tips sharpened and painted red to simulate dripping blood. "We all know you do… every single chance that eager beaver of yours gets!"

"That was uncalled for, Dolores!" Uncle Hawk Nose shouted, pounding the arms of his chair with his fists. "Apologize to your aunt, immediately!"

"Apologize for what? For having the balls to say out loud what everyone else already knows?" Dolores Angry Cloud hooted with cruel laughter. "We all know her legs spread faster than peanut butter on a slice of bread."

"Why, you jealous little viper!" Auntie Rosebud cried out. She pointed her right index finger at her ill-natured niece and angrily waved it about in the air. "I didn't make the journey all the way back here to New Mexico to be verbally abused by this… this… *sociopathic muff-diver!*"

"You say that like it's a bad thing," the punk rocker said in mock offense.

Auntie Rosebud abruptly yanked up her leopard-print blouse, exposing her braless breasts to everyone in the room. "Look at these tits! Just look at these tits!" she caterwauled madly. "Not one stretch mark! My mental health care provider told me I have the breasts of a twenty-year-old!"

Wenonah Winnebago let out a horrified scream of, "That's indecent!" and covered her eyes with her shaking hands.

Silent Wind was unable to maintain his silence any longer. "Great Titicaca!" he exclaimed, his eyes bugging out in amazement. He immediately began snapping pictures of the mammoth mammaries with his Instamatic camera.

"How glamorous," Randy Warpath stated with lethargic sarcasm, his nose turned up in disgust. "I'm sure Liz Taylor would be in awe."

"Who the hell gives a flying fuck about Liz Taylor?" Uncle Squatting Dog lashed out in his distinguishable Oklahoma accent. "Maybe if you weren't such a swish, Randy Warpath, you'd appreciate the beauty of the female breast instead of spending all your time filming the crab-infested crotches of those male hustlers you pick up on the streets!"

"Oh my, such masculine aggression," Randy Warpath remarked. "Self-loathing homosexuals are so tragic, don't you think? All that angry denial and repression of same-sex erotic desires must give you high blood pressure."

Uncle Squatting Dog leaped from his chair and assumed a fighting stance. "Are you calling me an Okla-homo? Back in my day, boy, I'd swab the deck with a sperm gargling limp-wrist like you and use your guts for fertilizer! If you were my son, I'd club you like a baby seal so hard that words describing the impact would appear out of thin air!"

Aunt Sioux-Ellen grabbed her husband by the wrist. "Squatting Dog, calm down. Remember your high blood pressure!"

"That… that bathhouse Bathsheba is a disgrace to all men with hair on their gonads!" Uncle Squatting Dog yelled to his wife as additional veins pulsated on his forehead.

Aunt Sioux-Ellen comfortingly patted the back of Squatting Dog's hand with her palm. "Not only a disgrace, dear, but a pervert and a menace to society. Ugh! Did you notice he's wearing face powder? *Face powder*, for God's sake! I always knew he'd turn out to be a transvestite. I even told his mother; but no, she wouldn't listen to me or take my advice to send him to a psychiatrist when he was a child. He exhibited unnatural tendencies even then."

"Thirteen weeks of boot camp, plus my fist, would knock that fairy dust right off his face!" Uncle Squatting Dog declared loudly, waving a clenched fist in Randy Warpath's direction as a threatening gesture.

Turquoise turned to Dolores Angry Cloud and, in a whisper, mockingly scolded her. "See the trouble you and your epitaph started, Dolores? All hell has broken loose now!"

Dolores Angry Cloud beamed with pride. "I know. Isn't it great!"

Turquoise shook her head and then spoke to her aunt. "Aunt Sioux-Ellen," she began, "I really think you and Uncle Squatting Dog are over-reacting. I mean, Randy's always been a little bit different. But, come on, just because he wears a silver wig and face powder doesn't make him a transvestite or a pervert or a menace to society. He's an artiste."

Aunt Sioux-Ellen shook her head in dissension. "An 'artiste?' Oh, for God's sake, don't be so naïve, Turquoise! Transvestites are mentally ill people with abnormal sexual urges and deviant behaviors. I'm well informed, young lady; I've read all about sick individuals like him in a 1948 study conducted by world-renowned sexologist, M. Bolism. These degenerates dress in women's clothing to give themselves *erections* and then they sell their bodies on street corners at night to other degenerates!"

"Filthy freaks!" Uncle Squatting Dog barked out, his face contorted in disgust, and his anger-filled eyes glued to his silver-wigged nephew. "They should all be impaled on wooden stakes!"

Aunt Sioux-Ellen gave Turquoise one of her know-it-all smiles. "Trust me, Turquoise, people like your cousin, Randy, have diseased minds and need to be locked up in mental hospitals for their own good, and for the safety of our children!"

A shocked look grabbed hold of Turquoise's face. "The safety of our children? Are you serious? It's blowing my mind how judgmental and unenlightened you really are. Randy isn't a danger to children. But, what *is* dangerous, Aunt Sioux-Ellen, is your narrow-minded, homophobic, archaic way of thinking!"

"I suggest you keep out of this, Turquoise," Aunt Sioux-Ellen snapped, her smile turning into a rictus of revulsion, and then freezing into a gremlin's glare. "You're just as bad as your pervert cousin, working at that disgusting sex shop teepee your half-baked grandparents own."

Turquoise laughed "Oh, you mean 'that disgusting sex shop teepee' where Uncle Squatting Dog bought his inflatable mulatto love doll with the hermaphrodite sex organs and battery-operated, remote control deep throat?"

Aunt Sioux-Ellen gasped. "Liar! I don't believe one word of it! This is just another one of your radical leftist vowel movements." She quickly turned and looked at her husband, who was staring at his shoes in grim silence.

Dolores Angry Cloud cracked an impish smile. "It's the truth, auntie. I was helping out in the shop that day when your husband came in and bought it. I'm sure the credit card transaction is still on file if you'd like to come down to the Squealing Squaw and see it for yourself."

Aunt Sioux-Ellen cocked her head back in defiance. "I don't believe you any more than I believe Turquoise. You and your cousin speak with forked tongues. But if it's true that your uncle bought such a thing, I can assure you, Dolores, that he only bought it for target practice!"

"This is just a little Peyton Place and you're all Chupacabra hypocrites!" Turquoise shouted.

With his nerves reaching a boiling point, Mister Pannowahoo pounded his fist upon the top of the desk like a judge's gavel, and a stone cold silence immediately fell upon the room. The nettled lawyer loudly cleared his throat several times as his eyes blazed with vexation. "I'm sure this astonishing display of family affection is an endless source of fascination to some; however, if no one has any objections, I would like to proceed—uninterrupted—with the reading of this will." He paused to glance around the room. Satisfied that he had everyone's attention, he began to read the will out loud: "I, Uvula Mae Moonwolf, being of sound body and mind, despite any and all rumors to the contrary, do hereby declare that this document is my last will and testament. In executing such document, I hereby declare that: One... I revoke all wills and codicils that I have previously made. Two... I am not currently married. I have no children now living, nor have I any deceased children who died and left issue. Three... I leave my entire estate to my beloved and faithful companion, Mister Nips."

Turquoise could scarcely believe what she just heard! As she watched her cousin, Randy Warpath, panning the room with his camcorder to capture the dumbfounded expressions on the relatives' faces, she pondered why she and the others had been asked to attend the reading of the will if her great aunt had left all of them out of it.

Irate, Uncle Squatting Dog squirmed in his seat and barked like a dog.

"Surely, you can't be serious!" Uncle Hawk Nose said to the lawyer. "She left the house, the money—everything—to one of her *cats*?"

Mister Pannowahoo nodded his head, and in his best Leslie Nielsen voice, replied, "I am serious, and don't call me Shirley."

To the astonishment of all—except for Turquoise—Dolores Angry Cloud burst into a fit of loud and uncontrollable cackling laughter. Turquoise instinctively knew that her punk rocker cousin would find great amusement in the absurdity of the situation. Turquoise would have been shocked if she hadn't.

The lid of Auntie Rosebud's left eye began to flutter, and Randy Warpath instantly zoomed in on it with his camera. "I've never heard of anything more preposterous in all my days!" she declared.

"The old woman was obviously off the reservation!" A disgruntled Aunt Sioux-Ellen bitterly remarked as she lifted her buttocks from the seat of her chair and stood up. "I always suspected she was one feather short of an eagle, if you catch my drift. But don't think for one moment, Mister Pannowahoo, that I won't have this cockamamie will contested!" She turned to her husband. "I've never been so humiliated. Come, Squatting Dog. We're leaving… now!"

"Everybody, please calm down!" Mister Pannowahoo shouted. "The will goes on to say that hidden somewhere within Chateau Catatonia is the Maltese Moccasin—a centuries-old, ceremonial moccasin encrusted with red garnets, amethysts, emeralds and blue sapphires. Each one of you will have twenty-four hours from the reading of this will, to search the mansion and grounds for this priceless treasure, and whoever finds the moccasin first shall become the sole heir to it." He chuckled. "*Sole.* Get it?" Clearing his throat again, he re-established his exterior of seriousness. "The rest of you will go home with *nihil*, which is Latin for nothing."

"How do we know there really *is* a Maltese Moccasin?" Uncle Hawk Nose asked, his voice oozing with suspicion. "If you ask me, I think it's a big hoax—something to send us all on a wild goose chase. It would be just like Uvula to cook up something crazy like that. She always did like getting the last laugh!"

Mesmerized by his jar of gallstones, Cousin Chappaquiddick began shaking it like a maraca, and appeared to be quite taken by the rattling sound it produced. "Dog food lid spelled backward is dildo of God!" he exclaimed, a smile beaming across his face. He was obviously quite proud of his ingenuity.

Wenonah Winnebago spoke in a louder-than-normal tone of voice in an effort to be heard above the noisy rattling of her cousin's newly invented rhythm instrument. "A hoax is the last thing we should be worried about! What if the moccasin has a curse on it? I've read about things like that in *National Geographic* while defecating, and they *always* have a curse on them!"

"Curse or no curse, *I'm* gonna be the one who finds that moccasin!" Dolores Angry Cloud loudly declared with arrogant confidence. "And after I get rich selling it, I'm moving to the West Coast and building a rotating, fifty-thousand seat, clitoris-shaped amphitheatre, The Clitorium, for my lesbian punk rock band, Dystopian Cesspool, to perform at!" She flashed her middle finger at everyone in the drawing room and then sneered.

"Ugh! Do I detect a carpet-muncher in this room?" Aunt Sioux-Ellen mockingly asked, her voice laden with revulsion. She gave Dolores Angry Cloud one of her proverbial looks-that-could-kill looks.

"A carpet-muncher?" Jambalaya Jetson cried in a fit of pique. "I'll have you know that I vacuumed in here this morning!" She raised her nose in the air in an aristocratic manner and turned away as if to dismiss the scowling woman.

"What happens after twenty-four hours if no one finds the Maltese Moccasin?" Turquoise asked the lawyer.

Mister Pannowahoo removed his eyeglasses and looked Turquoise in her turquoise-blue eyes. "According to your great aunt's will, if none of the ten potential heirs succeed in locating the moccasin within the allotted period of time, it shall be bequeathed to Mister Nips, the Siamese cat."

"I hate cats! They're evil little creatures!" Wenonah Winnebago blurted out. She shifted her gaze to Mister Nips, who was busy giving himself a tongue bath on top of his late mistress' casket. "Every time a cat licks its anus, it summons the devil!"

With a heart-stopping crackle and a deafening boom, a massive bolt of lightning zigzagged its way down from the heavens, scoring a direct hit on the old chemical plant across the street from Chateau Catatonia. A massive explosion ensued, sending debris hurtling through the air. The blast shook the walls of the mansion for several seconds, startling Turquoise and the others. They gasped, simultaneously, as the windowpanes rattled and the light bulbs in the crystal chandeliers flickered. The fur on the cat's back bristled, and he leapt from the casket and scampered from the room. Above the fireplace, a large, commissioned oil painting of Mister Nips trembled before going askew.

Like a herd of panicked bison, the Moonwolf Clan, along with Mister Pannowahoo and Jambalaya Jetson, stampeded over to one of the drawing room's arched, leaded glass windows looking out onto the chateau's magnificent view of the blazing chemical plant.

"Shango, the great god of thunder and lightning, has been angered," Jambalaya Jetson announced with fearfulness in her voice. "This is not a good sign. I can smell death and destruction in the offing!" She turned and fled from the room.

"The only thing I can smell is the sweet aroma of a lawsuit," commented Mister Pannowahoo, his words, like little gifts to himself, wrapped in blissful bows of germ-carrying American currency. A hint of a litigation-induced smile brought a serene glow to his normally solemn face as he reached into his pants pocket to retrieve his cell phone. "If you'll all excuse me, I need to phone in to my law firm and consult with my partner."

He let out a little grunting sound in response to his phone's inability to pick up a signal. He then trudged over to an antique mahogany desk in front of the other window, upon which sat a relic of a black rotary telephone, and attempted to place his call the old-fashioned way.

"Damn it!" he yelled to no one in particular, slamming the Bakelite handset of the phone into its cradle with disgust. "The phone is dead." He then embarked on a mission to grumble about "good-for-nothing technology" while continuously clicking the two black plungers in the phone's cradle in a fruitless attempt to procure a dial tone.

Squeezing between Dolores Angry Cloud and Wenonah Winnebago to get a better view from the window, Turquoise spied an odd and somewhat disconcerting sight: A longhaired man of advanced years—his shamelessly unclad body spasmodically jerking in an unnatural manner—was silently ascending the scrub-covered hill and drawing nearer to the chateau. Creeping slowly like a spider up a wall, he appeared to be in a daze.

Part Three
Naked Lunch

"Holy jizzin' Geronimo!" Turquoise interjected. Her lower jaw dropped slightly "Unless my eyes are deceiving me, there's an old guy wandering around out there with no clothes on!" She pointed to the elderly exhibitionist. "He's coming this way!"

Speaking in her best Boris Karloff voice, Dolores Angry Cloud intoned, "They're coming to get you, Turquoise. They're coming for you. Look, here comes one of them now!" Her words were followed by a deep, maniacal laugh.

With the reflections of the flames flickering in her dread-laden eyes, Wenonah Winnebago's body began to judder as she rapidly plummeted into anxietude. "This is no time for buffoonery!" she wailed. "What's the matter with you, Dolores? And the same goes for the rest of you! Don't you all realize that every single person in this house could be in mortal danger? My God, a chemical plant just blew up across the street, and here we are, just standing here watching it burn like it's some sort of Irwin Allen disaster film! That man could be injured! I'm surprised none of you are popping any popcorn! I really think we need to evacuate!"

Fed up with her cousin's high-strung ranting, Dolores Angry Cloud scowled. "I don't give a rat's asshole what you really think, Wenonah! No one's stopping you from evacuating if that's what you want to do. But don't go giving me orders, wacko! I'm not leaving this house without that Maltese Moccasin!"

Wenonah Winnebago cowered in response.

Another rumble of thunder shook the chateau. It was followed by the sounds of glass breaking and blood-curdling screams as a geriatric hippie, reeking of patchouli and chemical acridity, smashed through the other window of the drawing room. He wore nothing but a *Don't Trust Anyone Under 60* pendant around his neck and a hungry look on his ashen face. Mutated by the chemical fallout that had rained down upon the nudist colony, his eyes gave off a mysterious greenish glow, and his mouth dripped with disgusting foaming drool.

"Tune in! Turn on! Eat brains!" he cried out.

"Crispy Christ on a cross-shaped cracker!" Turquoise screamed, a look of terror dawning like the Age of Aquarius on her face.

The hippie grabbed Mister Pannowahoo, and sunk his dingy teeth into his throat, tearing out a substantial chunk of flesh. From the gaping wound, blood sprayed up into the air like a geyser of gore. He then ripped open the crotch of the lawyer's gabardine trousers and proceeded to cannibalize his defenseless genitalia, instantly rendering him a neuter prosecutor.

Stunned and unable to accept what her eyes were showing her, Turquoise froze for a moment, unsure how to react. *This surely has to be a bad dream*, she thought, trying to make sense of the absurd situation. *It's too ghastly to be for real!*

"Draft-dodging, commie, pinko creep!" Uncle Squatting Dog boomed as he and Silent Wind sprang into action and grappled to pull the voracious hippie from the profusely bleeding legal eagle. Slamming his fists into the nightmarish non-conformist with delight, the former Marine Corps officer echoed the words of General George Patton while he engaged in combat. "Perfect discipline! Calculated risks! A pint of sweat! Real Americans love the sting of battle!"

"God bless America! I think I might have a hand grenade in my handbag!" Aunt Sioux-Ellen shouted to her husband, while frantically rummaging through the considerable contents of her camo print purse.

"When you launch a grenade, you launch a dream!" Uncle Squatting Dog responded in between grunts as he and Silent Wind wrestled the longhaired assailant to the floor. Turquoise snapped out of her state of shock. She grabbed the toppled desk chair from the floor and began bashing it against the head of the flesh-eating hippie; while Dolores Angry Cloud repeatedly kicked his gyrating genital with her twenty-eyelet Doc Martens leather boots, shouting, "Anarchy rules!"

"Oh, you're all going to be famous for fifteen minutes," said Randy Warpath, phlegmatically, as he stood on a chair and filmed the carnage and pandemonium. "Maybe even sixteen."

Minutes later, the battered geezer lay lifeless on the floor, alongside the partially devoured Rudy Pannowahoo, who was, by all accounts, in an equally deceased state. Like a monstrous menstruation, a foul-smelling, foamy substance discharged from the hippie's gaping mouth, staining the carpet an inky black.

Uncle Squatting Dog wiped the sweat from his brow. His eyes twinkled with patriotism, and his chest puffed up like a rooster. "Feel the exhilaration of victory!" he crowed, still channeling his war-mongering hero.

For good measure, Dolores Angry Cloud gave the dead hippie's penis one final kick, forceful enough to detach it from the sagging, twitching torso from which it had protruded, and send it flying across the room. The dismembered member landed at Wenonah Winnebago's feet, where it oozed onto her orthopedic shoes a yellowish, sap-like substance from both of its ends.

With her neuroses rising, Wenonah Winnebago leapt through the broken window, shrieking like a reamed banshee. The moment her feet hit the ground, she took off running across the grounds of the estate like an anabolic steroid-injected racehorse bolting from its starting gate. Halfway to the tall iron gates at the end of the flagstone path, there came a loud crackling sound from the sky, and Wenonah Winnebago was fatally flattened into a great gooey mess by a falling Chinese space station that scored a direct hit upon her.

The aftermath of the impact was not a pretty sight, and Turquoise turned her face away from the broken window, her stomach threatening to hurl. "She's dead! Squashed like an insect under the heel of a shoe! My God, what a horrible way to die!"

"Yeah, well, good riddance to her," responded Dolores Angry Cloud, craning her neck to get a better look at the gore. "She was more annoying than a garden gnome wedged up the ass. Hey, Turquoise, you *gotta* take a look at *this* shit!"

With a copiousness of reluctance, Turquoise once again looked out the window and her eyes encountered the nightmarish and sickening sight of nearly one-dozen old hippie men and women—all garbed in nakedness—gathered around the smoldering wreckage of the space station. To her ultimate horror, they were hungrily feasting upon the still-warm remains of Wenonah Winnebago. Some were even fighting over pieces of her anatomy like wild animals fighting over a scrap of raw meat.

"Oh my God!" Turquoise exclaimed, the gorge rising in her throat. "They're eating our cousin, Wenonah! Or, should I say, what's left of her!"

Dolores Angry Cloud groaned as the rest of the relatives flocked to the window to view the horrendous sight. "Fucked-up hippies and their fucking flower children. I always said those crab-infested motherfuckers would eat anything, including raw sewage! This proves it!"

Once again, the sound of breaking glass filled the room as a naked woman sporting a rainbow-colored Afro smashed through the other window.

With her nipples spraying out streams of corrosive yellow venom, she grabbed hold of Auntie Rosebud's bare breasts and attempted to gnaw on them.

Clutched by terror, Auntie Rosebud opened her mouth and emitted a horrified shriek that could only be described as the mating call of a hyena in heat and an air-raid siren. It wreaked havoc on the eardrums of everyone in the room and shattered a Waterford crystal vase on the mantel of the fireplace.

Turquoise gasped in horror. Uncle Hawk Nose rushed to his wife's aid, and cried out, "Sweet Jesus! Not the breasts! No! No! Those puppies set me back thirty-seven hundred dollars!"

"I'll save you, Auntie Rosebud!" Cousin Chappaquiddick cried out as he courageously dashed across the room to help Uncle Hawk Nose disengage the breast-munching mutant. "Take that!" he yelled as he bashed in the back of the head of the crazed cannibal with his mayonnaise jar of prized gallstones.

Blood sprayed his face, blinding his eyes. And then, from the yawning wound, burst a scaly, snakelike creature that wasted no time in coiling itself around the neck of the idiot savant like a boa constrictor from hell. He desperately gasped for a breath of air and flailed his arms, and then he was dead. The hippie released her grip on Auntie Rosebud and began feasting on Cousin Chappaquiddick's freshly dead carcass.

Breaking out in a cold sweat, Auntie Rosebud clutched her chest. The color drained from her face and she gasped, "My... heart..." before crashing to the floor like an Acme safe in an old *Roadrunner* cartoon.

"Rosebud! Rosebud!" cried Uncle Hawk Nose, as he scrambled to check his wife's wrist for a pulse. His face grew grim. He then pressed his ear against her chest to listen for a heartbeat. "The Great Spirit has taken her from me!" Tears welled up in his eyes and he broke into a fit of sobbing. "My Rosebud is dead, and I haven't even installed the new sex trapeze yet. I'll have to become a necrophiliac now!"

Uncle Squatting Dog and Silent Wind pounced on the feeding hippie and began striking her with their fists. They were both ultimately sprayed in the face by her poisonous nipple jets and instantly rendered sightless. They released their grip on the woman and cried out from the searing pain. With their eyeballs burning as if scorched by the fires of hell, they writhed about on the floor, clutching their eyes, and terrified by their sudden blindness.

A naked hippie with a navel-length tangle of a gray beard and braided hair down to his peace sign-tattooed derriere burst through the window and sunk his teeth into Aunt Sioux-Ellen, who was still scouring through her purse in search of her hand grenade.

"Subversive degenerate!" she screamed as her ravenous attacker tore bloody chunks of flesh from her face and throat, gobbling them with gusto, before dragging her outside where a mob of mutants tore her limb from limb and cannibalized her.

Uncle Hawk Nose was the next victim claimed by the rainbow-haired grotesquerie.

Turquoise made a beeline to the pocket doors, followed by Dolores Angry Cloud and Randy Warpath, still filming the gruesome action. She slid the doors open, only to discover that the hallway was swarming with a horde of salivating disciples of Timothy Leary, on the hunt for human meat to satisfy their hunger.

"We're trapped!" cried Turquoise as she slammed the doors shut on the charging creeps. More of them were now pouring into the drawing room through the broken windows. "What are we going to do?"

"Quick! Up the spiral staircase!" Dolores shouted. "There's a door at the top. It's our only chance to escape!"

As she ascended the winding iron steps with the greatest of haste, Turquoise glanced down and saw the drawing room was riddled with dozens of rampaging, man-eating hippie freaks, drooling and growling as they smashed apart the bourgeois furnishings and stripped the flesh from the bones of her relatives with their piercing incisors. She also noticed that Great Aunt Uvula's casket was void of a corpse.

A hungry pack of flesh-eating hippies had begun to climb the spiral staircase, their sights set on Turquoise and her two cousins. With each step they took, the overloaded staircase groaned and rocked from side to side, threatening to rip away from its anchors and collapse.

"Fasten your seatbelts," said Randy Warpath, mimicking Bette Davis' voice. "It's going to be a bumpy night!"

The three cousins kept a tight grip on the iron scrollwork hand railing as they continued their way up the pitching staircase. The top step brought them to a small metal platform, connecting the spiral staircase to the wall in which was an old batten door.

Turquoise turned the white porcelain knob to open it, but she found that it was locked. An expression of panic swept across the contours of her high-cheekboned face. "We're all going to die," she announced, her voice grim.

"Oh dear," Randy Warpath retorted; his pale face seemed to grow even paler. "This is all so terrible. Whatever are we going to do?"

Dolores Angry Cloud's eyes suddenly lit up. It was clear that an idea had popped into her head. "Turquoise, do you still have that copper IUD up your cooter?"

Bewilderment momentarily replaced the fear that Turquoise's eyes conveyed. She slowly nodded her head. "What? Are you kidding me? This is a fine time to discuss contraceptives, Dolores!"

"Your IUD is our only hope for survival!" Dolores Angry Cloud snapped. "Just reach up there, yank that goddamn thing out, and give it to me. Quickly!"

Turquoise looked horrified by her cousin's peculiar directive. "Are you out of your mind, Dolores? You want me to pull out my IUD? Right here? Right now?"

"Don't be a teratoma, Turquoise. Just do it!" the punk rocker commanded, an authoritative tone saturating her voice. "I need the wire from it to pick the lock on this door. Or would you rather be eaten alive? And I don't mean in a good way."

"Don't look," Turquoise told Randy Warpath, who appeared to be rather uncomfortable at the very thought of it.

He cringed and then looked away. "Oh honey, you couldn't pay me enough money to look."

Embarrassed, Turquoise pulled down her panties with reluctance and assumed a squatting position. She then reached up under her skirt and inserted the middle and index fingers of her right hand into her lady-bits, feeling around for the two dangling strings attached to her intrauterine device.

"Stimulate your cervix! It's the gateway to life!" shouted Dolores Angry Cloud, barking out her words like a crazed Lamaze coach. "Lubricate and dilate! Lubricate and dilate!"

"Oh dear God," Randy Warpath groaned, his eyes rolling up to the apex of their sockets until they resembled a pair of cue balls. In a dramatic voice, he bleated, "Death, take me now!"

"This is beyond mortification!" Turquoise grumbled as she navigated her fingers through her nether regions.

"Hurry up!" Dolores Angry Cloud ordered, impatiently. "And stop your bellyaching. It's giving me gas." She opened her mouth and expelled a loud belch to prove her point.

At last, Turquoise located the strings she had been searching for, and after a half-dozen gentle tugs, the IUD popped out like a genie long-corked in a bottle. She quickly handed it to her foot-tapping cousin, who was waiting with her palm up.

Wasting no time, Dolores Angry Cloud uncoiled the copper wire from the T-shaped birth control device, inserted a small length of it into the keyhole, and began jiggling it up and down. Her lips pulled into a grin at the sound of the first pin clicking inside the barrel.

The voracious hippies were now more than halfway up the staircase, their hands and faces stained with the still-warm juices of their unfortunate victims. Tiny bits of raw flesh were stuck between some of their teeth, and from their rancid, salivating mouths drifted the sickening metallic odor of blood, the sour stench of gallbladder bile and the muddy smell of viscera.

Undaunted by the rapidly approaching jaws of death, Dolores Angry Cloud continued to pick the lock with the copper wire. As Turquoise watched her work, she noticed beads of sweat were forming on her cousin's forehead and her hands were starting to tremor. She could feel her own adrenaline surging and her heart began beating like a jackhammer. A loud snarl made her turn her head with a quick jerk, and she saw the cannibals coming close to reaching the platform. Within a mere matter of seconds, she and her cousins would be turned into a three-course meal.

"Hurry up with that lock, MacGyver!" Randy Warpath urged.

With all the skill of a master burglar, Dolores Angry Cloud defeated the lock and threw open the door. She made a mad dash into the attic, immediately followed by Turquoise and Randy Warpath, who was quick to slam the door shut behind him and re-lock it before the nefarious non-conformists could gain entry.

No sooner had Turquoise breathed a sigh of relief, than an unexpected sight met her eyes. In the center of the cobwebbed room, standing on a stone pedestal engraved with strange sigils, was a life-size statue of a hideous crone. It seemed to be watching her, with its haggard face and its cruel smile. Its sunken eyes, like reservoirs of malevolence and decay, met her own and set sail an armada of chills along her spine.

Dolores Angry Cloud joined Turquoise in staring at the statue. "What the fuck is *that?*"

Turquoise shrugged. "I guess it's someone's idea of art."

"Well, it's an ugly piece of crap, whatever the hell it's supposed to be," the punk rocker replied, caustically. "I can see why it was hidden away up here in the attic! Get a load of the face on that thing. Man, that's pretty fucked up!"

There was something disturbingly familiar about the sculpture, and upon closer inspection, Turquoise realized that, beneath its layers of decrepitude, the statue's features bore an uncanny resemblance to the face of her Great Aunt Uvula.

"Like I've always said, one person's art is another person's human decomposition stain," Randy Warpath commented, nervously, while eyeing the rattling door, upon which the growling hippies were pounding and clawing in their fevered attempt to gain entry to the attic.

"How long do you suppose that door is going to keep those things from getting in here?" Turquoise asked.

Dolores Angry Cloud shook her head and shrugged her shoulders. "Your guess is as good as mine. But I suggest we don't waste any time finding something to barricade that door with. And after that, we seriously need to scrounge up some stuff that can be used as weapons in case those fuckers *do* manage to get in… pitchforks, ice picks, neck braces, anything. With all the junk that's up here, we should be able to find *something* useful. Also, look around for some empty glass jars and kerosene so we can make Molotov cocktails. I love making Molotov cocktails!"

Like an anxiety-fueled scavenger hunt, the rush to find improvised weapons commenced.

Turquoise discovered an old steamer trunk serving as a depository for Great Aunt Uvula's impressive collection of white enamel bedpans, and she armed herself with one of the vintage receptacles. She reckoned it could function as both a protective shield and as an instrument to bash in what was left of the acid-fried brains of the flesh-eating hippies.

To the shock of Turquoise and her cousins, a trap door on the floor suddenly popped open with a squeak and a bang. Their jaws dropped and their eyes bugged out in disbelief as a woman armed with an antique Winchester rifle emerged. It was Great Aunt Uvula. Her white lace burial attire had been replaced by a high-waisted pencil skirt into which was tucked a pink angora sweater, the fabric stretched to its limits by the cone-shaped cups of a 1950's-style bullet bra that protruded like nuclear warheads.

"Just who the hell are you people and what are you doing in my attic?" she asked, eyeing each of them with suspicion. "This area of the house is off-limits to everyone but me!"

"I'm Turquoise, granddaughter of Fukowee and Loona Moonwolf, and these are my cousins, Dolores Angry Cloud and Randy Warpath. We're your nieces and nephew," Turquoise explained. "We came to Chateau Catatonia for the reading of your will. A bolt of lightning struck the chemical plant, causing a huge explosion that somehow mutated the hippies at the nudist colony. They've turned into flesh-eating freaks, and the entire house is under siege! We've taken refuge from them here in the attic."

"They're right outside the door. You can hear them trying to claw their way in," Dolores Angry Cloud added, nodding in the direction of the attic door. "They've killed everyone in the drawing room and devoured their bodies. We're the only ones left alive."

Great Aunt Uvula seemed to be more interested in Turquoise's face than in what Dolores Angry Cloud had to say. A glint of ruefulness appeared in her eyes. "Turquoise. Turquoise Moonwolf. Yes, I should have known by those mystical, turquoise-colored eyes of yours. I only saw you once, and that was on the day you were born, just before they took you away from me. But I always felt in my heart that you would grow up to become a beautiful woman with an intrinsic warrior spirit, like me. I can tell just by looking at you that I was right."

Puzzled by the woman's odd remarks, Turquoise frowned in confusion and cocked her head to one side. "I'm afraid I don't understand, Aunt Uvula."

"I'm not your Aunt Uvula."

Turquoise's confusion doubled. "You aren't? Then who are you?"

"I'm your mother."

Those three little words launched a shockwave through Turquoise's body and sent her head spinning in much the same way as Grandfather Fukowee's home-brewed firewater did. Never in her life had she heard anything so shocking or riveting, except maybe for the time she found out that Monrovia Sterling—winner of the annual Miss Pregnant Chupacabra Beauty Contest and part-time sales clerk at the S&M Green Stamps redemption center—secretly possessed a two-foot long tail that curled at the end. But even that paled in comparison.

"I think the old bat's lost her mind," Dolores Angry Cloud whispered into Turquoise's ear. "Death can do that to some people, you know."

Turquoise was flabbergasted and not quite sure what to make of the disorienting revelation. "My mother? But that can't be. My mother was Bald Beaver, wife of Mad Cow. My grandparents told me they both died in a freak uphill skiing accident in Los Alamos when I was a baby. There's no way I could be your daughter. You're mistaken."

A serious look came over Great Aunt Uvula's flawless face. "It's time you knew the truth, Turquoise. There was no Bald Beaver, no Mad Cow, and no freak uphill skiing accident. That was a story invented by Loona and Fukowee when they adopted you. They wanted to shield you from the painful truth that your mother is a murderess."

"Great thundering buffalo balls!" Turquoise exclaimed. She could scarcely believe what she was hearing; it all sounded so incredibly incredible. "That means my entire life has been a lie! So, if Bald Beaver and Mad Cow never existed, and you're actually my mother, then who is my real father and where is he? Is he alive? I must know the truth!"

"Your father's name is Waka Jawaka. He deserted me after the little cat food incident made the front page of the *Coyote Gulch Gazette*. Like a typical man, he just couldn't handle my notoriety, the son of a bitch. I haven't seen him in many moons, but the last I heard he was a demented taxi driver with a weird hairdo and a penchant for stockpiling weapons."

Turquoise shook her head as if to shake off the shock. "This is all so extraordinary! I'm floored to find out you're actually my mother! It's so hard to believe! But tell me, Great Aunt Uvula, I mean, Mother, how did you come back from the dead? I saw your body laid out in the casket downstairs. We all did. Are you a ghost or one of the walking dead? And how did you keep from aging? You don't look to be any older than I am!"

"Yes, I must say, you look positively swanky for a moldering corpse," Randy Warpath complimented, zooming in on Great Aunt Uvula's face with his camera. "Death certainly becomes you."

Great Aunt Uvula smiled for her close-up. "Thank you ever so much. However, I can assure you, dearies, that I'm very much alive. You see... I suffer from a rare form of catalepsy that puts me into prolonged trance-like states that are indistinguishable from death. It can be most annoying. As for my agelessness, my housekeeper, Jambalaya Jetson, is a mambo—a Vodou high priestess." She turned to the hideous statue on the stone pedestal and smiled. "Through her powerful sorcery, this here statue of yours truly was created. Take a look at the face—its flesh of stone fissured by the passing of my years; its fairness fouled by every sin I've ever committed. As you can see with your own eyes, the statue grows old and horrible and dreadful, while I remain forever young and radiant; my beauty unblemished by time."

An outcry of "Shit! Shit! Shit!" exploded from Dolores Angry Cloud's mouth. "I guess this means the search for that Maltese Moccasin is off. What a waste of time! I might as well go home and beat my meat."

Great Aunt Uvula aimed her rifle at Dolores Angry Cloud and growled, "Not so fast, Dolores! Nobody's going home *or* beating their meat! I can't very well allow you and the others to simply walk out of here alive after discovering my little dark secret. Your knowledge is a threat to my survival, and that's a risk I'm not prepared to take! So you see, I have no other choice but to eliminate all three of you. It's nothing personal, mind you."

"How very uncordial," Randy Warpath observed.

Great Aunt Uvula winked her eye. "I promise it'll be quick and almost painless."

"That's a fine how-do-you-do," Turquoise groused. Before she could say another word, she was staring down the barrel of the Winchester. Oddly, with death looking her in the face, she found herself more incensed than afraid, which filled her with a sense of wonder. She ascribed it to her intrinsic warrior spirit. "First you tell me you're my mother, and then you tell me you're going to blow my head off! Don't you have any maternal instincts? Surely, you wouldn't kill your own daughter—your own flesh and blood—would you?"

Great Aunt Uvula grinned. "Your flesh and blood will make a delicious pate for Mister Nips and the other pusses of the chateau." Her face then twisted with anger, and as she squeezed the trigger, she said, in her best Leslie Nielsen voice, "And don't call me Shirley!"

Part Four
The Maltese Moccasin

A shot rang out like an eardrum-assaulting clap of thunder, and Turquoise was thrown back by the impact of the bullet. She landed on her buttocks on the dusty floor with a thud. Dazed, she looked down, expecting to see blood gushing from a bullet entry wound, and was surprised not to see a single drop of red. She then realized that the bullet had merely struck the bedpan clutched in her hand, leaving a dent in the metal. She breathed a sigh of relief.

There suddenly came the sound of a loud, splintering crash as the hungering hippies smashed their way through the attenuated door and advanced into the attic. They captured Great Aunt Uvula before she could escape down her trapdoor in the floor, and viciously clawed the screaming woman until her skin was slashed into a roadmap of blood-oozing highways, all leading to hell. They then took her down and piled on top of her like a flock of horned-up priests on an altar boy, mercilessly ripping into her with their razor-sharp teeth.

Her terrified screams were soon replaced by the sickening sounds of mastication, slurping, gulping and burping as her mutilated and brutalized body steadily disappeared, morsel-by-morsel, down the greedy gullets of the homicidal hippies.

Repulsed, Turquoise looked away, her gaze landing on the statue of Great Aunt Uvula. Its hideous, antiquated face was undergoing a curious transformation into an unblemished, youthful version of itself. But, seconds after its mysterious age-reversal, cracks began to appear on the statue—a few at first, and then dozens, and then hundreds. Emitting a sound that resembled a woman's scream, the statue split apart and crumbled to the floor, where it disintegrated and then vaporized into nothingness.

On top of the pedestal, where the statue had stood, was the legendary Maltese Moccasin, its multifaceted jewels twinkling like a starry night! Turquoise was quick to snatch it up, leaving the life-saving bedpan in its place. It filled her delicate hand with a warm, tingling sensation, which felt most odd to her, yet at the same time, quite pleasurable.

Seeing the moccasin in Turquoise's hand, Dolores Angry Cloud flashed her cousin an angry look. "*I'll* take that moccasin," she growled, attempting to yank the precious prize out of Turquoise's hand. She quickly released her grip on the shoe and pulled her hand back, wincing. "Ouch!

That motherfucking moccasin just gave me an electrical shock!"

"Bitch, that's probably because Turquoise was the first one to find it—not you," Randy Warpath said in a near-whisper, so as to not attract the attention of the hippies. "It's rightfully hers, and hers alone. So keep your paws off of it."

Dolores Angry Cloud frowned and gave a grunt of concession.

A sudden clamor of paws stampeding up the spiral staircase erupted, and a slew of cats appeared at the doorway to the attic like a plague. Without warning, they lunged at the feasting freaks, their eyes radiating with the same greenish glow as their mutated human counterparts. With foam dripping from their yowling mouths, they began clawing out eyeballs and tearing off strips of wrinkled hippie flesh with their teeth. Their surprise ambush quickly turned into a full-fledged orgy of carnage, rivaling the goriest of gorefests.

Seizing the opportunity to flee to safety while the cannibals were preoccupied battling the attacking cats, Turquoise and her two cousins absconded down a secret staircase below the trapdoor from which Great Aunt Uvula had emerged, unsure as to where the cobweb-shrouded, dust-blanketed steps would lead them. The deeper they descended, the quieter the mayhem in the attic became until the echo of their hurried footsteps was the only sound that remained. It did little, however, to put Turquoise's mind at ease.

At the bottom of the secret stairs was a door leading to the kitchen of the chateau. Its mid-century appliances and fixtures gave it the appearance of being frozen in time, and the faint aroma of grease hung in the air. In the center of the room was an industrial-sized meat grinder, massive in its proportions; and from metal hooks spread out across one wall hung an interesting array of kitchen implements, which included several hacksaws, a three-piece set of meat cleavers, an old hand-cranked skull saw, a pitchfork, and a flathead shovel. Ominously dangling from a wooden beam running across the ceiling was a large meat hook, not unlike the kind used in slaughterhouses.

A feeling of unease grew inside Turquoise's gut as her eyes scanned the kitchen. Her unspoken words screamed with realization in the back of her mind. *This is the room where she committed that atrocity! This is where that man's body was dismembered and ground into pate-style cat food!* She began to wonder if any other unfortunate victims met a similar gruesome fate at the hands of Great Aunt Uvula. (Turquoise found it difficult, if not impossible, to think of that woman as her mother.)

An old Kelvinator chest freezer standing next to a pantry brimming with tins of cat food caught Turquoise's eye, and the suspicious reddish-brown drip marks down the front of it set her imagination ablaze. She imagined it to be filled with human body parts, neatly wrapped in white butcher paper like little ghastly bundles of gore. Compelled by her nagging curiosity, which was growing by the moment, she willed her reluctant feet to carry her in the direction of the disturbing appliance. With her heart pounding in her ears like a piston inside a cylinder, she ever so slowly lifted up the lid, dreading the horrible secret she was convinced it contained.

There suddenly arose the ear-piercing screech of a cat as Mister Nips jumped out of the empty Kelvinator, nearly stopping Turquoise's heart. Before his paws could land on the linoleum floor, he snatched the Maltese Moccasin from Turquoise's hand with his mouth. Within the proverbial blink of an eye, he took off running like the proverbial bat out of hell.

Turquoise immediately gave chase, pursuing the larcenous feline through the kitchen, past the meat grinder, down the hallway, and into the devastated, blood-splattered drawing room. Dolores Angry Cloud and Randy Warpath followed closely behind.

"Give me back that moccasin!" Turquoise shouted angrily at the cat. "You four-legged shit dispenser!"

With the leather shoe still clenched firmly between his teeth, the contemptible Siamese took a running leap into Great Aunt Uvula's open casket. After several moments of tug-of-war, Turquoise victoriously wrestled the moccasin away from the hissing cat, and Dolores Angry Cloud slammed the lid of the casket shut, trapping Mister Nips inside of the satin-lined box.

Frantic clawing noises emanated from the casket, followed by the frenetic voice of Jambalaya Jetson. "Let me out of this casket, immediately!" the housekeeper demanded. The sound of a clawing cat changed over to the sound of pounding fists. "Heed my warning! I will put a Voodoo curse on all three of you if you don't release me at once and return that moccasin to me! I'm the only one who knows how to control its power!"

Dolores Angry Cloud jumped up onto the casket and sat on its lid, preventing Jambalaya Jetson from escaping. "Shut up, pussycat, or else I'll nail this lid shut."

Jambalaya Jetson replied with dead silence.

Turquoise gazed upon the sparkling jewels of the Maltese Moccasin in her hand. "I wonder why the moccasin didn't zap Mister Nips—I mean Jambalaya Jetson—like it did Dolores?" she pondered aloud.

"Probably because she's a Voodoo woman," Dolores Angry Cloud replied. "She possesses supernatural powers." She turned to Randy Warpath and balled up her fist. "And if you don't get that fuckin' camera out of my face, you'll be videotaping your teeth marching out of your mouth," she added, in a sulfurous tone.

"That was absolutely brilliant—a riveting performance," declared Randy Warpath, his voice unruffled. He continued filming, despite his cousin's animosity. "The raw emotion… the brutal honesty. Your screen presence is nothing short of magnetic."

"I'm warning you, asshole!"

"This low-budget cinéma vérité is destined to be a cause célèbre at the annual Chupacabra Film Festival. I think I'll call it, *Chronicle of a Carnivore*."

Turquoise raised her index finger to her lips. "Shhh! I thought I heard something."

From out in the corridor came the scurry of pattering feet on the ugly carpeting. It increasingly became louder, and more ominous. And then, much to the horror of Turquoise, Dolores Angry Cloud and Randy Warpath, a horde of several dozen growling cats amassed outside the open pocket doors of the drawing room like an angry mob, their eyes alight with an eerie greenish glow, teeth bared, ears back, and tails swishing.

"That sure is a lot of pussy," Dolores Angry Cloud quipped. Despite her marginally humorous remark, her words were laden with trepidation.

Randy Warpath struck a petrified pose. His mouth opened, as if to speak; however, no words were forthcoming—only a faint, mouse-like squeak.

"I don't like the way those cats are staring at us," Turquoise said, with a tremble in her voice. "Do you think we should make a run for it?"

"It's highly doubtful that we'd be able to outrun them," Dolores Angry Cloud rejoindered, stripping Turquoise of any last vestiges of hope. "They'd have their sharp, little teeth and claws buried in our flesh before we got halfway across the room."

A tiny, nearly inaudible squeaking noise again came from the back of Randy Warpath's throat.

The growling of the cats all at once grew louder, and they began to slowly advance into the drawing room, their movements typical of felines stalking their prey. The fur along their backs bristled as the entire platoon of four-legged predators assumed a pre-pounce crouch complete with butt-wiggle. Outside the broken drawing room windows, scores of other feral cats with glowing eyes had converged. They, too, were hungrily eyeing the three cousins, and poised to strike.

"Are we having fun yet?" Dolores Angry Cloud asked, sarcastically, as if to laugh in the face of doom.

"More fun that a Roto-Rooter up the cooter," Turquoise replied.

Randy Warpath finally found his lost voice box. "We're trapped with no way out," he declared, the seeds of despair germinating in the bleak landscape of his tense words. "I feel just like Dorothy Malone in *The Last Voyage*."

A burst of evil laughter rang out from the confines of the casket, and Jambalaya Jetson's threat of a curse began to reverberate hauntingly in the back of Turquoise's mind. It became apparent that the imprecation of the Voodoo woman was about to come to fruition.

Turquoise Moonwolf seldom shed tears, but she felt one streaking down her cheek at that moment. Despite her clan's motto: *Today is a good day to die, but tomorrow would be much better*, she had no fear of dying, but the sudden realization that she would never again see her beloved Grandmother Loona or Grandfather Fukowee ripped apart her heart, far deeper and more painfully than any cat's claws could ever rip apart her body.

Turquoise shut her eyes and readied herself for death as the voracious cats moved in for the kill. "Oh, how I wish we were all safely back at the Squealing Squaw teepee right now instead of this horrible   place!"

Part Five
Where the Fukowee

The pungent aroma of sagebrush, along with the sensation of a warm breeze gently caressing her face, prompted Turquoise to open her eyes with curiosity. She was quite startled to find herself, along with Dolores Angry Cloud and Randy Warpath, standing outside the Squealing Squaw Trading Post, the Maltese Moccasin still clutched in her hand. From up in the cloudless sky came the soothing grunt of a turkey vulture in flight. A black-tailed jackrabbit scampered across the lonely highway and disappeared into a nearby clump of mesquite. A black swallowtail butterfly flitted among the pink blooms of a nipple beehive cactus. But not a single cat was in sight.

"How on earth did we get here?" Turquoise asked, looking around at her unexpected surroundings. Her mind felt like a canoe in the rapids of confusion. "Just a few moments ago we were in the drawing room of the Chateau Catatonia. This must be a dream."

"If it is, then I'm having the same dream as you are," spoke Dolores Angry Cloud. "If you ask me, I'd say the Maltese Moccasin transported us here when you wished for it. Jambalaya Jetson *did* say it had powers!"

"A shoe that grants wishes?" Turquoise sounded unconvinced. "I've heard you say some crazy things before, Dolores, but this one really tops the teepee!"

"Then just how do you explain how we got here?" Dolores Angry Cloud asked. "None of us walked out of that chateau and hopped on the next train to Chupacabra."

Turquoise shrugged her shoulders. "I don't know. But there has to be a rational explanation for all of this. There just has to be!"

"Oh, this is just all too much." Randy Warpath began to wobble like a Weeble. "Don't be silly. I'm not going to faint. I'm not the type," he said, imitating Joan Crawford in *Forsaking All Others*. He then promptly fainted.

After reviving him, Turquoise and Dolores Angry Cloud helped him into the sunbaked, teepee-shaped tourist trap, where Grandmother Loona was busy reading a year-old copy of *The Chupacabra Daily Times*. The newspaper's headline, in bold black letters, read: CHUPACABRA TOURIST STABBED TO DEATH BY ARMLESS ATTACKER.

Grandmother Loona shook her head and mumbled to herself, "Story no make sense; Chupacabra has no tourists." She glanced up from her newspaper with a look of surprise. "Turquoise! I thought you not returning from Coyote Gulch until tomorrow." She pointed to Randy Warpath. "What's wrong with the *berdache* there? He not look too well."

"Grandmother, that word is considered offensive in this day and age," explained Turquoise. "Randy Warpath prefers to be called a two-spirit."

Grandmother Loona rolled her eyes.

Randy Warpath tilted his head back. "Accuse me, if you will, of melodramatic embroidery. But if I don't look too well to you, it just might be because I was bullied and threatened by a psychopathic Marine and his harpy of a wife; narrowly escaped being cannibalized by over-the-hill hippies; was nearly gunned down by a narcoleptic woman in a bullet bra that threatened to poke out eyes; came inches away from being lunch for a legion of demonic felines; and then, for the icing on the cake, had all of my atoms dematerialize without warning and rematerialize in a different location—all in the same afternoon... and without even a chance to freshen up my lip gloss."

Grandmother Loona shook her head, unsympathetically. "You always were over-sensitive to things." She then shifted her gaze back to Turquoise. "So what did you inheritate?"

Turquoise held up the Maltese Moccasin for her grandmother to see.

"A shoe? You inheritated a shoe?"

Turquoise nodded her head. "It's not just any old shoe, Grandmother. It's a Maltese Moccasin. Dolores is convinced that it has the power to grant wishes."

Grandmother Loona gasped and took a step back. "There is powerful medicine in the Maltese Moccasin! It is a sacred gift from the ancestors. Use it wisely, Granddaughter."

Dolores Angry Cloud was jubilant. "You see? You see? I told you so! But if you still need convincing, all you need to do is make another wish and see if it manifests. Just think of the fortune you could make with that thing! Go ahead, Turquoise. Wish for something cool!"

Turquoise stared at the dazzling gems of the magic-filled moccasin, and then, with embarrassment, revealed that she could not think of anything to wish for. She blamed "being put on the spot" for her inability.

Dolores Angry Cloud ruminated for a moment, and then spoke. "Everybody in town knows you secretly have the hots for Billy Jack. So why don't you wish for him?"

Turquoise glared at her cousin, irked and regretting having confided her secret in the bodacious blabbermouth. But, then again, she should have known better than to trust her with such sensitive information. Dolores Angry Cloud had a well-known habit of letting cats out of their bags, spoiling surprise parties and giving away the endings of movies. In high school, she once mortified Turquoise by revealing to the archery team that Turquoise had a mole in the shape of Elvis Presley on the left cheek of her buttocks. And then there was the time she blabbed in town that Cousin Kakawanga, following the advice of a topless lady psychiatrist in Gallup, routinely inserted a decapitated Barbie doll into his rectum to reduce anxiety. The humiliation that ensued drove him out into the desert, where he remained for forty days and nights, surviving on a diet of grubs and bird droppings, and sticking cactus spines in his eyes, before being eaten alive by a wendigo.

"But Billy Jack isn't a real person," Turquoise argued. "He's just a fictional movie character."

"What the hell does that matter?" Dolores Angry Cloud retorted, snappishly. "Don't be such a mooncalf. You hold the power to make him real, right there in your hand. So, go for it, cuz! This is your chance to have that Billy Jack, who makes you drool. That is, unless you'd rather settle for that Billy Balls, who makes you cringe."

A look of worry erupted on Grandmother Loona's face like acne on a teenager. But, before she could cough up a word of caution, Turquoise had already shut her eyes and silently wished for Billy Jack to appear.

The screen door of the teepee suddenly blew open as if propelled by a hurricane-force gust of wind, and a pimple-faced man with a staggering snout and a feral Jewfro stood in the open doorway, appearing rather dazed. Wearing a pair of brown, double-knit, polyester slacks, a blue turtleneck shirt, and nerd glasses, he looked anything *but* Turquoise's ass-kicking heartthrob.

"Who are you?" Turquoise asked the mysterious stranger, doing her best to conceal her disappointment.

"I'm Billy Jack," he replied, his eyes scanning the surroundings with obvious perplexity. "Billy Jack Lipschitz… from Teaneck, New Jersey. Are you guys Indians? So tell me, what is this place?

How did I get here? *Oy gevalt!* There must have been something un-Kosher in that pickled herring!"

Turquoise was gobsmacked. "Oh no! Something went terribly wrong!" she cried. "He's definitely *not* the sexy Billy Jack that I wished for! He doesn't look like a half-breed Green Beret or a hapkido master. He doesn't even have an Indian Joe round dome hat with a beaded hatband!"

Billy Jack Lipschitz looked insulted. "Well, of all the *chutzpah!*"

"When you made the wish, you spoke the words, but they were hollow because you were filled with doubt," Dolores Angry Cloud explained to Turquoise. "That's probably why the moccasin sent you the wrong Billy Jack. But don't worry, cuz. All you need to do is wish him back to where he came from, and then, before you can say, '*wigwam, thank you ma'am,*' he'll be gone. Then you can wish for something better."

"Not so fast!" cried Grandmother Loona. "I know well of the Maltese Moccasin. Its medicine only gives three wishes, and no more. You've already used up two of them, Turquoise, and have only one remaining. Give good thought to it before you make it!"

"I'm usually not one to *kvetch*," Billy Jack Lipschitz chimed in, "but all this *mishegoss* has made me hungry." He turned to Grandmother Loona. "So, Bubbe, you got anything around here that a guy can nosh on?"

At that moment, there sounded the loud roar of a flushing toilet, and Grandfather Fukowee emerged from the bathroom, a dripping toilet plunger in his hand. "Toilet backed up again. Must be evil spirit." He looked Billy Jack Lipschitz up and down, and then handed the toilet plunger to him. "Here. Make self useful."

Appalled, Billy Jack Lipschitz turned to Turquoise and asked, "Who is this *yutz?*"

Turquoise replied, "He's my Grandfather Fukowee."

"Oy, that's what I'd like to know myself," came the response from the befuddled man as he shook his Jewfro. "Where the Fukowee?"

"Have you decided yet how you're going to use your last wish?" Randy Warpath inquired of Turquoise.

"Remember, Turquoise, it's your final wish," Dolores Angry Cloud interjected. "Whatever you do, don't blow it on something nauseatingly sentimental like world peace or the end of famine and disease."

"Hmmm. What about a million dollars?" Turquoise suggested.

Randy Warpath nodded his head, approvingly. "Oh, I think that would be really wonderful," he opinioned in his typical tepid fashion.

Dolores Angry Cloud rolled her eyes and grunted. "Ugh! Everyone always wishes for a million dollars. You need to be a little more original. More radical!"

"A million dollars is a perfectly good wish," argued Randy Warpath, "especially if Turquoise invests it in my film. I think it would be a nice gesture after that traumatizing, psychologically scarring ordeal I've just been through, don't you? It was just so horrendous."

"Why should she give any money to *you?*" Dolores Angry Cloud snarled. "*I'm* the one who picked the lock and led us all to safety! Fuck you and your stupid film."

Expressionless, Randy Warpath replied, "Oh… well, in that case, I think Turquoise should request a five-hundred-piece collection of hand-painted cookie jars in the shape of teacup poodles. That's what *I* would wish for."

"That is silly wish," Grandmother Loona contended. "Turquoise should wish for pink 1955 Cadillac Fleetwood, like in the Graceland museum."

"Well, she does have a mole on her ass in the shape of Elvis," Dolores Angry Cloud once again divulged, bringing great embarrassment to Turquoise.

"Such a *yenta*," Billy Jack Lipschitz observed.

"What good is old car?" Grandfather Fukowee asked, angrily. "Turquoise needs something practical, like x-ray vision. But I not complain if she ask moccasin for Ann-Margret."

"I wish mass murder was legal!" Dolores Angry Cloud hollered.

Billy Jack Lipschitz cleared his throat and then revealed to all that he had secretly wished to be an amputee since childhood. "I've always felt like I should have been born without a left leg," he confessed. "There isn't a single day that goes by that I don't obsess over it. Oh sure, I've thought about slicing it off with a chainsaw to satisfy my peg-leg fetish, since none of the doctors I've seen would agree to amputate a healthy leg. But I just can't bring myself to do it. Blood makes me faint. But it wouldn't hurt for the girl over there with the shoe to be a *mensch* and make my lifelong wish come true, you know, to make up for all the inconvenience she's caused me."

"I'll gladly cut off your left leg and any other parts of your anatomy, for a few Benjamins," Dolores Angry Cloud offered. "My motto's always been: If you've got the backing, I'll do the hacking."

"Enough of crazy leg talk!" Grandmother Loona ordered. "Cut off body parts later! Right now Turquoise has important wish to make. Wish for pink Cadillac!"

Grandfather Fukowee scolded his wife. "Don't tell Turquoise how to wish, old woman! It is her decision to make, and she will ask moccasin for x-ray vision."

"A pink Cadillac!" shouted Grandmother Loona in defiance, her eyes filled with daggers.

"What about my teacup poodle cookie jars?" Randy Warpath whined.

"X-ray vision!"

"Pink Cadillac!"

Before Turquoise knew it, everyone in the teepee had encircled her like a swarm of buzzing locusts, and was shouting out their demented wishes to her like a frenzied chant.

"Cookie jars!"

"Pink Cadillac!"

"Amputation!"

"X-ray vision!"

"Mass murder!"

Turquoise's ears started to ring like discordant bells. She feared, at any moment, her head might begin spinning around like Linda Blair's in *The Exorcist*. She shut her eyes tightly. She parted her lips to speak, and the sound of silence fell over the teepee as everyone waited with baited breath to hear what wish Turquoise had decided upon.

The words began to slowly roll off of her tongue. "I wish… I wish… I wish this cockamamie story would hurry up and get to…"

THE END

NO HAPPY MEDIUM
Part One
Running Beaver

"And in local news," came a man's voice over the transistor radio on the checkout counter of the Squealing Squaw Trading Post, "Weasel County deputies are currently investigating a string of brazen armed robberies this week that targeted a number of local business throughout the Chupacabra area. Business owners and residents are being advised to take extra precautions and report any suspicious activity or persons immediately. If you have information about these or any other crimes, please contact New Mexico Crime Snitchers at 555-BLAB. We now have some breaking news out of Washington. The president stunned the nation by tweeting this morning that he blames his historically low poll numbers on the existence of the numerical system. At a press briefing this afternoon, the White House Press Secretary defended the president's tweet by saying..."

Dolores Angry Cloud grabbed the radio and angrily flung it against a nearby wall. Upon impact, it smashed into smithereens, and caused a meticulously arranged assemblage of Up Yours butt plugs and Silver Bullet multi-speed vibrators to tumble from their shelf. They hit the wooden floor with a rapid succession of thuds before rolling off in different directions.

"Fuck that fossilized defecation!" she screamed at the broken radio's pieces of plastic casing and transistor-based circuitry that were scattered about on the floor. "That forked tongue fuckweasel is as useless as taste buds in an asshole! Where's John Hinckley Jr. when we need him?" Her minatory words caused the safety pin that was piercing her lower lip to oscillate in an interesting fashion.

Grandmother Loona looked up from tomorrow's edition of *The Chupacabra Daily Times*. Its headline, in bold black letters, read: CHUPACABRA MAN HOSPITALIZED AFTER SEXUAL ASSAULT ON NON-CONSENTING PORCUPINE. She looked down at the remains of the radio, and then shook her head at Dolores Angry Cloud before returning her eyes to her newspaper.

"It's nice to see you in a cheerful mood for a change," Turquoise remarked to her Mohawk-haired cousin as she started for the back of the shop to fetch Grandmother Loona's ceremonial corn broom and a dustpan.

At that moment, William Cyrus Ballschmieder— Chupacabra's scruffy town drunk and one-eyed pervert—stumbled his way into the trading post, his missing left eye covered by a black patch like a pirate, and his right eye glazed and out of focus. He clumsily reached into the front pocket of his disheveled trousers and withdrew an old straight razor, which he unfolded and held up in the air for Turquoise to see.

"You see this here razor?" he asked. His words were slurred and his breath reeked of Old Panther Piss whiskey. His intoxicated body swayed slightly from side to side like a pestilent weed in the wind. "This old cut-throat razor belonged to my old cut-throat father. It was the only thing that good for nothing rattlesnake left me when he died."

Turquoise rolled her eyes as she swept up the pieces of the annihilated radio. "Billy Balls, I have a lot of work to do and haven't got time for your drunken nonsense. So would you please take your razor and leave this teepee before you scare away all of our customers?"

"I'm not leaving this here teepee until you accept my heartfelt proposal of matrimonial union... or at least agree to letting me have a piece of ass. If you don't, I'm going to take this here razor and lop off my ear like that Vincent van Gogh guy and give it to Boobs Callahan over at the Mother Trucker all-night truck stop. And then you'll be sorry."

Turquoise shook her head "Oh, Billy Balls. That's just crazy."

Ballschmieder hiccupped and his head bobbled a bit, reminding Turquoise of a dashboard hula dancer's hips. "Never underestimate the craziness of the human mind… especially mine."

"Drop dead."

"Ooh, you're a vulva-licious vixen!" Ballschmieder's free hand dove down the front of his trousers and he began fondling his rapidly engorging member. "I love it when you talk mean to me, Turquoise! Mmmm, it excites old Billy's loins! Come here, you little bucking bronco, and let this old barebackin' buckaroo ride you off into the sunset!"

Baring her teeth, Dolores Angry Cloud pointed to the door. "Listen, Buckaroo Brainless, my cousin told you drop dead. If you're smart, which everyone in this one-horse town knows you aren't, you'll take her advice. Now, if you don't haul your sorry pocket pool-playing ass out of this trading post in five seconds, the garbage men will be hauling it out of here in a ninety-six gallon trash bag tomorrow morning!"

Waving his straight razor in Dolores Angry Cloud's direction, the teetering Ballschmieder inarticulately grumbled, "I might not be a gynecologist, Dolores, but I sure know a cunt when I see one!"

"And I might not be a proctologist," Dolores Angry Cloud shot back, "but I know an asshole when I see one! Now, I'm warning you, get your moldy old ass out of here, Billy Balls, before I take that goddamn razor and cut off your crab-infested…"

All at once, there came a loud, blood-curdling scream from the bathroom, causing Grandmother Loona to once again peer over her newspaper.

Turquoise, her infuriated cousin, and the perverted town drunk all turned their heads to look.

The door to the bathroom burst open and a middle-aged, blonde woman came barreling out with her beige polyester stretch pants and white granny panties down around her ankles. Her face was flushed with a look of unparalleled horror. Inside the unoccupied bathroom, the wooded seat of the toilet was violently banging up and down as if controlled by a pair of invisible hands.

"I am never stepping foot inside this trading post again!" cried the flustered female as she ran toward the exit. "Your toilet physically attacked me!"

And, as quick as a flash, she was out the door and gone.

With his salivating tongue hanging limp from his mouth like a panting dog in the heat of summer, William Cyrus Ballschmieder dropped his straight razor on top of the counter and drunkenly zigzagged his way out of the teepee after the bare-bottomed woman. "Hot damn!"

The banging of the toilet seat abruptly stopped. It was replaced by an eerie silence.

"That is third time this week bathroom scare away customer," Grandmother Loona griped. "One lady say ghostly hand reach up from bowl of toilet and give her rectal exam. Another say ghost appear in mirror and moon her. Business slow enough as is—no can afford to lose more customers!

At that moment, Grandfather Fukowee entered the trading post, all wild-eyed. "Just saw running beaver go by!" he announced. He shook his head. "Not good sign. Means six more weeks of drought. Time for rain dance again."

"That wasn't running beaver," Grandmother Loona contradicted him. "That was customer."

Dolores Angry Cloud snickered. "A *former* customer. And her beaver sure looked like it was running to me."

"Well, she no had time to wipe," said Grandmother Loona. "Evil spirit in the bathroom scare woman away."

Grandfather Fukowee shook his head, gravely. "This not good. Not good at all. We are losing too much wampum. What we going to do?"

"We tried burning bundles of sage and tobacco, but smudging ceremony not work," Grandmother Loona replied. "Evil spirit not want to leave!"

Turquoise picked up the receiver of the telephone on the counter and began dialing a number.

"Who you gonna call?" Grandfather Fukowee asked. "Ghostbusters?"

"The next best thing," Turquoise answered. "I'm calling TOPS."

Grandmother Loona looked puzzled. "TOPS?"

Turquoise nodded her head. "Toilets Only Paranormal Specialists. You know, Mason Hawkins—the ghost-hunting plumber with his own reality television show on channel zero. He has special training for situations like this."

Dolores Angry Cloud erupted like a volcano. "I fucking *hate* television! And I especially hate those fake-ass reality shows like his! They rot your brain from the inside out. I'd personally like to kill every fucking person on TV—starting with those irritating mimes, those cock-sucking televangelists, and all those old bastards who keep falling and can't get up. They all deserve to die! Every one of them! Television has nothing whatsoever to offer the intellect. I want to watch abortions, autopsies, and live executions!"

Grandfather Fukowee took a close look at the nose ring dangling from Dolores Angry Cloud's nostrils like a doorknocker. "If I pull ring in your nose, does that turn off blathering mouth?"

She rudely responded by grabbing the crotch of her red tartan bondage pants and giving it several upward yanks.

The old man frowned, temporarily adding more crisscrossing lines to his leathery, weathered forehead. "You got cooties down there?"

"If you want to see cooties," Dolores Angry Cloud snickered, "just wait until those coke-snorting paranormal phonies get here."

"I snorted coke once," Grandmother Loona confessed.

Stunned, Dolores Angry Cloud's eyes widened. Her mouth gaped. "I don't believe it, Grandmother! *You* snorted coke?"

Grandmother Loona nodded. "Oh, it's true, Dolores. It was back in the Seventies when everybody was doing it. I was young and curious so I decided to give it a try myself. You know, just to see what everybody was raving about. Well, a friend gave me some coke at a party and I snorted it. Let me tell you, it was terrible experience! The ice cubes kept getting stuck in my nose!"

"Okay. Thank you. We'll see you then." Turquoise hung up the telephone. "I have some good news, everyone. The plumber from TOPS said he'd be here in one hour with his cameraman, makeup artist and spiritualist medium, Yvonne. Our problem will soon be over!"

Grandmother Loona shook her head, doubtfully. "I have heap bad feeling about this. Something tell me our problem is just beginning."

* * *

"Lavatory hauntings are far more common that most people realize," Mason Hawkins told Turquoise and her relatives.

As he spoke, Hayley the makeup girl dabbed a cosmetic sponge all over his goateed face and applied powder to the crown of his shaved head to reduce the glare from his chrome dome. Her twin brother, Harley the cameraman, scurried about the teepee, setting up recording equipment and securing camera cables to the floor with strips of duct tape.

"Most of these disturbances are what we in the business call, 'residual energy imprint hauntings,'" Hawkins continued. "To put it in simpler terms, they're nothing more than energy from emotionally charged events, like murders or suicides, which somehow gets imprinted on the environment. Like a recording of the past, it replays over and over." He held up a hand mirror to inspect Hayley's cosmetological artistry. "I am convinced, however, that what we're dealing with in your case is an intelligent haunting."

"What does 'intelligent haunting' mean?" Turquoise asked.

"It means that your bathroom has been taken over by a sentient spirit that interacts with the living as if somehow trapped between this world and the next. Are you familiar with the term, 'poltergeist?'"

Turquoise shook her head from side to side. Her grandparents and Dolores Angry Cloud followed in suit.

"It's a German word for 'noisy spirit,' the paranormal plumber explained. "Poltergeists typically like to make a racket, levitate and throw objects, hide things and play havoc with electrical devices. They've also been known on occasion to physically attack the living. The spirit that has attached itself to your toilet is a type of poltergeist that we at TOPS refer to as a 'bowl-tergeist.'"

"Oh no!" Turquoise cried out. "This is a crisis!"

Grandmother Loona plunged her face into the palms of her hands and began to sob uncontrollably. Tears streamed down her leathery cheeks like raindrops rolling down the sides of a buffalo hide teepee. Grandfather Fukowee put his arm around his weeping wife in an effort to console her.

"Now, there's no need for anyone to lose their composure. As sure as my name is Mason Hawkins, my gifted psychic and I will unclog your toilet of that paranormal blockage and flush it right down the drain. Rest assured, we're professionals!"

At that moment, the fashionably late Miss Yvonne made her grand entrance, a cardboard box filled with paperback copies of her latest book, *Mediumship for Imbeciles*, in her arms. She waited with a tapping toe and an air of conspicuous impatience as Turquoise hurriedly folded up the straight razor left behind by William Cyrus Ballschmieder and slid it into the front pocket of her jeans. Miss Yvonne then plopped the box down on the checkout counter, turned her head, and did a quick visual scan of the trading post.

"Copies of my best-selling book, which was ghostwritten by an actual ghost, are available at fifteen ninety-nine each, plus tax," she announced, with a trace of a French Canadian accent. "Of course, you will all want autographed copies. For an extra twenty dollars, I'd be more than happy to personally sign them for you."

Dolores Angry Cloud picked up one of the books from the box and scrutinized the front and back covers. A look of disgust materialized upon her face like a rabbit from a magician's hat. Rolling her dark eyes, she tossed the book back into the box as if it were discarded trash, clearly unimpressed.

"This is enough to gag a maggot. I'll catch you guys later," she said, as she headed toward the door. "I'm going home to rewire that electric chair I bought at the Salivation Army store." Contorting her facial muscles to produce a monstrous expression, she gave Miss Yvonne a middle-finger salute, and then she was gone.

The psychic medium shut her eyes and the carrot-colored curls on the top of her head fibrillated like moths in the throes of a bug-zapper electrocution. She extended her arms out to the sides like a savior nailed onto an invisible cross. "I'm picking up strange vibrations," she announced, slowly moving her head from side to side, while Hayley diligently dabbed powder on the shiny regions of her face. "They're getting stronger by the minute."

"No need to worry," Grandmother Loona reassured the woman. "It's only Silver Bullet multi-speed vibrators. Big shipment come in this morning. You look like vibrator type. I give you special discount."

Miss Yvonne's eyelids flew open. "I beg your pardon!" she hissed. "I can assure you that, unlike some people, I have *never* had to resort to artificial stimulation by penile-shaped devices."

A low, menacing growl resounded from within the bathroom. It quickly rose to a terrifying roar, which was not unlike that of a constipated bull moose. Startled, Miss Yvonne let out a loud gasp and broke a fingernail, and Mason Hawkins dropped his mirror onto the floor.

On the cracked surface of the glass, Turquoise thought she saw the hideous reflection of a demonic face. It possessed humanoid features, but was covered with scaly skin like a reptile. It bared its teeth at her and then, in an instant, it was gone. Turquoise wondered if anyone else in the teepee had noticed it, or was it merely a manifestation of her over-active imagination or perhaps a trick of the light?

"Bowl-tergeist not sound very happy," Grandfather Fukowee observed.

Before the old man could say anything more, there came another roar. It was much louder and even more ferocious than the first.

The plumber immediately reached into one of the pockets of his blue denim overalls and whipped out an electromagnetic field detector.

With his other hand, he motioned for Miss Yvonne to follow him, and then together they dashed into the bathroom to confront the thunderous entity. Harley followed right behind them with a large video camera perched atop his right shoulder and his right eye glued to the viewfinder.

No sooner had the TOPS team set foot inside the bathroom, the multi-colored lights on Mason Hawkins' EMF meter lit up and the device began to buzz wildly.

"The energy in here is off the charts!" the plumber exclaimed.

Filled with curiosity, Turquoise and her relatives congregated outside the open door of the bathroom, alongside Hayley who was on standby for any emergency touch-ups. They watched as Miss Yvonne placed her hand upon the tank of the toilet and commanded the bowl-tergeist to identify itself. The seat of the commode suddenly flew open with a bang and the water in the bowl began to churn.

"The entity attached to this toilet is definitely male," the psychic medium declared with certainty. "I'm also sensing an enormous amount of negative energy," she added, her voice taking on a rather ominous tone.

Taking no chances, Mason Hawkins armed himself with a nearby toilet plunger. "Who are you?" he shouted into the toilet bowl. "Why haven't you crossed over into the light?"

Miss Yvonne emitted a strange moaning sound and began moving her head in a slow rotation. She shut her eyes and appeared to enter a deep state of concentration. "Everybody, hush. I'm on the verge of telepathic contact with the other side. Yes, yes, I can hear you, spirit. Please reveal yourself to me and tell me why you haunt the bathroom of this trading post." She paused for several moments and then reopened her eyes. The rotation of her head came to an abrupt halt. "The spirit has told me his name. He said it was Jimmie… Jimmie Yellow Snow."

Grandmother Loona raised her hand to her mouth and gasped with horror upon hearing the dreaded name rolling off of Miss Yvonne's tongue. "Jimmie Yellow Snow was very evil ancestor! He stole silver ring from old Gypsy woman at carnival, and as revenge, she put dreaded curse of snapping turtle on him. He go crazy and bite off people's fingers each time moon over Chupacabra was full. Angry mob lynched him fifty years ago, right here on same spot where teepee now stands."

The churning of the water in the toilet bowl grew more violent as if in direct response to Grandmother Loona's narrative. An odd chill permeated the air like the harbinger of ill tidings, prompting Mason Hawkins to shout out with glee, "A cold spot! A genuine cold spot! Zak Bagans, eat your heart out!"

Without warning, the turbulent water in the toilet bowl shot up into the air like a geyser, and then formed itself into a long human arm with a large, claw-like hand. Its transparent fingers grabbed the plumber by his throat and lifted him nearly one foot from the floor.

"Whoa, dude!" the cameraman ululated as he zoomed in for a close-up shot of the unnatural occurrence before him. "That's totally bitchin'!"

Horror-stricken, Turquoise and her grandmother gasped and took a step back.

The trembling lips of the make-up girl parted like the carnivorous leaves of a Venus flytrap and from her mouth was expelled a scream, which seemed to infuriate Miss Yvonne.

"Shut up, Hayley!" she hissed, spittle flying from her mouth, her words like shards of glass in an acid bath. "Shut the fuck up! I'm the only one who screams on this goddamn show! It's stipulated in my contract!"

Miss Yvonne's truculent words were immediately followed by one of her signature shrieks, causing the hair at the nape of Turquoise's neck to bristle. Bursting with drama, she pulled down on the chrome handle of the toilet in a desperate effort to flush the foul phantom, but it was to no avail.

"Evil entities are no match for my expertise with a plumber's helper!" Mason Hawkins cried out, empathically, while furiously plunging the toilet with the rubber suction cup of his unclogging apparatus. "I command you, Jimmie Yellow Snow, to depart this toilet at once!"

As Turquoise observed the pair of paranormal experts in action, a static-like tingling sensation tickled her scalp and raced down the back of her neck and upper spine. Mass quantities of goosebumps erupted on her arms. She wondered if her grandparents were experiencing the same things.

Miss Yvonne snapped her fingers three times as if signaling a waiter in a restaurant and demanded that Harley give her a close-up shot so that the details of her face could be appreciated. "You should know by now that I am entitled to a minimum of six close-up shots per episode. It's stipulated in my contract!"

As soon as the camera moved in for a close-up, the pretentious psychic began to shout, wildly, at the spirit. "Go into the light, Jimmie Yellow Snow! Go into the light! Jesus Christ, Janis Joplin, and seventy-two virgins are waiting for you in the light!"

A look of vexation crossed the plumber's greasy features. "How many times must I explain it to you, Miss Yvonne, that the seventy-two virgins line only works when you're dealing with Muslims? This bowl-tergeist is an Indian who thinks he's a turtle, you dumb twit!"

"How dare you call me a twit. You are a jackass with a head like a bald-pated testicle. I gave up a promising career as a movie actress to be on this two-bit television series." Miss Yvonne turned up her nose, snobbishly. "We both know that *my* talents are the only reason the viewers tune in each week to watch it."

"Talents? Is that what you call them?" Mason Hawkins dispensed a mocking snicker as he continued plunging the obstinate toilet, beads of sweat forming on his brow. "Yeah, well, your horizontal performances in the celluloid epics, *Dracula has Jizzin' from the Grave*, *Intercourse with the Vampire*, and *Rosemary's Boobie,* ain't exactly the crown jewels of the theater world, sweetheart!"

"For your information, *The Daily Snatch* called my performances 'riveting!'"

"I played the leading role in the Chupacabra High School production of *Autopsy of Jane Doe*," Turquoise blurted out with pride, eliciting an eye roll from Miss Yvonne. "Not to toot my own horn, but Mister Farshtinkener—the head of the theater arts department—*did* rave about my acting ability. He said I was very convincing. And he had Cotard's syndrome!"

"You played the part of a corpse," said Grandmother Loona. "You had no lines."

Mason Hawkins flashed Turquoise a quizzical look. "What's Cotard's syndrome?"

"Oh, it's a rare neuropsychiatric disorder," Turquoise replied. "It causes people to think they're dead and putrefying."

At that fateful moment, the bowl-tergeist decided to give a riveting performance of its own. The toilet began to tremble like a creeper smitten by the violence of the wind, and like an aquatic orgasm, the hostile limb of water promptly exploded into thousands of airborne droplets, drenching Hawkins, Miss Yvonne, and the cameraman, and covering the bathroom floor with an immense puddle. A thunder-like boom immediately ensued and a roll of toilet paper mysteriously launched from its holder on the tiled wall. It sailed across the room like a two-ply projectile, bouncing off of Grandfather Fukowee's forehead and knocking him to the floor with its intense force.

While helping her dazed grandfather to his feet, Turquoise was taken aback by the strikingly scaly texture of the old man's hands. She was sure they weren't like that earlier, and found it a rather queer thing. She remarked how they felt inordinately rough to the touch.

Shaking her head in disgust, Grandmother Loona made a grunting noise. "I warned him that that would happen if he didn't stop fondling his totem pole. But the old fool never listens to me. He's as stubborn as a constipated, one-ball mule, and with a skull twice as thick."

Turquoise's face expressed her incredulity as she watched her grandfather's hands sprout tubercles and his fingers turn into webbed claws. His facial features seemed to take on a frightful reptilian appearance, with the whites of his eyes bearing mottled-camouflage coloration. His neck elongated, and within a mere matter of seconds, his mouth morphed into toothless massive jaws with a sharp hooked beak like that of a snapping turtle.

"My goodness, Grandfather. What a big beak you have!"

Grandfather Fukowee tilted his head back, and from out of his mouth came a loud hissing sound. His tongue, which had shriveled into a pink worm-like appendage, wriggled.

"All the better to bite your finger off, my dear," he said in an odd and maniacal tone of voice. His words, however, were not his own. Turquoise instinctively knew they belonged to the evil spirit of Jimmie Yellow Snow.

"Look out! He's possessed by the bowltergeist and extremely dangerous!" Mason Hawkins cried out.

Grandmother Loona glowered at her husband. "Just my rotten luck. Why you not get possessed by a beefcake like Chief Thundercloud or Iron Eyes Cody?"

Mason Hawkins warned everyone to exercise extreme caution, and assured all of them that he was well versed in spirit possessions, old Gypsy curses, and the internal workings of a toilet.

"Stand back while I un-devil this misfortunate geezer!" he commanded, sounding quite infallible.

"Careful, dude! This shit's gettin' gnarly!" Harley shouted, as Mason Hawkins sprung into the air and body-slammed Grandfather Fukowee with all of his weight in an attempt to deliver him from evil.

Right on cue, Miss Yvonne let loose a loud demoniacal scream that made Turquoise's eardrums quiver, and the hair on the back of the shop's stuffed buffalo mascot stand on end.

Horrified, Turquoise watched as the two men struggled and rolled about on the floor of the trading post with Mason Hawkins bellowing out exorcism prayers from the *Rituale Romanum*, and Grandfather Fukowee hissing like the angry turtle he had become. They knocked over the stuffed buffalo and smashed the window of a display case. The sound of breaking glass echoed ominously throughout the teepee. They then crashed into a Captive Couture Bondage Boutique display, sending to the floor a bevy of Styrofoam heads modeling such fashion gems as black leather hoods with huge bat ears, black leather puppy muzzle masks, and black leather head harnesses with attached cheeseburger-shaped ball gags.

Fuming, Grandmother Loona scolded her husband for destroying the trading post and demanded that he stop embarrassing her.

The impromptu rite of exorcism came to an abrupt end when the possessed sexagenarian twisted his head and clamped his powerful jaws down upon the plumber's thumb, biting off the entire digit. Bellowing with pain, Mason Hawkins released his grasp on the old man and grabbed his maimed hand, which was shooting jets of blood into the air like a ghastly lawn sprinkler. His horror-filled eyes nearly popped out of their sockets.

"Oh my God! My thumb!" he screamed as blood ran like a river of gore down his arm, staining the sleeve of his shirt bright red. "He bit off my thumb! Somebody help me! Call an ambulance before I bleed to death!" His teeth began to chatter and his body started to shake. Cold sweat profusely poured out from his pores. He moaned in pain, and his lips started to take on a bluish tint.

Miss Yvonne was livid. "How dare you upstage me!" she growled at her hemorrhaging co-star, her voice seething with petulance. "You bastard!"

Turquoise dashed to the telephone on the counter and dialed 911. While she was arranging for an ambulance, Grandfather Fukowee set his sights on the make-up girl, who was trembling with fright. Letting out a fierce hiss, he lunged at her with his claws ready to slash and his beak hungry for another finger. Her face went pale as a sun-bleached sail, and she fainted on the spot, triggering a heated reaction from Miss Yvonne.

"Don't you *dare* pass out now!" the enraged psychic screamed. "After this ordeal, my make-up needs retouching, and my hair is out of place. Hayley! God damn it! Wake up this instant and perform your duties, otherwise I'll see to it that you're fired!"

Grandfather Fukowee knelt down beside the unconscious girl and picked up one of her limp hands. His jaws opened and his pink, worm-like tongue wriggled. "Mmmm, such delicate little fingers you have there," he remarked, his voracious mouth salivating as he spoke. "I bet they taste as delicious as they look."

With a loud clunk, Grandmother Loona conked her husband over the head with one of the Silver Bullet multi-speed vibrators. One blow to the noggin was all it took to knock him out cold. He keeled over and hit the ground with a thud, eliciting a sigh of relief from everyone in the teepee.

"Cowabunga, dude!" the cameraman exclaimed, while still filming the action.

"Vibrator is a woman's best friend," Grandmother Loona declared to the camera with a stimulated smile on her furrowed face. She triumphantly petted the dented phallic device as if it were a housecat.

With her phone call completed, Turquoise hung up the receiver and promptly instructed Mason Hawkins not to worry; the paramedics would be there in two hours. Her words, however, fell upon deaf ears, for the plumber had lapsed into a state of hemorrhagic shock and was unconscious.

"Turquoise! Fetch me the straight-jacket from utility closet," directed Grandmother Loona, her voice riddled with urgency. "And hurry, before your grandfather wake up and start snapping!"

"You keep a straightjacket in your utility closet?" Miss Yvonne looked positively appalled.

"You ask stupid question, paleface woman." Grandmother Loona rolled her eyes. She shook her head. "It old family heirloom. Where else you keep it?"

With the straight-jacket fetched, Grandmother Loona grabbed her husband's arms, stuffed them into the ape-length sleeves of the white canvas garment, and then wrapped them around his body. As she hurriedly secured the straps behind him, Turquoise covered his head with one of the kinky leather bondage masks to prevent any further finger biting in the event that he regained consciousness. With the assistance of Harley, they dragged Grandfather Fukowee's restrained body across the teepee and locked him inside the utility closet, while Miss Yvonne stood by, uselessly, and watched.

The unheralded bang of a gunshot rang out from behind Turquoise, causing her startled body to jolt; screaming and pandemonium instantaneously followed. Turquoise pivoted on her heels, and her jaw dropped.

"Great thundering buffalo balls!" she gasped.

Her eyes widened. Her hair, black as a raven in the dead of night, stood on end. She could barely believe what her eyes were showing her. It had to be a dream, and a terrible dream at that. It seemed too bizarre, too unbelievable to be real…

But it was.

Part Two
Snapped

Standing in the doorway of the teepee, armed with revolvers, were conjoined twin brothers and former Chupacabra mayoral candidates, Russ and Ross Gonzalez. Like Chang and Eng of P.T. Barnum circus fame, they were joined at the torso by a band of flesh, cartilage, and livers fused in the ligament connecting their sternums, giving them the appearance of hugging. They each wore on their head a black, Che Guevara-style beret bearing the image of a two-headed Siamese cat.

"Death to the fascist hemorrhoid that festers in the rectum of democracy!" they shouted in unison.

A scowl erupted on Grandmother Loona's face. "God damn it, Gonzalez brothers! Why you shoot hole in roof of teepee?"

"The Gonzalez brothers no longer exist," proclaimed Russ Gonzalez. "There is no Russ. There is no Ross. We have changed our names to Tania to symbolize our rebirth as revolutionaries of the SLA—the Siamese Liberation Army! Now, hand over all the money from the cash register and no one will get hurt."

"Cash register is empty," Grandmother Loona explained. "Business very slow. We not make any sales today. But you can have that box of books there on the counter. They were ghostwritten by an actual ghost."

"Hey!" Miss Yvonne shouted with indignation. "Now just you wait a God damn minute! Who the hell…"

"Shut up!" Ross Gonzalez growled, waving his gun in Miss Yvonne's direction. "We don't want any of your lousy books! We want your money and your valuables—that means wristwatches, rings, gold chains, weapons grade plutonium...you get the idea. Now, hand over the loot, and don't give us no costume jewelry crap!"

"If you value your lives, you'll do as he says," Ross' brother warned. "We're desperate revolutionaries."

"Why are you so desperate?" Turquoise asked, as she removed the sterling silver ring with the turquoise-inlaid turtle from the middle finger of her right hand and handed it over to the robbers.

"We need to raise ten thousand dollars for a costly surgical procedure to separate us," Russ Gonzalez replied as he took the ring and stuffed it into his pants pocket. "Operations aren't cheap. In case you haven't noticed, medical care in this country is highway robbery. Now, hurry up with the money! We haven't got all God damn day!"

Ross Gonzalez nodded his head. "That's right. We've got other places to rob, you know."

Turquoise gasped with realization. "So, *you're* the ones responsible for the recent rash of robberies in Chupacabra! I had no idea you were the perpetrators! I thought you guys were running for mayor."

"Our career in American politics prepared us for a life of crime," Russ Gonzalez replied, beaming with pride. His tone suddenly became tempestuous. "Now, for the last time, empty out that cash register and hand over the money! This is your final warning! We won't hesitate to gun down every single person in this fiberglass teepee!"

"You always did have a Chippewa on your shoulder," Grandmother Loona avowed as she rang up "No Sale" on the cash register to pop it open. She removed the moneyless drawer and held it up for the revolutionaries to see. "Look for yourself. No money. Drawer empty, look I told you."

"There must be *something* of value in this teepee other than one stinking ring!" Russ Gonzalez eyed the padlocked door of the closet that imprisoned Grandfather Fukowee. "What have you got locked up behind that door over there?"

"Nothing that would do you any good," Grandmother Loona replied. "It's just utility closet containing stuff not worth stealing."

"Don't lie to us, Loona!" Russ Gonzalez snapped. "I've got a sneaking suspicion there's something of great value behind that door, otherwise you wouldn't have that padlock on it! Nobody's going to break in to steal brooms and mops!"

"I bet that's where these crazy Injuns keep all their cold hard cash hidden," Ross Gonzalez surmised, licking his lips. "We're one step closer to getting that operation we've always dreamed of. Mmmm. I can almost feel the scalpel now!" His demented eyes twinkled with anticipation.

Losing his temper, Russ Gonzalez aimed his gun at Grandmother Loona. "Unlock that door, old woman, and be quick about it! You've got until the count of ten and then…"

"Okay, okay." Grandmother Loona reluctantly reached into the pocket of her fringed buckskin smock and pulled out the key. "Don't say I not warn you." With a turn of the key, she popped open the padlock and then quickly moved away from the door.

The Gonzalez brothers yanked the door open and a look of bewilderment befell their faces. Turquoise and her grandmother gasped in horror, and Miss Yvonne pressed her knuckles to her cheeks in drama queen fashion until they turned white and belted out a windowpane-shattering scream.

On the wall at the back of the utility closet, dusty rays of sunlight peered like a voyeur through a large, gnawed hole leading to the outside. Lying on the floor, in tatters, was the heirloom straightjacket, its straps chewed completely through. And to make matters even worse, Grandfather Fukowee was nowhere in sight.

"Oh no! He's gone! Fukowee's gone!" wailed Grandmother Loona, her eyes fixed on the empty closet and harboring a look of calamity. She turned to her granddaughter. "What we gunna do?"

Growing restive, the gun-toting brothers waved their guns in the air and demanded to know what the hell was going on.

With distress in her voice, Turquoise relayed to them how an ancestral spirit with a Gypsy curse had taken possession of her grandfather and, through mysterious supernatural means, transformed him into a human snapping turtle. "We locked him in that closet after he bit off one of Mason Hawkins' fingers. He must have used his beak to gnaw through the straightjacket and make a hole in the wall to escape through."

"We saw him running off into the desert as we were coming up the road," said Russ Gonzalez. "We didn't know that was your grandfather."

His brother shook his head. "We thought it was Mitch McConnell."

"We have to find him quickly and get him to an exorcist before he attacks anyone else! It's a matter of life and death!" Turquoise stressed. "Will you help us?"

"I don't think you understand, Miss Turquoise. We came here to rob this place, not to help you," Ross Gonzalez laughed. "Turtle or not, your grandfather's no concern to us. The only thing my brother and I care about is acquiring enough money to pay for our separation surgery so we can lead normal lives." He looked at his brother. "Isn't that right, Tania?"

Russ Gonzalez gave his head a quick nod and replied, "That's right, Tania. We're sick and tired of going through life having people gawking and laughing at us like we were weird. It's not good for one's self-esteem. We need to split up."

"Sounds like good idea." Grandmother Loona pointed to the exit. "Why don't the two of you split now?"

"We have no intention of leaving this teepee empty-handed," Russ Gonzalez announced. "We're taking a hostage with us. Armed robbers such as ourselves need a getaway vehicle, so we're also taking that black van that's parked out front. Now, give us the keys, or everyone dies!"

Without hesitation, Harley pulled the keys to the van out of the front pocket of his jeans and tossed them to the conjoined twins. "Dudes, be careful with her, okay? She's like full of high tech paranormal equipment that's ultra sensitive and quite expensive."

The brothers' eyes lit up upon hearing the "E word." It was like music to their ears. They swiveled their faces to look each other in the eye, and simultaneously shouted with elation, "Jackpot!"

A soft moan filled the air as the passed-out make-up artist began to come to. She slowly raised herself into a sitting position. "Where am I? What happened?" she enquired in a groggy sounding voice as her eyelids lifted, filling her eyes with the startling image of the Siamese Liberation Army revolutionaries standing before her, fingers poised on the triggers of their guns. With a groan, her face went pale, her eyes rolled up in their sockets, and she once again fainted.

"Why do you need to take a hostage?" Turquoise asked, unable to hide the nervousness within her voice.

"Well, for one thing, my brother and I don't drive, so we have to abduct somebody who can operate the van for us," Russ Gonzalez answered. "Hostages also make for good bargaining chips."

"And human shields," his brother added, a contemptuous smile curling the corner of his mouth.

Turquoise overheard Miss Yvonne whispering excitedly to the cameraman. "This could be the opportunity of a lifetime, being abducted by the Siamese Liberation Army, indoctrinated with revolutionary thinking, trained to be an urban guerilla, and then acquitted on the basis of brainwashing. Why, the publicity would make my name a household word and catapult my acting career into super stardom!"

Miss Yvonne struck an exaggerated glamour pose that was unintentionally comical, bordering on Norma Desmond deranged. "I'm ready for my abduction, Mister DeMille!" she announced eagerly to the conjoined twins.

"The name is Tania!" they growled in unison; rage spanning their unshaven faces.

In an attempt to redeem herself, Miss Yvonne wasted no time in apologizing for her faux pas. Smiling seductively, she then undid the top two buttons of her blouse and batted her false eyelashes at the Gonzalez brothers, trying her best to exude sexuality.

"Third rate gold-digging tramps like you don't have what it takes to be revolutionaries in the Siamese Liberation Army!" Russ Gonzalez spat out with disdain.

His brother nodded his head in agreement and added, "There's only one person in this teepee worthy of an abduction—and that's Turquoise Moonwolf!"

Turquoise felt oddly flattered and her cheeks began to blush.

Flabbergasted, Miss Yvonne's lower jaw dropped open and she instinctively threw her hands to her hips. "*Turquoise Moonwolf?*" she cried, her voice vibrating with disbelief and wounded pride. "Are you kidding me? She's a nothing! *I'm* a celebrity—a huge media sensation! My fallopian are utopian! The paparazzi adore me! Try using those heads on your shoulders. Your feeble attempt at a revolution will go absolutely nowhere without me. I have connections in high places and a higher thinking capacity than your two brains put together. Don't abduct *her*! Abduct *me*! Don't you realize that I'm your ticket to international infamy, you stupid sideshow freaks?"

Enraged by the psychic medium's unbridled insolence, the conjoined twins simultaneously shouted, "Eat lead, bitch!" and squeezed the triggers of their revolvers—each firing off a round of ammunition at Miss Yvonne. One bullet grazed the inside of her thigh, while the other blew off the lower portion of her right ear, knocking her off her Gucci clad feet. She screamed like a madwoman as the blood spewed forth, rapidly forming sticky puddles of red on the floor around her.

"*Zut alors*! You sons of bitches! You shot me! I can't believe you fucking shot me!" Miss Yvonne darted her face to the stunned-looking cameraman, whose mouth was hanging open, speechless. "Don't just stand there, you drooling idiot. Get a close-up of my bullet wounds!"

Russ Gonzalez motioned to Turquoise with his gun that it was time to go. The braided beauty hugged her sobbing grandmother, kissed her on the cheek, and promised her that everything would be all right. The old woman responded with a nod and a downhearted smile; however, Turquoise could tell by the anguish in her grandmother's glistening eyes that she doubted Turquoise's reassuring words. Turquoise doubted them as well.

"Get your ass in gear!" the Gonzalez brothers barked in unison at their newly acquired hostage. "Together, we shall destroy capitalism and replace it with surrealism! The revolution is waiting!"

Shining like black obsidian under the blazing New Mexico sun, the 2003 GMC Savana 2500 with the TOPS acronym stenciled on the rear side windows in large, yellow, army-style letters started up with a roar as Turquoise turned the key in the ignition.

A man's voice, rife with a nasal twang and all the sleaziness of an unscrupulous used car salesman, suddenly blurted out from the speakers of the radio. "I'm Cletus Cooter, and I'll save any soul from eternal damnation for just ninety-nine ninety-five. No ups, no extras. Ain't that right, my purty little Honeydew?"

The breathy voice of a sobbing Southern Belle replied, "That's right, Cletus. No one does it better than you do, sugar-britches. Praise the lord!" After a brief pause to sniffle, she continued. "As many of you good Christian folk out there in radio-land already know, I—Honeydew Mellins—used to bare my flesh for drooling men with excited loins and fists filled with Satan's money. Yes, brothers and sisters, I was led down the path of sin and shame by the devil himself. But Cletus Cooter saved my soul from eternal damnation. Now I only bare my flesh for the Father, the Son, and the Holy Spirit." She paused to once again sniffle, and then erupted joyously, "So praise the Lord and give Cletus a call today. He can save you, too!"

"Brothers and sisters, the devil has many sins for sale: the sin of alcohol, the sin of drugs, the sin of gambling, and sins of the flesh. I say, stop giving away your money to Satan, and give it to me—the Reverend Cletus Cooter—so that I may save your soul from eternal damnation!"

"Praise the Lord!" Honeydew Mellins whooped, shaking a tambourine.

"Remember, friends—no ups, no extras. This Sunday, let our Cathedral of Divine Ostentation be a catheter to drain away your sins!"

The preacher's words were immediately followed by a catchy, banjo-propelled jingle with the chorus: "If you need an exorcism from that demon, Darwinism, go see Cletus, go see Cletus, go see Cletus…"

Turquoise suddenly felt the cold steel of a gun pressed against the back of her head.

"Turn off those sanctimonious charlatans!" growled the agitated Gonzalez brothers from the backseat.

Fearing for her life, Turquoise did as she was told. She quickly switched the radio to a classic rock station, where Grace Slick's soaring voice was belting out an exhortation to "feed your head." With music soothing the savage beasts, Turquoise took a deep breath to steady her nerves and stepped on the gas pedal.

As she sped away down the highway of uncertainty with the Siamese twins looming over her shoulders, she silently bid farewell to the rapidly shrinking teepee trading post in the rear view mirror, unsure if she would ever lay eyes upon it again.

* * *

"What am I supposed to do with *this* thing?" Turquoise asked, her eyes darting back and forth between the highway in front of her and the latex mask of North Korean Supreme Leader, Kim Jong-un, dropped into her lap by her conjoined captors in the back seat.

"Put it on before we arrive at the Dice and Vice Casino," Russ Gonzalez instructed as he pulled a realistic-looking Vladimir Putin latex mask over his head. "That place is ripe for the robbing, but they've got security cameras everywhere. Therefore, it's imperative that we hide our true identities so no one can identify us."

"But, you guys are the only Siamese twins in all of Weasel County. Don't you think that's sure to give away your identities—with or without the masks?"

"Listen and learn, comrade," Russ Gonzalez enjoined, his voice slightly muffled by his mask. "Before embracing the path of revolution, Tania and I faked our own deaths. No one can point a finger at you if they think you're already dead."

"That's pretty ingenious," Turquoise complimented as she made a right turn onto Red Herring Highway. No sooner had she passed the bustling Mother Trucker all-night truck stop with its giant yellow M atop a towering steel pole, a look of fret appeared on her face. "But what about all the armed guards at the casino? That place is crawling with them! They're not going to let us rob the place and walk out with all the money just like that. What if they shoot at us? Shouldn't we be wearing bullet-proof vests or something?"

Ross Gonzalez had been staring with an intensifying look of loathing at the Donald Trump latex mask handed to him by his sibling. "How come *I* always get stuck having to wear the stupid Donald Trump mask?" he complained. "It's not fair, Tania. Why can't *I* be Vladimir Putin once in a while instead of that putrid, tangerine-colored asshole?"

Russ Gonzalez shook his head. "Because that putrid, tangerine-colored asshole is the kind of asshole that other assholes look at and say, 'now *there's* an asshole!' Besides, I'm the general of this army, so it's only fitting that *I* wear the Putin mask. Now, stop your damn bellyaching and put on the fucking mask."

Grandfather Fukowee suddenly appeared from behind the twisting branches of a large manzanita bush and darted out onto the highway. Turquoise reactively slammed her foot down on the brake pedal and jerked the steering wheel to the left to avoid turning him into road kill. The smoldering tires screeched like the claws of a demon across a hellish chalkboard as the rear end of the van fishtailed wildly out of control. The Gonzalez brothers emitted a prehistoric-sounding grunt as the vehicle flattened a mustard-colored road sign reading ABSOLUTELY NOTHING NEXT 22 MILES, and literally scared the crap out of a nearby armadillo, in copious amounts. Turquoise let out a scream and held onto the steering wheel for dear life as the van overturned and rolled over several times, filling her ears with the sounds of crunching metal and breaking glass.

While her body was being battered and bruised by the flipping van, her heart-pounding panic vaporized, leaving her feeling as though she were floating in a dream. Nothing seemed real. The past and the present and the future melted into one shapeless, meaningless blur, and her life flashed before her eyes like an out of control reel of celluloid from a bizarre Federico Fellini film. For a brief moment, Turquoise's rattled brain even convinced her that she was the main character of a tasteless paperback novel penned by a mad author with a mind as twisted as the burning wreckage she would soon find herself trapped within.

Part Three
Amok in the Muck

A startling symphony of beeping and buzzing from the flashing ghost-detecting devices in the back of the TOPS van devoured the deathly silence that hung heavy in the air after the out of control vehicle had come to an abrupt stop. Steam billowed from under the crumpled hood like a cloud of ill omen.

Turquoise stared forward through the cracked windshield in numb horror, unsure if she were dead or alive. She gradually became aware of something warm and wet on her cheek. She released her fingers that were still tightly locked around the twisted steering wheel, and tilted the rear view mirror down to confront her reflection. A stream of blood from a jagged cut above her left eyebrow was coursing in a rivulet down the left side of her face like a streak of bright red war paint running in the rain. She wiped it from her cheek with her hand and stared at it as it glistened on her fingers and palm.

Oh, shit.

Moments later, a dull throbbing pain replaced her numbness. It stormed the inside of her head with relentless cruelty. She shut her eyes and wrinkled up her nose, but that did nothing to alleviate her headache from hell.

Well, I guess that proves I'm still alive.

Wincing, she slowly turned her head to the right and gasped with shock. The gorge rose in her throat and she quickly turned her head away and fought with herself to keep from vomiting in her lap.

Slumped over in the blood-drenched front passenger seat like a poster child for seatbelt safety was the lifeless body of Russ Gonzalez, the Vladimir Putin latex mask still covering his head, albeit slashed in several spots and splattered with gore. Bloody chunks of cartilage and liver dangled from a yawning hole in his sternum where his conjoined twin had been attached before the crash violently tossed them about and ripped them apart from each other.

Turquoise looked over her right shoulder. The sight of Ross Gonzalez's mangled and decapitated corpse sprawled across the bench seat behind her in a puddle of blood with guts hanging from his sternum filled her eyes with horror, and her stomach with nausea. His head was nowhere to be seen.

It wasn't a pretty sight, to be sure, but Turquoise felt, that in an ironic way, the two Tanias had achieved in death what they had longed for in life— to be separated. And in a peculiar sort of way, she actually felt happy for them.

Hit by the sudden realization that she was no longer a hostage of the Siamese Liberation Army or in danger of being pumped full of bullets by some trigger-happy rookie cop with a "shoot first and ask questions later" policy, a sense of relief washed over Turquoise. She unbuckled her seatbelt—thankful that she, unlike the Gonzalez brothers, had worn one—and pulled up on the handle of the door. However, it was jammed and would not open. She tried it again, but to no avail.

Flames suddenly burst from under the hood with a roar. They were accompanied by a thick volume of black smoke that rose into the air almost as quickly as the panic that rose in Turquoise's chest. Wasting no time, she climbed over the dead body in the seat next to her and tried the other door; but, like the one on the driver's side, it too was jammed.

With the smell of gasoline and death invading her lungs, and her heart pounding like a drumstick-wielding Keith Moon on Dexedrine, Turquoise raced to the back of the Savana 2500. Spotting her stolen silver ring on the floor, she snatched it up and returned it to its rightful place on her finger. She then escaped through the back doors of the van and ran like the wind in the direction of the all-night truck stop.

Grandfather Fukowee's claw-like hands suddenly seized her, causing her feet to grind to a halt, and a scream to rise in her throat. Still possessed by the spirit of Jimmie Yellow Snow and transformed by the curse of the snapping turtle, the old man spun his frightened granddaughter around to face him. An evil glow beamed from his eyes. He grabbed her by her wrists and hissed at her, while snapping his atrocious beak.

Gritting her teeth, Turquoise delivered a swift kick to her grandfather's gonads, sending a shockwave of acute pain surging through his body with such intensity that his mouth flopped open and his eyes crossed, uncrossed, and then crossed again. Recoiling in testicular agony, he released his hold on his dauntless granddaughter, grabbed his assaulted crotch with both claws, and yowled in a falsetto.

Turquoise once again took off running down the shoulder of the highway, her sights set on the truck stop in the near distance with its sign shimmering like a beacon of hope in the bright afternoon sun. She had advanced no more than a dozen feet before the turtle-man caught her by the braids and wrenched her to a halt. Like an instant replay, he spun her around and his claws clamped down upon her wrists, holding her captive.

"Let me go!" Turquoise yelled. "Unless you want another kick in the family jewels!"

"Don't play hard to get," said Grandfather Fukowee. "You turn Jimmie Yellow Snow on." He began moving his hideous head from side to side and wiggling his worm-like tongue in a strange mating dance. "It's the breeding season, Turquoise. Don't make me get aggressive."

Taking backward steps, he began pulling Turquoise toward the black muck of a nearby swamp in which he had recently taken up residence. She tried to rest herself free from his iron-like grip, but his claws tightened around her wrists.

"Are you going to kill me?" she asked.

"No. I have other plans for you," the old Indian replied.

"Where are you taking me?"

"To my lair in the swamp for a fuck in the muck!"

Turquoise gasped. The thought of her grandfather mating with her—even in the guise of a spirit possessed snapping turtle—filled her with copious amounts of disgust. She was now all the more determined to escape from the sexually aroused creature that he had become, and fought like a bucking bronco to regain her freedom. She was a strong girl; however, her strength was no match for Fukowee's paranormal-powered might.

Suddenly, the burning TOPS van exploded in a great ball of fire that shot skyward, sending bits of metal, pieces of glass, and other debris flying in all directions. Like a cephalic cannonball, Ross Gonzalez's detached head shot out of the flame-engulfed wreckage and flew through the air in Turquoise's direction. Spotting it in flight, the blue-eyed girl instinctively ducked and the airborne head crashed into Grandfather Fukowee's forehead with a loud crunch. The impact knocked him to the ground with a dull thud.

To Turquoise's astonishment, the possessed geriatric began to undergo a rapid physical transformation. His sharp, turtle-like beak and claws retracted and his gray, scaly skin turned smooth as his reptilianism gave way to the re-emergence of his human features. In less than thirty seconds, the metamorphosis was complete.

A strange hissing noise, unlike anything Turquoise had ever heard before, suddenly filled her ears. It grew louder by the second. Looking up, she caught sight of a blazing comet streaking across the cloudless sky. It was phenomenally immense and traveling in a westerly direction.

As it passed overhead, a peculiar tingling sensation engulfed Turquoise's body. She found herself unable to move a muscle, or even blink an eyelid. It was as if her entire body had turned to stone.

An ear-splitting sonic boom thundered out over the desert, and within a matter of seconds, the comet was out of sight. The mysterious tingling vanished, and to Turquoise's relief, she regained control of her body. She gazed down at her hands and wiggled her fingers as if testing them to see if they still functioned.

That was bizarre, she thought. *What the hell just happened?*

She looked over at the spot where her grandfather had fallen, startled to find his body gone. Her eyes scanned the landscape around her, but the old man was nowhere in sight. It was as if he had simply vanished into the thin air, along with the decapitated head of Ross Gonzalez. Turquoise was puzzled.

Where the hell did they go?

She then realized that the burning remains of the exploded van had also disappeared without a trace. Not so much as a scrap of metal, a shard of broken glass, nor a wisp of smoke remained. Her puzzlement blossomed into full-blown shock. She blinked her eyes and shook her head in an unavailing attempt to make sense of it all.

A dusty wind whistled an unearthly refrain, while a lone tumbleweed scurried across the deserted highway like a question in search of an answer. In spite of the heat of the day, an icy chill crept into Turquoise's bones.

What's going on here? Have I gone stark raving mad?

* * *

Upon her arrival at the normally busy truck stop, Turquoise was met by an overwhelming silence and a deepening sense that something was amiss. To her surprise, there was not a truck or a car anywhere in sight. Not even a single lot lizard.

Outside the truck stop's diner there stood an ancient telephone booth. Turquoise pulled the cracked glass door open, deposited the required amount of coins in the slot at the top of the coin-operated phone, and attempted to place a call to the Squealing Squaw Trading Post. Three high-pitched tones blared into her ear, immediately followed by a recording of a woman's voice informing her that the number she had dialed was not in service. The recorded message then instructed her to hang up and try her call again, which she did. However, she once again got the same recording.

What the hell?

Turquoise hung up, scooped up her change, and then dialed 911. The line rang. And rang. And rang. Turquoise sighed with impatience as five rings turned into ten, which turned into twenty.

Come on. Answer the damn phone!

Feeling disgusted, Turquoise was about to hang up when a man with a twang in his voice answered with a "hello" that sounded more like a question than a greeting.

"Hello? Is this 911?" Turquoise asked, unsure if she had reached a 911 dispatcher.

The man paused for a few moments. "Uh, yes ma'am. Uh, what all is the nature of your emergency?"

Turquoise heard what sounded like a female voice giggling in the background. "My name is Turquoise Moonwolf. I was kidnapped, and there was an accident and an explosion… I think. I mean, there was, but I don't know where it went. It's like… I mean… Oh, it's all too complicated to explain over the phone! I just need you to send some help."

"You sound like a pretty young thing to me. Why, I'd be more than happy to help you. That's my job. Now, where are you at?"

"I'm calling from the payphone at the Mother Trucker all-night truck stop on the Red Herring Highway."

After a long period of silence, the twanging man asked Turquoise if she were by herself, to which she replied, "yes."

"Good. Good. Help is on the way. Now, don't you go wanderin' off anywhere, you hear? You stay put at that there truck stop."

Before Turquoise could answer, there was a click and the line went dead. She hung up and walked over to the diner. Inside, the lights were on, but there was not a single soul in the place—no beehive-headed waitresses in their pink and white uniforms, and no greasy short order cooks in stained wife-beater undershirts. There were no grubby, coffee-guzzling long haul truck drivers with nostril-offending armpits, and none of the usual verminous grilled cheese-chewing locals.

A thick layer of light gray dust coated all the tabletops and chair seats, and cobwebs clung to every corner like hideous shrouds. The carcasses of small rodents and lifeless insects—all in varying stages of decay—littered the dirty floor, along with flakes of old lead paint and powdery pieces of crumbled plaster that had dropped down from the ceiling.

Confusion rained down upon Turquoise like a New Mexico summertime monsoon. The truck stop diner looked as if it had stood abandoned for years, yet it was bustling with customers just earlier that afternoon! Turquoise tried to make sense of it, but like her mysteriously vanishing grandfather and the disappearing wreckage of the van, any logical explanation eluded her. The only thing she could be sure of at that point was that something was wrong with this picture—something frightfully wrong.

Turquoise decided to wait for the police outside, and was halfway out the door when a peculiar sound, like a strange watery gurgling, perked up her ears. It seemed to be coming from the other side of the soda fountain, where a row of swivel stools with pitted chrome legs and red leather seats stood like silent sentinels.

"Hello?" Turquoise called out, her voice echoing eerily in the deserted restaurant. "Is there anyone here?"

Silence replied.

Curiosity stirred Turquoise into action. She cautiously inched her way across the diner in the direction of the soda fountain. As she drew closer to it, the watery gurgling once again filled her ears— only this time it was much louder.

To Turquoise's sheer horror, a trio of black, octopus-like tentacles suddenly shot up from behind the counter. At the end of each suction-cup-covered limb was a large bulbous thing, like a misshapen human head, with a grotesque gaping mouth displaying a circular row of barbed teeth. Reeking with the foulest of stenches, and dripping with bubbling, stomach-churning slime, the tentacles waved wildly before lashing out in an attempt to coil around Turquoise's body. However, before the creature could snare her for its lunch, her feet were in motion and she was out the door of the diner like a shot, colliding with a uniformed officer of the law whose nametag identified him as Sheriff Traylor Parks. The impact nearly knocked the oversized, black Stetson hat from his head.

"Whoa there, Missy! Who all are you running from?"

"Not a who all," Turquoise explained, breathlessly, "but a what all."

"Come again?"

Turquoise pointed to the diner and trembled. "I know this is going to sound absolutely crazy to you... I know it would sound crazy to me... but there's something freaking weird in that diner... some kind of thing... some kind of monster... I don't know. Whatever it was, it tried to kill me! I narrowly escaped with my life! Oh, Sheriff, you've got to believe me. It was the most horrible thing!"

"How horrible was it?"

Turquoise's body shivered. "It was more horrible than the thought of Donald Trump as president for life!"

Crimson rage suddenly came into the sheriff's face and his nostrils flared. "Don't ever let me hear you say a disparaging word about that man, Missy! He was the finest commander-in-chief this country has ever seen! Why, even our great national hero—Richard Milhous Nixon—pales in comparison! The Donald single-handedly took this country and transformed it from a freethinking nation of commie liberals and progressive parasites into a bleak, dystopian hellscape, where the banal horror of everyday life is marked by intermittent periods of senseless cruelty and violence!" He reached into his breast pocket and extracted a small notebook and pen, and spoke in a calmer voice. "Now, tell me, what did this alleged monster of yours look like? I need you to describe it for me while I write it down in this here book, and don't you leave out no details either."

Turquoise drew a deep breath to calm her emotions. "This thing was like some sort of mutated sea creature out of a tacky Japanese monster movie. I've never seen anything like it in my entire life! It was bizarre! It had these long, black tentacles, sort of like an octopus, but they had human-like heads with sharp teeth. That's what it tried to grab me with!" Turquoise wrinkled up her nose in disgust. "The whole thing was slimy and smelled like a backed-up sewer, and it made the most repulsive gurgling sound. This thing... it definitely isn't human, and it isn't any kind of animal either. If you ask me, it's something not of this world!"

Sheriff Parks crossed his arms and stared curiously at Turquoise. She could tell from the expression on his face that he did not believe any of what she had just told him.

"Have you been licking hallucinogenic toads, Missy?"

"What? Of course not! I'm telling you the truth, Sheriff!"

"Ain't no octopuses in New Mexico," the sheriff shook his head from side to side. "Now just you take a deep breath and calm yourself down, young lady. Are you the one who called to report a kidnapping and a vee-hicular accident?"

Turquoise nodded her head. "Yes."

"I see. Would it be a safe bet to say that you hit your head in that crash? Now, I ain't no doctor, but I've dealt with enough accident victims to know that brain injuries can sometimes cause folks to see all kinds of things that ain't really there... like giant, man-eating octopuses in truck stop diners."

"But it was there!" Turquoise protested. "I know what I saw. I didn't imagine it!"

"Okay, okay. Calm down, Missy. There's no need for you to go running amok. If it'll make you feel better, I'll go inside and have me a look around. But I can guarantee you that as sure as your braids are black, there ain't going to be nothin' in that building but a lot of dust and cobwebs."

"Okay, but be careful," Turquoise advised. "That thing in there is dangerous!"

"Don't you worry none, Missy."

If that chromosome-deficient, pasty-faced mongrel calls me 'Missy' one more time, I swear he's going to need a pair of forceps to pull that ridiculous cowboy hat out of his bacon-reeking asshole.

Sheriff Traylor Parks drew his Glock 22 sidearm and cautiously entered the diner, while Turquoise nervously waited outside with bated breath. Several minutes later, he emerged with a smirk upon his face and returned his gun to its holster.

"You can relax. There weren't nothin' in there except a whole lot of dust and cobwebs, just as I predicted there would be."

"What? That's impossible! Did you look behind the soda fountain? That's where the creature was lying in wait."

The sheriff nodded. "Yes ma'am. I sure did. But there weren't no octopuses behind there. I even looked in the kitchen and the warsh-room. No monsters. Nothin'!"

Turquoise peered through the dirty plate glass window of the diner. "I don't understand any of this. How could that—that *thing*—just disappear into thin air? And how could this diner be abandoned? When I passed by it, just before the van crashed, it was open and there were trucks and cars and customers…"

"You must have driven past a different truck stop. People do it all the time. A lot of them look the same, you know."

"No. It was this one. I'm positive. It was the only truck stop I drove past."

Shaking his head and crossing his heavily tattooed arms, the sheriff refuted, "Couldn't have been. This place went out of business years ago after that deadly swarm of EF-5 tornadoes tore through Chupacabra, destroying nearly everything in its path."

Ambushed by bewilderment, Turquoise turned and looked at the sheriff. "Tornadoes?"

He nodded his head. "Yes ma'am. It was the damnedest thing, too. Happened during one of the worst droughts these parts had ever experienced. I tell you, those twisters appeared out of nowhere and ripped through here with a vengeance! Nobody bothered to rebuild anything, so there ain't much standing between this place and Coyote Gulch, just a few old shacks here and there. Oh, and the old Penance Ministries church. Luckily the good Lord saw fit to spare that."

Bafflement creased the skin of Turquoise's brow. "What the hell are you talking about? I've lived in Chupacabra all my life and we've never had a tornado outbreak in this area, although my grandfather *did* almost conjure up a twister during one of his bungling rain dances."

Turquoise let out a little nervous laugh. However, the unamused sheriff slowly shook his head as if in pity and mumbled something to himself about brain injuries.

As a rust-ravaged metal sign over the gas pumps squeaked in the desert breeze, Turquoise stared off into the horizon, dumbfounded and speechless. What hidden meaning did all these curious and inexplicable things hold? Were they merely figments of her imagination, engendered, perhaps, by a blow to her head as the sheriff had suggested earlier? Was she trapped in a bizarre nightmare from which she would awaken any moment? Or had her mind taken a detour into madness? She began to ponder the possibility that she had died during the crash and was a spirit wandering the underworld. The more she searched her rattled brain for the answer, the more she felt like Lewis Carroll's Alice, after having plummeted down the rabbit hole into a bizarre world where nothing was real.

Turquoise's silent speculation was blown to smithereens by the sheriff's voice inquiring if she were all right.

"You're looking a little green around the gills there, Missy, if you'll pardon me sayin' so. I think it might be in your best interest if I take you someplace where you can get some help. I don't think your moccasins are laced all the way to the top, if you know what I mean."

"I know what you mean, and I'm not crazy!" Turquoise protested, in a feeble attempt to convince not only the sheriff, but also herself. Since the disconcerting vanishing act of the TOPS van and her grandfather, she was having growing doubts about her sanity. "I'm just having a very weird day, and more than anything I just want to go back to the Squealing Squaw Trading Post, where I work. My poor old grandmother must be worried sick about me!"

Sheriff Parks opened the rear door of his cruiser and motioned with his hand for Turquoise to get in. She climbed into the backseat, anxious to return to the trading post. He started up the engine and drove out of the parking lot onto Red Herring Highway. He picked up the microphone of his radio and depressed the transmit button.

"This is Sheriff Traylor Parks to dispatch. Be advised I am en route with a fifty-one fifty. Over."

There was a five-second pause, and a female's voice crackled over the radio speaker.

"Copy that, Sheriff. What is your ETA? Over."

"About fifteen minutes. Over."

"Ten four."

The sheriff turned off the radio.

"What did you mean by a fifty-one fifty?" Turquoise asked.

"Nothing for you to worry your pretty little head about, Missy," the sheriff replied, as he turned the car off onto a dusty, unpaved road leading to the long-abandoned ghost town of Nalgona.

"Hey! This isn't the way to Chupacabra!" Turquoise exclaimed as a battered stop sign slid past her window like a red omen of doom. "Where are you taking me?"

The sheriff did not answer.

Panicked, Turquoise pounded her fists on the metal screen that separated the front of the squad car from the rear. "Stop this car and let me out!" she cried, her demands falling on deaf ears.

The musky aroma of cannabis wafted through the car as Turquoise watched in astonishment while the sheriff casually light up a joint. After taking a couple of tokes, he offered her a hit, which she politely declined. He shrugged his shoulders, took another toke, and began humming a chirpy little tune that was both vexatious and hauntingly familiar to Turquoise's ears. She was unable to place it at first, but after a short while, recognition set in like gangrene.

Go see Cletus, go see Cletus, go see Cletus.

Part Four
Rattlesnake Necktie

"Why are we stopping here?" Turquoise asked as the sheriff pulled up in front of the remains of an old church with a sun-bleached sign that said: Penance Ministries/SFC Studios.

Sheriff Traylor Parks parked alongside an old Cadillac Eldorado with an Infant of Prague figurine attached to its grill and beeped his horn three times before turning off the ignition. "Now, there's nothing for you to worry about, Missy. The man and woman who run this here organization are kind-hearted, God-fearing, Christian folk. They'll see to it that you're taken care of good and proper."

As Turquoise stepped out of the squad car, the front doors of the church creaked open to reveal a smiling middle-aged couple standing in the doorway, waving hello.

The man was a portly specimen with a spray-on tan, a mouth like a puckered anus, and stubby fingers embellished with enough flashy gold rings to put a pimp daddy into a coma of envy. His thinning, dirty blond hair exhibited the inauthenticity of a bad comb-over, and the image of a Latin cross was tattooed on the center of his greasy forehead in black ink.

The woman at his side—a busty exercise in tawdriness—towered over him in her pink, rhinestone-speckled high heel shoes and platinum blonde wig that was teased up into a missile silo of synthetic fibers. Her eyelashes, encrusted with numerous layers of black mascara, resembled long-legged spiders dipped in tar. Her cheeks, whiter than the dunes of the White Sands Missile Range, were permanently stained with streaks of black from decades of rapture-induced running eye make-up, giving her a "cheaper than a whore at a clearance sale" look, which she wore with pride.

Turquoise instantly recognized the couple from their daily barrage of one-minute-long commercials, which television viewers throughout Weasel County had been mercilessly subjected to for years: They were none other than televangelist Cletus Cooter and his pole-dancing, Jesus-praising consort, Honeydew Mellins.

Cletus Cooter winked one of his bloodshot eyes at Turquoise as the sheriff escorted the Native American girl to the entrance of the church with his hand wrapped tightly around her upper arm. "Salutations, Turquoise," he greeted, his twanging voice sounding suspiciously like that of the 911 operator on the telephone back at the truck stop. "I'm the Reverend Cletus Cooter, and this here is

Miss Honeydew Mellins. We've been expecting you."

"Praise Jesus!" Honeydew Mellins exclaimed in a voice strangely similar to the one that crackled over the radio in the sheriff's car. Her heavily made-up eyes glistened with joyful tears. "It always fills me with great joy to welcome a lost sheep. This land of disenchantment can be so cruel to those who have strayed from the path of righteousness." She turned to Cletus, excitedly. "Oh, Cletus! Isn't she just a precious thing? She reminds me of one of those little Kachina dolls they sell in those roadside tourist shops—only life size!"

Cletus Cooter emitted a little grunting sound, as his head jerked up and down like a puppet, his reptilian gaze firmly fixed on Turquoise's almond-shaped eyes.

"I bought me a rattlesnake necktie at one of them places a few years back," the sheriff boasted, the pupils of his eyes dilated like black, Roswell-bound flying saucers.

With a wave of his hand, Cletus Cooter motioned for Turquoise to come inside. She complied and followed the preacher and his consort down a narrow, claustrophobia-inducing hallway to a small room that reeked of must and despair, with the lawman following closely behind like a shadow. An old and badly scuffed trestle table with four equally scuffed wooden chairs stood in the center of the room like depressing relics from the era of the Great Depression.

Cletus Cooter motioned with his hand for Turquoise to take a seat.

She sat down and her eyes drifted about the room, unsure if the toenail fungus green on the walls and ceiling was paint or mold. And then her eyes beheld an eerie sight.

On a cracked wall, above a veneer-peeling sideboard displaying a statue of Saint Denis holding his decapitated head, hung a massive oil painting featuring a bearded man garbed in a long blue robe. Lying on a bloodstained altar before him was the nude body of a ghostly-white woman, whom he was hacking into pieces with a large dagger with a ruby-encrusted handle while a trio of robed men with smiling faces carried away her head and dismembered limbs.

Intrigued, Turquoise rose from her chair and made her way over to the framed monstrosity in order to avail herself a better look. Upon closer inspection, she was taken aback to discover that the facial features of all four men in the painting bore a striking resemblance to those of Cletus Cooter.

"I can tell you're an admirer of fine art," Honeydew observed. "Cletus painted it himself, using a live model. It's his magnum opus."

Turquoise was unsure how to react, but didn't want to come off as rude. "It's uh, very unique. No home should be without one."

"It's his rendition of *The Levite's Concubine*—a story from *The Book of Judges*. Are you at all familiar with it?"

Turquoise shook her head.

"Once upon a time," Honeydew began, as if reciting a children's fairy tale, "there was a Levite—a Jewish man from the Tribe of Levi—who owned a female love slave known as a concubine. One day, the concubine—who was very unfaithful—ran away from the Levite and returned home to her father, who lived in Bethlehem. Well, the Levite wanted her back, so he went there to convince the concubine's father to return his daughter to him, which he gladly did. The journey home was a long one, so, before nightfall, the Levite and the concubine stopped in Gibeah, where an old man took them in for the night. In no time at all, a gang of godless queers surrounded the house where they were staying and pounded on the door, hell bent on raping the Levite. Can you imagine such a disgusting thing? Anyway, to make a long story short, the Levite decided that instead of fighting all those perverts and risk losing his honor, he would simply thrust his lady friend out the front door and let the mob of men have their way with her. Well, needless to say, those horned-up degenerates wantonly gang raped and beat her all night long."

Honeydew's eyelashes fluttered like the wings of a moth trapped against a windowpane.

"In the morning," she continued, "after enjoying a good night's sleep, the Levite awoke to find his concubine's battered and lifeless body on the doorstep. So what did he do? I'll tell you what he did: He threw her over the back of an ass, took her home, and cut her up with a knife into a dozen pieces—one for each of the twelve tribes of Israel!"

A chill crept up Turquoise's spine like a spider with legs of ice.

"How do you take your tea?" Honeydew inquired, running the tip of her index finger down one of Turquoise's braids.

Creeped out by her hostess' distracting digit, Turquoise shook her head. "I don't want any tea, thank you. All I really want is to just go home."

"Home is where the heart is," Honeydew stated, a mascara-colored tear running down her cheek. "And the baby Jesus wants to make his home in yours." She turned and headed for the door leading to the kitchen, her high heels clicking on the wooden floor.

Click, click…

Click, click…

Cletus Cooter smiled lovingly at his coiffed consort as she departed the room with a wiggle in her hips, and then he shifted his gaze back to Turquoise. "She brews it with holy water. It keeps the palace of the soul serene," he explained.

"I don't care what kind of water she brews it with. I really don't want any tea," Turquoise reiterated, the tone of her voice revealing her growing irritation and provoking a smoldering glare from the sheriff.

The preacher placed his hand upon Turquoise's shoulder. "Eleanor Roosevelt once said that women are like tea bags. You never know how strong they are until you put them in hot water."

With a sigh of fatigue, Turquoise returned her derriere to the scuffed wooden chair. The room went uncomfortably quiet, save for the faint ticking of a plastic Mary Magdalene wall clock.

Tick…

Tick…

Tick…

Turquoise cleared her throat. "So, what exactly is this place?"

"Penance Ministries—home of the Sin Fighting Crusaders, or SFC for short. It's where Honeydew and I carry out the things that God requires of us," Cletus Cooter replied. "It's the nerve center of our operations."

"Hmmm. That's odd. I thought the nerve center of your operations was the gold-plated Cathedral of Divine Ostentation, not a run-down building in a ghost town."

The preacher's face manufactured a puzzled look. "The gold-plated Cathedral of Divine Ostentation? I've never heard of such a place." He turned to the sheriff and inquired, "Have you?"

The sheriff, looking rather amused, shook his head to indicate no.

Cletus Cooter turned back to Turquoise, still sporting a puzzled look. "And just what on God's barren earth is this Cathedral of Divine Ostentation, if you don't mind me asking?"

Turquoise returned a puzzled look, wondering what sort of head games her host was playing with her. "As if you didn't know, it's that gaudy mega-church you built on sacred Indian burial ground and from where you and Mellins broadcast your phony faith-healing show every Sunday morning."

"Mega-church? Faith-healing show? Young woman, I know nothing of these things about which you speak. I fear the devil has made your mind his playground. Have you, by any chance, engaged yourself in the licking of hallucinogenic toads?"

"Of course not!" Turquoise growled. "I've never licked a toad in my entire life—

hallucinogenic or otherwise! And I wish people would stop asking me that stupid question!"

The sheriff cleared his throat, leaned over, and whispered into the preacher's left ear. "What did I tell you? Fifty-one fifty."

Cletus nodded his head and whispered back, "You were right about this one. The little wheel is turning, but the hamster is dead."

The clicking sound of Honeydew's high heels heralded her return from the kitchen. In her hands was balanced a silver-plated tea tray upon which sat four teacups with matching saucers arranged around a teapot in the shape of Charles Manson's head, complete with maniacal eyes and forehead swastika. Next to it was a plate containing cross-shaped cookies, each with four strategically placed drops of red jelly to symbolize the blood from Christ's crucifixion wounds.

Wow! This is some really weird shit, Turquoise thought as she stared in near disbelief at the head honcho of the Manson family's likeness in blue and white porcelain. *But everything is weird today, like some kind of riddle without an answer.*

"Mmmm—my favorites!" grunted the sheriff as he grabbed a handful of cookies and stuffed them into his salivating mouth like a starving mongrel.

"The world if filled with ugly truths and beautiful lies," Honeydew Mellins said while pouring some of the hot tea into Turquoise's cup from the spout protruding from Manson's temporal lobe. "Which one are you?"

Turquoise put down the cookie she had been nibbling on and took a sip of the tea to wash down the crumbs of crucifixion that had lodged themselves in her parched throat. "I really don't know what you mean."

"I asked you a simple question, Turquoise. Which one are you? Well? I'm waiting for an answer."

Turquoise pondered the bewigged woman's odd enquiry for several moments and then replied. "I'm neither an ugly truth *or* a beautiful lie. I am what I am, and that's all that I am. I'm Turquoise Moonwolf. No more. No less."

She took another sip of tea.

A look of loathing invaded Cletus Cooter's eyes like a swarm of angry hornets, and with his right arm outstretched, he pointed his finger accusingly at Turquoise. "You're one of those filthy stygiophiliacs, aren't you?"

Like a bird dropping from out of the blue, the question took Turquoise by surprise and wrapped her in a cocoon of perplexity. "A stygio what?"

Forcing his words past the stranglehold of his revulsion, the preacher replied, "A heathenish harlot whose satanic sexual organs are aroused by thoughts of hellfire and damnation!"

Turquoise was dumbfounded. However, before she could string together any words of rebuttal, Honeydew Mellins picked up the Charles Manson teapot, erupted with a cry of "Whore of Babylon!" and proceeded to pour a steaming, amber-colored stream of hot tea directly onto Turquoise's hand.

"Owww!" Turquoise screamed loudly, immediately grabbing hold of her scalded hand with her other hand in an ineffectual effort to quell the harrowing pain. "You fucking crazy bitch! You deliberately burned my hand with that God damned tea!"

Cletus Cooter's eyes went ablaze with fire and brimstone. "Sinner! Blasphemer!" he hissed like a demented hedgehog. "Thou shalt not take the name of the Lord thy God in vain; for the Lord will not hold him guiltless that taketh His name in vain!"

"And in a house of God where miracles are wrought!" Honeydew Mellins added in an appalled voice, a solitary teardrop glistening upon her cheek.

"By your words shall you be justified, and by your words shall you be condemned!" Cletus Cooter continued. "I realize you were raised by savages in a heathen environment, but that's no excuse for blasphemy. Sin cannot go unpunished."

With his eyes wild and filled with bloodlust, the sheriff drew his gun and aimed the barrel between Turquoise's eyes. "Do you want me to shoot her in the head?" he asked with excitement mounting in his voice.

"That's very sweet of you, Traylor," said Honeydew Mellins, as she wiped away the tear from her rouged cheeks, "But you've already reached your quota for this month. Plus, as you well know, that's not how the Lord—our rock and our redeemer—has instructed us on how to deal with sinners at Penance Ministries."

With his head hung like a scolded puppy, the sheriff grumbled under his breath and returned his gun to its holster.

"Screw all of you!" Turquoise exploded.

"Repent, savage!" the heated preacher demanded. "And be baptized in the name of Jesus Christ for the forgiveness of your sins!"

Anger swirled like a vortex in Turquoise's gut; it coursed through her veins, more searing than the tea that had blistered her hand, and bubbled violently inside her brain like a magma chamber on the verge of a volcanic orgasm. She had taken all she could take from these weirdos and could endure no more. Knocking her chair to the floor, she rose to her feet. It was time to go on the warpath.

"I've had my fill of this bullshit, and I'm not taking any more of it!" she vociferated with vexation, her hands balling up into fists of rage. "I've been kidnapped, preached at, threatened with a gun, insulted and scalded. Your toxic tongue can call me and my people 'savages,' but the real savages are the sanctimonious, fork-tongued piranhas of religion that devour reason and poison everything they come into contact with!"

"Discipline," Cletus Cooter began, like a schoolteacher calmly addressing his class, "produces a harvest of righteousness. Blessed is the one whom God corrects." Without warning, and much to the delight of Honeydew Mellins and the sheriff, he smacked Turquoise across the face with the back of his hand, sending her thumping to the floor. "You can now add 'corrected' to your laundry list of grievances."

"Yes! Yes!" Honeydew Mellins cried out in an orgasmic fashion while reaching up under her blouse and pinching her perky nipples between her fingertips. "Strike her again, Cletus! Again! Again! Oh, heavenly rapture! Yes! That's it! That's it! God wants to see some blood! He wants to see some bruises! My holy receptacle of

Christ is tingling. My Jesus juice is starting to flow! The Lord truly works in mysterious ways!"

"You fucking lunatics! You're all mad!" Turquoise cried out from the floor, all the while rubbing her sore cheek. "Certifiably crazy! Just wait until I sell my story to the *National Enquirer*. I'm sure they'd love to hear how I was brought to this hellhole against my will to be psychologically and physically abused by insane cult leaders. This sham of a religious organization will be under federal investigation so fast your heads will spin. Kidnapping is a first degree felony in New Mexico, and I'll personally see to it that your asinine asses get thrown into jail cells or padded rooms where they belong!"

Looking flabbergasted, Honeydew Mellins stood akimbo, hands on her hips and elbows out. "Never in all my years as a woman of the cloth have I ever encountered such ingratitude."

"Ingratitude?" Turquoise asked with a grating tone of anger in her voice. "You actually expect me to be grateful? For what… Pouring hot tea on my hand? I'm sorry; was I supposed to thank you for that?"

"It's all a part of the soul saving process, Turquoise. You see the blisters on your hand as a symptom of a second-degree burn; however, we view them as a sign of God's displeasure with you. No one ever said being dragged out of hell and returned to the path of salvation was easy—or without pain. You must have faith that Cletus and I only have your spiritual interest at heart! We want to cleanse you of all unrighteousness so that you, too, nay inherit the kingdom of God."

"Amen!" Cletus Cooter blurted out, his arms lifted high and his sweaty palms turned up as if drawing down invisible spiritual forces from the cracks in the yellowed, plaster ceiling.

"I don't want your salvation!" Turquoise screamed. "I don't want your cleansings! All I want is for you to let me go home! If you don't, I swear I'll…"

The preacher smiled and spoke in a calming voice. "There's no need for melodrama or threats. No one here is holding you against your will, Turquoise. You're free to leave this place any time you wish, if that's what you truly desire."

Free to leave. The words were succulent and rang in Turquoise's ears like a Liberty Bell. Despite her mistrust of Cletus Cooter, she savored each delectable vowel and every scrumptious consonant as mouth-watering thoughts of returning to the fiberglass teepee and to her beloved and abundantly dysfunctional Moonwolf clan warmed her insides with a gleam of hope.

Turquoise picked herself up off the floor, anxious for her ordeal to at last come to an end. All at once, a wave of dizziness came over her and sent her staggering to and fro like a drunkard. She paused for a moment to allow the disquieting sensation to pass. But, instead of subsiding, as she had hoped, it only intensified. The room began to spin out of control, and Turquoise shuffled over to the badly scuffed trestle table and grabbed onto the edge for support.

What's happening to me? Did these Bible-thumping crackpots slip me something?

Echoes of distorted laughter escaping from the mouths of the televangelists and the trigger-happy sheriff confirmed Turquoise's growing suspicion that her holy water tea had indeed been laced with some sort of mind-altering drug. She shut her blurry eyes, held on tight, and fought to remain conscious.

But it proved to be a battle she could not win.

Part Five
Unparalleled

When Turquoise awoke, groggy and none too focused, she found herself in an unfamiliar room, strapped to a stainless steel autopsy table with the hot glare of an overhead spotlight assaulting her turquoise-colored eyes.

Where the hell am I? Why am I strapped to this table?

Turning her face away from the blinding light, her eyes fell upon a black video camera mounted on a tripod. In front of it stood a stainless steel utility table, upon which sat a large, ruby-handled dagger that bore a disturbing resemblance to the one in Cletus Cooter's macabre painting. Its blade was speckled with what appeared to be dried blood.

A leathery brown book, which Turquoise instinctively knew was bound in human skin, sat inches away from the dagger, an inverted cross and the words, *Morum Mala Facta*, stamped in gold on its front cover. Turquoise was in no way proficient in Latin, but she remembered enough of it from high school to be able to translate the book's title into English. It said: *Bible of Evil Deeds*.

Alarmed by her precarious predicament, Turquoise twisted her body and struggled against the leather straps with all her might, but they continued to hold her down rigidly upon the table. She paused for a moment as if to build up her strength and resumed her endeavor to free herself from the unyielding restraints.

"Help!" Turquoise yelled, her words shrill with panic. "Someone help me!"

A faceless voice from the other side of the room crept into Turquoise's ears. It was the voice of a young woman and had an all too familiar ring to it.

"I would like to help you, but as you can see, I'm a bit tied up at the moment."

Turning her head in the direction of the voice, Turquoise was shocked to see her cousin, Dolores Angry Cloud, strapped to a large wooden cross in the corner of the room, a crown of thorns upon her head.

"Dolores!" Turquoise gasped. "What are you doing on that cross?"

"You're mistaken, hun. My name isn't Dolores. It's Indigo."

"Indigo?"

"Yes. My parents were New Age mystics and named me after the color of their Third Eye charkas."

"Stop it, Dolores! This is no time for one of your featherbrained jokes. Can't you see that this is a desperate situation we're in?"

"You poor thing. Have you been licking hallucinogenic toads?"

Turquoise rolled her eyes and responded with a groan. "Not you too, Dolores!"

"My name is Indigo Lackawanna. I was the lead singer of the lesbian punk rock band, Lez Valdez and the Piranha Pariahs, before those religious whack-jobs kidnapped me and tied me to this fuckin' crucifix. But if you insist on calling me 'Dolores,' far be it from me to use up what little time you have left by arguing with you about it."

Why is Dolores claiming her name is Indigo and acting like she doesn't know me? Turquoise wondered. "What do you mean by 'what little time I have left?'"

"Wake up and smell the coffin!" Indigo replied with a harsh laugh. "You're the reverend's new SFC Studios superstar!"

"Huh? What are you talking about?"

"Cooter and that tacky whore of his are sexual sadists and serial killers, among other things. They want everyone to think that SFC is the abbreviation for Sin Fighting Crusaders. But it isn't. It really stands for Snuff Films for Christ. That's how those two make their money—by offering pay-per-view live streaming of murder and mutilation on the dark web. And the sickos who get off on that shit—some of them celebrities, cops, judges, politicians—pay them up to ten thousand dollars to watch it!"

A jolt of unparalleled horror raced through Turquoise and she struggled even harder to free herself from the leather straps holding her to the table, but it was to no avail. "Oh, my God! This can't really be happening. I'm going to wake up any minute and find out this was all a nightmare. Aren't I?"

"That's only half of the story," said Indigo. "After Cooter and Mellins torture and kill their snuff stars, they cut up their dead bodies into a dozen pieces with the dagger that's on the table next to you, and then they feed them to a teratoma that lives at the bottom of that pit over there." She pointed across the room to a large opening in the floor, from which a repugnant smell arose.

"A teratoma? Isn't that one of those rare tumors that have hair and teeth and stuff?"

Indigo nodded. "That's precisely what it is. But this one also has tentacles and is massive… I mean really massive… like the size of a grizzly bear—and twice as vicious. Honeydew gave birth to it."

"Oh, my God!"

Indigo commenced a mocking snigger. "God had nothing to do with it. That thing is the demonic product of that demented bitch's incestuous union with her son, who just happens to be that lowlife Sheriff Traylor Parks." Indigo spat on the floor. "That whole family's nuts. They pray to that creature in the pit as if it were some kind of deity, you know. Not only does it unravel their sanity, more and more with each feeding, it demands their eternal servitude. It's evil."

Beads of cold sweat had gathered on Turquoise's forehead like raindrops on the bloom of a doomed flower. Mounting terror turned the blood in her veins into rivers of ice. She felt as helpless as a butterfly trapped in a nightmarish web of surreal horror, yet refused to resign herself to what seemed surely to be her inevitable fate of gore.

As Turquoise squirmed and struggled for her freedom, she pondered what unfathomable atrocities Cletus Cooter and his conniving consort might have in store for her, a barrage of terrifying images, like snippets from the worst of bad horror movies, inundating her mind.

Exhausted, she paused for a moment to collect her strength. "I always knew the world was full of crazy people, Dolores… I mean Indigo, but never in my wildest dreams did I think any human beings could be *that* crazy!"

"Never underestimate the craziness of the human mind," the girl on the cross replied, her words eerily echoing those spoken by the intoxicated William Cyrus Ballschmieder earlier that day while threatening to slice off his ear.

Like a light bulb switching on, it suddenly occurred to Turquoise that she had slipped the one-eyed pervert's straight razor into the front pocket of her jeans after his drunken departure from the teepee.

The straps holding Turquoise to the autopsy table with her arms at her side were unyielding and without mercy. But, with a determined effort, Turquoise managed to twist her hand just enough to slide two fingers into her pocket and pull out the razor. Exercising the utmost caution to prevent dropping the shaving device, she opened it, positioned it just right, and began sawing through the leather straps with its blade while Indigo looked on intently.

If this works and I get out of here alive, Turquoise thought as she worked with urgency and diligence, *I'm going to give that Billy Balls a great big kiss the next time I see him... but only after his weekly teeth brushing.*

Each second that passed seemed to drag on like an hour until finally Turquoise had cut through the first leather strap that held her captive. With her upper body now free, she bolted into a sitting position and hurried to slice through the strap pinning her legs to the table. There suddenly came the sound of advancing footsteps from multiple pairs of feet outside the door to the snuff studio—among them the clicking of high heels. Turquoise's adrenaline surged, causing her heart to pound like the galloping hoof beats of the Four Horsemen of the Apocalypse.

With a final cut of the blade, her legs once again tasted freedom. She leapt off the cold, metal table and rushed across the room to the wooden cross from which Indigo Lackawanna hung like a crucified hell-raiser in black Doc Martens boots. Wasting no time, she hacked through the thick rope wrapped around the ankles of the punk rocker, bringing a faint glow to the pallid features of the trussed-up girl. The rope fell to the floor like a defeated viper.

"Hurry," Indigo urged, her words wrapped in a desperate whisper.

Turquoise was about to free Indigo's wrists from the transverse beam of the wooden structure when the door burst open and she heard Cletus Cooter's voice, with its grating twang, gleefully announce, "It's show time!" She turned her head and was appalled to see him standing there, draped in the same long, blue robe worn by the creepy Levite in his macabre painting. He was flanked by the sheriff on one side, and by Honeydew Mellins on the other.

His eyes met Turquoise's and the barracuda grin on his face abated. In his eyes a storm of ire raged.

Upon discovering that Turquoise was no longer restrained and was attempting to free Indigo, a shriek flew out of Honeydew's mouth like a rabid bat from a caliginous cave. "This is an act of heresy! Get back on that table, sodomite! This is no way for the leading lady of *Death is a Many Splendor Thing* to behave!"

"Drop the razor, rabble-rouser!" barked the sheriff, his sidearm drawn and pointed at Turquoise. "Now, step away from the girl on the crucifix and keep both of your hands up in the air where I can see them!"

Turquoise did as he ordered.

"Traylor, use that rope over there to hogtie this heathen," Cletus Cooter instructed, "and then we can get on with the sacrificial rite."

With his eyes and gun locked on Turquoise, the sheriff made his way over to the crucifix and crouched down to pick up the rope from the floor. Without warning, Indigo unleashed a cry of "Pig!" and delivered a knockout blow to the back of the sheriff's head with the heel of her booted foot. With a grunt, the stunned lawman lurched forward and then landed, face down, in a heap like a two hundred pound slab of pork belly. His gun flew from his hand and skittered across the floor like a hockey puck in Turquoise's direction. She darted to the gun and snatched it up before Cletus Cooter and Honeydew could get to it.

"Don't make me shoot you," Turquoise cautioned, pointing the gun at her two captors.

"Release that punk rocker from that cross right now and let us both go!"

"Shoot them!" Indigo screeched. "What the fuck are you waiting for, girl? Do the world a favor and exterminate that pair of filthy cockroaches!"

Like a slithering snake, Cletus Cooter slowly advanced toward Turquoise and a startling smile stretched across his lips. "That would be a mistake, Turquoise. You and I are shrouded in the Divine Plan that the good Lord has purposed for us. Surrender yourself to God's will."

"Don't come any closer, Cooter!" Turquoise warned, her voice rising to a fevered pitch. "I swear to the Great Spirit I'll pull this trigger and blow your twisted brain right out of your head!"

"Just do it!" Indigo screamed.

Cletus Cooter laughed. "I wear the armor of God, the breastplate of righteousness, the sword of the spirit, and the butt plug of deep, deep faith. I'm on a mission from God. Bullets cannot stop me!" And with that being said, he lunged at Turquoise, his hands extended like claws.

Turquoise squeezed the trigger of the gun, sending a bullet sailing into the preacher's right shoulder. Blood spurted from the wound like red wine from a hole in a cask; however, the man did not flinch. His face showed no indication of pain and he continued to come at Turquoise. She squeezed the trigger again and fired off another bullet, which ripped a hole into the preacher's chest. His mouth burst open in a silent scream and his body spun in a grim pirouette. Bleeding profusely, he staggered across the floor, slipped on a slick puddle of his own blood, and fell headfirst into the reeking pit where the foul and monstrous teratoma waited, salivating and ravenous for human flesh.

"God bless David Parker Ray!" were Cletus Cooter's last words as his body plummeted to the bottom of the pit. It landed with a loud thud. Within a matter of seconds, the sound of sharp, chomping teeth puncturing skin and ripping flesh from bones drowned out the preacher's waning moans of pain. Turquoise's insides rippled with a feeling of nausea, coupled with a strange elation.

"Vengeance is mine, sayeth the Lord!" screamed Honeydew Mellins, as she snatched up the ruby-handled dagger from the utility table.

Turquoise turned her head and gasped. The teary-eyed televangelist was barreling down at her like a rampaging rhinoceros, her garishly painted eyes glazed over by a chilling look of derangement, and the silver blade of her dagger flashing in the light and precariously poised for a stabbing.

Without hesitating, Turquoise aimed the gun at the charging woman and squeezed the trigger several times. *Click! Click! Click!* To her horror, she realized the gun was out of ammunition. She threw the useless sidearm at Honeydew and it bounced off her mammoth mammaries and landed on the floor.

The tip of the plunging dagger had come within inches of puncturing a not-so-pretty hole in the side of Turquoise's neck when she grabbed Honeydew's wrist and pushed her arm back, preventing the stab. As the two women battled for control of the dagger—a struggle between the forces of good and evil—Indigo repeatedly yelled for Turquoise to "kill the bitch!"

Honeydew was putting up a good fight and Turquoise was astonished—almost impressed—by the older woman's strength. She was relentless… as well as insane. Like ammonia and bleach, it was a hazardous combination.

Turquoise's adrenaline pumped. Her breathing grew rapid. Beads of sweat formed on her forehead and were dripping down into her eyes, causing a slight burning sensation and a blur in her vision. But she refused to allow Honeydew Mellins the occasion to overpower her, for that would mean certain death.

Turquoise rammed Honeydew's lower back into the autopsy table, dislodging her blonde bouffant wig, which took a nosedive to the floor, uncovering a hairless scalp into which had been carved the numbers 666. Honeydew made a guttural sound deep within her throat and leaned into Turquoise with all her might, aiming the tip of the dagger at the young woman's wildly beating heart.

In a desperate attempt to preserve her own life, Turquoise called upon her inner warrioress. Evoking every ounce of strength she possessed, she twisted the dagger around, and drove it into her assaulter's right breast.

Honeydew let out an ear-shattering howl as copious amounts of blood and silicone blasted out of her body like the gelatinous contents of an exploding jelly doughnut. Clutching her rapidly deflating breast, she fell backward onto the autopsy table and continued howling in burning pain.

"You cursed little bitch! Look what you've done! I'm deflating! Deflating!"

Turquoise plucked the quivering dagger from Honeydew's bleeding bosom like Arthur drawing his legendary sword from the stone. She then raced over to the crucifix. Using the sharp blade originally intended for her pay-per-view demise, she sliced through the ropes that secured Indigo's wrists to the wooden beam.

Basking in the exhilaration of her reacquired freedom, Indigo Lackawanna wrapped her tattooed arms around Turquoise in a quick, but robust, hug of gratitude before removing the crown of thorns from her head and vengefully forcing the painful headpiece onto Honeydew Mellins' bald head, drawing blood. She then presented the slowly rousing sheriff with another fierce kick to the head, sending him back into the oblivion of unconsciousness. Crouching like a beast of prey, she fished his car keys from out of his pants pocket, stood up, and beamed with satisfaction.

Jingling the ring of shiny keys in front of Turquoise's face, Indigo flashed an almost-impish grin, prideful of her recent acquisition. "To the pig-mobile!" she thundered.

* * *

"Floor this mother!" Indigo shouted, her eyes of sepia blazing, her chest rising and falling at a rapid rate. "The faster we haul our asses out of this hellhole of a ghost town, the better!"

Turquoise responded to her passenger's request by jamming her foot down on the gas pedal of the sheriff's car. She held onto the steering wheel with a death grip as it shook wildly under her hands, the tires spinning dirt into thick clouds of dust. Outside the driver's side window, miles of disused, wooden utility poles with wires coming from nowhere and leading to nowhere whizzed by so fast they looked like a picket fence as the gravel road led back to the faded asphalt of the Red Herring Highway.

"Rock and roll!" Indigo cheered, in between tokes on a marijuana cigarette she had discovered in a see-through plastic sandwich bag while snooping through the glove compartment.

At the battered stop sign at the highway junction, Turquoise made a right turn, heading in the direction of her beloved Chupacabra. She tossed her head back, feeling almost giddy. Freedom never before tasted so delicious.

Her euphoria, however, was destined to be short-lived, and it withered away into a bramble patch of uneasiness when she overtook the abandoned truck stop that harbored the hellish beast of unknown origin.

As the building waned in her rear-view mirror, so did Turquoise's disquiet. She let out a sigh of relief. Monsters of both the human and non-human varieties were now far behind her, and a polychromatic sunset was beginning to paint its soothing colors on the western horizon. A smile found its way onto her face, for she knew that with each mile marker she passed, she was drawing closer to the Squealing Squaw teepee.

"It won't be long before we're back home, Dolores!" Turquoise realized her faux pas and grimaced. "I'm sorry; I keep forgetting. I meant to say Indigo."

Indigo shook her head and giggled. "Who the hell is this Dolores person you keep mistaking me for? She'd better be one cool bitch!"

"Dolores Angry Cloud. She's my cousin and best friend in the whole world. And yes, she's definitely one cool bitch... *and* a lesbian! You're the spitting image of her, like an identical twin. Same exact face. Same exact hair. Your voice is even the same as hers. It's the weirdest thing!"

"Wow! That *is* weird, but kind of cool at the same time. You want to know what else is weird, Turquoise? I've never met you before today; yet, somehow I feel like I've known you all my life. Isn't that crazy?"

"Not as crazy as almost getting snuffed by that pair of evangelical psychopaths back there and fed to a giant teratoma," Turquoise replied.

The sparkle in Indigo's eyes dimmed. "I would have preferred *that* over what those demented lowlifes did to me."

"What did they do to you?" Turquoise enquired, almost afraid to ask.

"They lured my band to their church of horrors one Sunday under false pretenses. They claimed their SFC Studios were holding auditions for a punk rock version of *Jesus Christ Superstar*. Well, their Sunday Mass turned into Sunday mass murder. They drugged us and locked us in filthy cages like animals, using electric cattle prods on us. One by one, they tortured and murdered my band mates to make their snuff films and then dismembered them and fed the body parts to their pet in the pit."

"Holy shit!" Turquoise exclaimed.

"*Un*-holy shit is more like it. The only reason I didn't meet the same fate as the others was because Cooter and his son used me as a baby factory, raping me on that crucifix several times each day, knocking me up, and then auctioning off the babies to pedophile priests and wealthy cannibal socialites. They called it 'dike conversion therapy' and said it would save my soul."

"That's abominable!"

"Sometimes, for the sheer fun of it, they'd inject me with some kind of medicine to induce an abortion, which they would film. And then, with the camera rolling, they'd put a loaded gun to my head and force me to…" Tears welled up in Indigo's eyes, and she began wringing her hands. "Oh, God! They'd force me to eat my aborted fetus!"

"Holy fuckin' buffalo balls!" cried Turquoise, almost veering off the road, gorge rising in her throat. "Those sick son of a bitches!"

Indigo did not comment. Instead, she stared out the passenger window as if in a trance, her abysmal silence speaking louder than words.

After regaining her composure, Turquoise spoke, hoping that her words would offer some amount of comfort to the traumatized girl in the seat next to her. However, in the back of her mind she knew there was nothing she could say that would.

"It's all right, Indigo. I know what you went through was a nightmare beyond any horror story. But that's all behind you now. The best thing to do is to try and forget it. The main thing is you and I made it out of there alive. We beat death!"

Indigo slowly turned her head and stared at Turquoise with vacant eyes. "Did we?"

* * *

"I don't believe my eyes!" Turquoise thundered in disbelief as she pulled up to the spot where the Squealing Squaw Trading Post once stood. "Where the hell is the teepee?"

"From the looks of things, I'd say your teepee is over there… and over there… and over there…" Indigo replied, pointing to all sorts of debris that were scattered about.

Turquoise climbed out of the stolen sheriff's car, immediately followed by Indigo. A desert breeze sailed through her braided hair, as she stood, mystified and akimbo, surveying the broken bits of this and the mangled scraps of that, which were strewn profusely over the desert floor. Remnants of rubber adult novelties and marital aids, melted and rotted from years of exposure to the grueling desert sun, dotted the arid landscape with simulated genitalia and orifices for as far as the eye could see. Little clumps of insulation clung to the spines of cacti like pink cotton candy. Before Turquoise's feet lay a piece of a splintered wooden sign with faded red letters that partially spelled out: THE SQUEALING SQUAW TRADING POST.

A single tear dribbled down Turquoise's cheek, making her feel like the iconic crying Indian (who, in real life, wasn't an Indian) in the old "Keep America Beautiful" commercials. Bafflement clawed at her brain.

"What the hell happened here?" Turquoise mumbled to herself as she looked around, frowning in confusion. "I thought the sheriff was just messing with my head when he told me that tornadoes destroyed Chupacabra. But he said that happened years ago. The Squealing Squaw was here this morning, just like the rest of the town. Everything was normal. Well, as normal as can be expected for Chupacabra. And now… now it's all gone! Wiped out! How is this possible? Have I lost my mind?"

"Are you all right, Turquoise?" Indigo's face was draped with concern. "You're looking really flummoxed."

"You'd be flummoxed, too, if *your* teepee suddenly disappeared."

Just then, the flash of something silver caught Turquoise's attention, and she angled her way toward it, curious. There, on the ground, surrounded by rubble, was Grandfather Fukowee's prized tomahawk, which he had inherited from his grandfather, Crooked Canoe. Its shining metal blade and hand-carved wooden handle were intact. Turquoise picked it up and lovingly held it in her hands. Another teardrop streamed from her eye, moistening the contours of her cheek.

With an eight-cylinder roar, like a bat out of hell, the Cadillac Eldorado with the Infant of Prague statue affixed to its grill came barreling down the highway and screeched to a halt beside the stolen squad car. The passenger door flew open and Sheriff Traylor Parks bolted from the vehicle, his revolver in hand. He pointed his gun at a stunned Turquoise and Indigo while Honeydew Mellins observed the action from the driver seat of the Caddy, her dagger-deflated right breast wrapped up in a blood-soaked bandage like a miniature mummy.

"Freeze!" shouted the sheriff. "I'm placing the two of you under arrest!" He strutted toward Turquoise and Indigo and cracked a grin. "I bet you thought you was pretty clever, Missy, smuggling in that concealed weapon of yours, killin' the fine Reverend Cooter, and absconding with the other prisoner." He snickered. "Murder. Assault on an officer. Automobile theft. Well, let me assure you both, your crimes won't go unpunished. The long arm of the law always catches up with you. Now, both of you, off with them clothes, and be quick about it!"

Turquoise's mouth dropped open, agape in disbelief. "You're fucking nuts!"

Indigo promptly gave the sheriff a middle finger salute. "Filthy pig!" she hissed. "You can kiss my ass!"

"You heard me, bitches. I said start stripping. And after you get all naked, I want you to lay down on the ground, on your backs with your legs spread and ready, and bleat like sheep!"

Horror-stricken, Turquoise watched as the sheriff's crotch suddenly sported a massive, pulsating bulge. It rapidly swelled to alarmingly epic proportions, stretching the fabric of the lawman's pants to its limit in an apparent effort to escape the rigor of its confinement. Unable to hold back the ballooning boner any longer, the zipper burst open and out popped the furled flesh of a peculiar pecker that exhibited a shiny greenish tint. As it uncoiled into a lengthy, tentacle-like appendage covered in dozens of tiny suction cups of darker green, the glans at the end of the freakish penis mushroomed into a grapefruit-sized human head, upon which formed a face resembling that of Donald Trump.

Turquoise's stomach churned. The hairs on the back of her neck bristled. She had experienced many strange adventures throughout her life; but for unparalleled horror, this one was eminent beyond comparison. She knew she had to act fast. With her life hanging in the balance, she crossed the first two fingers of her left hand for luck, cocked her right arm back, and hurled her grandfather's tomahawk at the sheriff's monstrous member with all the might she could muster.

The primitive blade whirled through the air and struck its intended target, slicing through the shaft, close to where it connected to the lower belly, instantly amputating the sheriff's penis. It dropped to the ground and bounced one time like a rubber chew toy before finally coming to rest, blood oozing from both ends like sap from a wounded tree.

Bellowing in agony, the sheriff dropped his gun and clutched his blood-spurting, sexless groin with both hands. The color drained away from his cheeks and he fell upon the ground, his body flipping and flopping like a beheaded chicken.

Honeydew shifted the Eldorado into drive, hit the pedal to the metal, and aimed the car at Turquoise and Indigo, each of whom let out a shriek and took off like rabbits running for their lives. Loud crunches and crackles filled the air as the whitewall tires rolled over the bits and pieces of the tornado-ravaged trading post.

Turquoise's foot caught on a rock and sent her sprawling toward the ground. She landed face down with a thud, the breath knocked from her lungs, and tiny lights flashing like exploding stars before her eyes. She cursed her luck and gritted her teeth, expecting any second to feel her bones crushed by the rapidly approaching vehicle.

The crunching and crackling came to a sudden stop, replaced by the furious whir of rear tires without traction. The odor of scorched rubber wafted through the air, prompting Turquoise to look up in curiosity. To her pleasant surprise, she discovered the Cadillac motionless, its left front tire helplessly trapped in a deep rabbit burrow.

Seizing the opportunity, Indigo made a mad dash to the immobile automobile and ripped the Infant of Prague statue from its grill. She repeatedly bashed it against the driver side window until the glass shattered. She then yanked open the door, climbed inside the car like a rabid animal on the attack, and began pummeling Honeydew's head with the statue.

"Die! You fucking bitch!" she screamed as she pummeled. "Die! Die! Die!"

Blood sprayed the interior as the replica of child Jesus broke Honeydew's nose, knocked teeth from her screaming mouth, and popped out an eyeball with its golden globus cruciger.

With her vengeance satiated, Indigo climbed out of the car, exhausted and splattered with gobs of gore. Breathing heavily, she gave Turquoise a thumbs-up and ambled toward her. Her blood-painted lips stretched into a smile of satisfaction.

With a roar of the engine and a squeal of the tires, the Eldorado screeched out of the hole, and with a thud worthy of a cringe, mowed down the punk rocker. A battered and monocular Honeydew Mellins detonated with insane laughter as she threw the car into reverse and ran over the girl again.

Turquoise's legs broke into a terror-fueled sprint, and she ran as fast as they could carry her. She knew her chances of outrunning the car was slim to none, but the thought of becoming the next human speed bump did not exactly appeal to her senses.

There suddenly came a high-pitched pulsing hum. It was unlike anything Turquoise had ever experienced. It was eerie. Unearthly. It grew louder and louder, threatening to deafen Turquoise's ears, until finally a blue port-a-potty materialized from out of nowhere a few yards in front of Turquoise. Its door swung open and a man wearing a brown suede fedora upon his head and an abnormally long, multi-colored scarf around his neck stepped out and wagged his hand furiously for Turquoise to hurry inside. He bore an uncanny resemblance to Billy Balls, except his face had no beard stubble, and he wore no eye-patch.

Turquoise raced toward the port-a-potty as the Eldorado sped toward her like a shark moving in for the kill. She could hear Honeydew's mad laughter growing louder as the car roared closer. With only seconds to spare, she made it to the port-a-potty and rushed inside. The man with the scarf around his neck quickly shut the door and pushed a small button on a panel on the wall. A loud and cyclic wheezing sound arose.

"Welcome aboard!"

Panting like a spent hound, Turquoise looked up and around. "What on earth is that strange noise?"

"Oh, that's nothing for you to fret about," the man replied, his voice thick with an English accent.

"It's simply the engines firing up in dematerialization mode." He grinned and offered Turquoise a Jelly Baby from a white paper bag.

Turquoise shook her head to decline. "Dematerialization?"

"Indeed! The opposite of materialization, as every fan of science fiction knows. It's the relatively simple process of converting from the material to the immaterial. Cup of tea, love?"

"No thank you. I've had enough tea for one day."

Turquoise gazed around at her surroundings in amazement. The interior of the port-a-potty was not at all what she had expected to find. Rather than being a closet-size building containing a toilet, it was a spherical, observatory-like structure, curiously immense in size, and packed with futuristic-looking instrument panels replete with copious dials, switches, and flashing buttons in every color of the spectrum. Not a single toilet was in sight.

"What is this?" Turquoise asked. "Some kind of interplanetary craft?"

With a gleam in his eyes, the man took Turquoise on a tour of the place, and explained, "After decades of inventing brilliant but useless marvels like powdered water and artificial smog, I decided to convert an inconsequential port-a-potty into a machine capable of traveling forward and backward in time, as well as between parallel universes. I call it, the Thunderbox."

"Wow!"

"Wow, indeed. The very nature of its design affords me a multitude of advantages, including the ability to bring along my own toilet whenever I travel through time and space, denying sewer divers and rival scientists insights to my stools."

"That's incredible!" Turquoise exclaimed. "You've been to the future?"

Smiling, the man nodded. "Indeed I have! And I must say, I remember the future as if it were yesterday. Oh, good heavens, where are my manners?" He extended his arm and shook Turquoise's hand. "Professor Ballschmieder at your service. But you can simply call me the Professor. Everyone throughout this sector of the galaxy does."

"I don't suppose anybody ever calls you... Billy Balls?"

"Billy Balls? That's a most interesting sobriquet. But, good gracious, no."

Turquoise introduced herself and thanked the Professor for saving her life.

"All in a day's work," he replied, modestly.

He then led Turquoise into his study, which smelled of old books and pipe tobacco. His gobsmacked guest sat down upon one of two maroon-colored chairs, and it let out a little squeak the moment her butt cheeks came into contact with the seat. The Professor proceeded to pour a generous amount of blackberry brandy into two snifters and handed one of them to Turquoise before his butt cheeks elicited a squeak from the seat of the other chair.

Turquoise took a sip of the sweet spirit. "You mentioned something about traveling between parallel universes. I've heard of those before, but I thought they only existed in science fiction."

The Professor's eyes twinkled. "Ah, well, yesterday's science fiction has a curious habit of becoming tomorrow's science fact. Wouldn't you agree? A parallel universe—and there are quite many of them, I might add—is a universe that exists separately from our own, and in most cases occupies the same timeline. It's a mirror world, if you will, where time moves in different directions and/or where mirror versions of ourselves live different lives, make different choices, and experience different fates."

He lit his pipe, and continued. "The concept of parallel universes—call them quantum universes, interpenetrating dimensions, alternate realities, or whatever you wish—is far from being new. In fact, in the early eighteenth century, Sir Isaac Newton—a brilliant fellow Englishman and a most remarkable chap—wrote about them. He and I had many invigorating discussions on that subject before he went off his trolley from all that mercury poisoning, poor old sod."

Turquoise drank some more brandy, and mulled over the Professor's words. "So, basically, what you're saying is there's a different me, a different you, and a different everyone else all existing at the same time in these similar, yet different, worlds?"

The Professor nodded his head. "I do say, my dear, you catch on rather quickly!"

"A parallel world!" Turquoise cried with excitement as if a light bulb had switched on in her brain. "That would explain why everything and everybody's been so different! It's all starting to make sense to me! This is a parallel world where Dolores Angry Cloud isn't Dolores Angry Cloud, and you aren't Billy Balls. It's why the truck stop was deserted and why everything in Chupacabra…" Her excitement came to an abrupt halt. "But wait a minute, Professor. If this *is* a parallel world, then how did I get here, and where is the other Turquoise Moonwolf—my mirror image?""

"When that comet passed over the earth yesterday," the Professor explained, "it generated a phenomenon known as a wormhole—a kind of tunnel that connects two points in space-time, thus allowing one to travel in time, to different locations throughout the universes, and even to parallel worlds. Or, to put it more simply, a wormhole is a transcendental bijection of the asymptotic projection of the Calabi-Yau manifold manifesting itself in a maximally symmetric Lorentzian manifold with negative scalar curvature.

The Professor packed some more tobacco into his pipe, and paused before lighting it.

"According to the Thunderbox's anomaly-detecting instruments, the wormhole remained open for less than a millisecond. But that's all it takes for one to suck you into its vacuum and spit you out in a parallel world, like the one you're in now. As for your parallel world counterpart, naturally, she would have switched places with you. At the exact moment in time when you were propelled into her world, she was propelled into yours. It would be impossible for the two of you to co-exist within the same dimension of space and time without throwing the space-time continuum out of balance. Why, such a thing, if it were possible, would unravel the very fibers of the universe!"

The Professor sucked deeply on the stem of his pipe and then gazed deeply into Turquoise's eyes.

"So, tell me, Turquoise—what is my parallel world counterpart like?"

"Oh, that one-eyed, booze-reeking varmint, Billy Balls, is nothing at all like you, Professor," Turquoise replied. "You're a gentleman, very handsome, and a respected scholar. And he's…well, let's just say his IQ test came back negative."

"You mean to tell me that my mirror image is an indescribably benighted mental midget and a conglomerate of intellectual constipation?"

Turquoise suddenly felt a tingle in her loins that yearned to be fulfilled. "Oh, Professor, you really do have a way with words."

The Professor looked pleased. "Would you care to hear more?" he asked.

Turquoise wet her lips with her tongue in anticipation. "Ooh, yes please!"

After clearing his throat, the Professor continued, "This Billy Balls misdemeanant sounds to me like a lamentably ignominious Neanderthal and a classic example of the inverse ratio between the size of his sub-literary brain and his cretinous mouth. How was that?"

With her face flushed with arousal, Turquoise replied, "That was great! Your command of the English language is very… stimulating."

The Professor tipped his fedora and smiled. "Why, thank you. I'm always happy to oblige a lovely young lady with an obvious penchant for onomatophilia."

"Yoko Ono what?"

"Onomatophilia," the Professor ingeminated. "The definition of the word means a naughty attraction to words. I assure you it's nothing to be ashamed of or embarrassed by. Your condition is a known paraphilia, and one that—to put it in scientific terms—winds up my willy. Care for a bit of rumpy pumpy?"

Unable to contain her desire to make love to the verbose man of science, Turquoise replied affirmatively.

The Professor pressed a mysterious button on the band of his wristwatch, and within seconds, a heart-shaped bed materialized in the center of the room. Covered in luxurious red velvet, it had the appearance of a super-sized box of Valentine chocolates. Giving Turquoise a wink, the stimulated scientist proceeded to perform a provocative striptease, removing all articles of his clothing, except for his fedora hat and floor-length, knitted scarf. He then jumped into bed.

Relieved to find the Professor's anatomy to be relatively normal—no slithering, external intromittent organs of Lovecraftian horror— Turquoise slipped out of her clothes and joined the Professor on the giant heart, eager to give herself over to the pleasure of his touch. She soon found herself entangled in the far-reaching threads of his unending scarf, and enjoying the titillation of it. Her naked flesh tingled like a thousand butterflies.

It was an unequivocal WTF moment for Turquoise when the Professor showed off his sexual prowess with the unexpected insertion of a vast quantity of Jelly Babies into her love canal. But she soon found herself in head-spinning heaven when he began performing Jelly Baby-lingus on her with his roving tongue. She shut her eyes and moaned with delight. *Whoever thought gelatin-based gummy candies could be so incredibly erotic?*

After the last of the Jelly Babies had been consumed with gusto, the Professor positioned himself between Turquoise's parted thighs, and with the vigor of a man half his age, began copulating—or as he euphemized it: "doing the horizontal greased weasel tango."

"Oh, Professor. Talk dirty to me," Turquoise moaned in a state of elated bliss, her eyeballs rolling around in their sockets. "The dirtier, the better!"

"Oh, you *are* a cheeky monkey," the Professor replied, an impish grin on his face. "Very well. Let's see." He gave the matter a few seconds of thought before shouting out, "galactic bulge!" and thrusting his manhood deep into Turquoise's palpitating poonanie. "Thermal coupling!" He thrust his penis into her again. "Quantum tunneling!"

"Oh yes!" Turquoise cried out. "That's it! More! More!"

Driving his member in and out like a jackhammer, the Professor deliriously shouted, "Double-slit experiment! Transversal time dilation! Vacuum polarization! Stimulated emission! Molecular disintegration!"

Poised at the edge of an orgasm, Turquoise's body trembled. "Oh, God! Oh, God! Don't stop now!"

The Professor tweaked Turquoise's oscillating nipples, and with the next plunge of his pecker, bellowed out, "Tribo-physical waveform macrokinetic extrapolator!"

Turquoise screamed with pleasure as climax after climax rocked her to near senselessness, and ripped her to exquisitely satisfied shreds. Beads of cold perspiration formed on her forehead. Her braids unraveled. Stars danced behind her eyelids.

The Professor pressed his lips against Turquoise's and groaned as he reached the pinnacle of his own orgasm in her depths. His body, slick with the dew of amour, rocked and rolled. His pelvis shuddered. His fedora quivered. Self-luminous, gaseous, celestial bodies of great mass, producing energy by means of nuclear fusion reactions, danced behind his eyelids.

Spent but blissful, he rolled onto his back and panted like a pooch. "Sweet Fanny Adams, that was jolly good. I'd even venture as far as to say it was the dog's bollocks! Mister Willy's never had a shagging like that before. You really put a smile on the old todger. Tell me, Turquoise, was it as ace for you as it was for me?"

It was then that his ears detected a snore rumbling out of Turquoise's mouth. He turned his head and discovered she was fast asleep.

"Well, bugger me gently!" he exclaimed under his breath. "I blinded her with science!"

* * *

Roused from her dreamy slumber by an accelerating roar, Turquoise opened her eyes of blue and found herself alone on the heart-shaped bed. The Professor was nowhere in sight.

"Professor?" Turquoise called out.

There came no reply.

Turquoise climbed out of bed and began putting her clothes on. And that was when she observed the strangest of sights: The room and everything within it seemed to be growing in size and then shrinking, growing and shrinking, again and again. She blinked her eyes as if to reset her vision.

I must be seeing things!

Moments later, the peculiar cycle of increase and decrease stopped, as did the roaring sound. Turquoise finished getting dressed and made her way back to the console room, where she found the Professor monitoring a large wall-mounted computer screen while tinkering with a set of dials on a control panel below it. Hearing her approaching footsteps, he turned his head in her direction and greeted her with a smile and a cup of hot tea.

"Good morning, Professor. What was that strange sound I heard a little while ago, and why did the room seem to be expanding and contracting?"

"Good morning, love. I assure you it's nothing to fret about. It's quite a normal thing, under the circumstances. I do say, Turquoise, you look positively radiant this morning! I don't know about you, but certain anatomical regions, near and dear to me, are still experiencing seismic waves from our little slap and tickle."

Turquoise wore a look of confusion. "Our little what?"

"You know what I mean—our little bouncy-bouncy, frickle-frackle," the Professor winked his good eye. "Humpy-squirty, boppin' squiddles."

"What on earth are you talking about?"

"Waka-waka, stuffin' the muffin," said the Professor, continuing to wink his eye. "A bit of bam bam in the ham. You know, squishin' the gibbly bits. Oh, don't be such a daft American. How about a two-ball in the middle pocket?"

Turquoise's eyes lit up as she realized what the Professor was referring to. "Oh, I get it now! You mean the sexual intercourse we had last night! Why didn't you just say so in the first place? I wish you Englishmen would speak English."

"Oh, you are a cheeky little monkey. I trust you slept well."

"To be honest with you, Professor, I don't think I've ever had such a good night's rest before. I must have really needed to catch up on some zees. I feel like I've slept for a hundred years!"

The Professor grinned. "That's because you did!"

"What?"

"You see, whilst making myself a cuppa this morning, the end of this interminable scarf of mine managed to get itself caught on the time transducer lever. I gave it a good tug to free it, and as a result, it plunged us one hundred years into the future. That's what produced the time propulsion roar and the expansion-contraction phenomenon you experienced. You see, the atoms in the molecular structure of the Thunderbox and everything within in, including you and I, were simply readjusting to the centenary precipitation into futurity and undergoing a fourth dimension synchronization. It's nothing more than a bit of a nuisance, really."

"I see," said Turquoise. "It's a good thing this contraption goes backward in time, as well as forward. All you have to do is put the lever in reverse, right?"

The Professor cleared his throat, removed his fedora, and scratched the top of his head. "I'm afraid, in the process of withdrawing my fashion accessory, I inadvertently did a mischief to the lever. To put it in more scientific terms: I really buggered it up. Broke that joystick right in two! From the looks of it, I'd say it was beyond repairable."

"Ricocheting coyote nuggets!" Turquoise cried, as panic swept through her body like a blizzard of chaos. "You mean we're stuck in the future? There's no way to get back to the twenty-first century?"

Patting Turquoise's arm, the Professor smiled reassuringly. "Now there, Turquoise, it's nothing to get your knickers all in a knot about. Really, it's not as alarming as suddenly hearing banjo music playing in the middle of your prostate exam. But seriously, the future's not so bad. In fact, as any time traveler in the know will tell you, the twenty-second century is when the *real* party starts!"

"Oh my God! What are we going to do?"

"Well," the Professor began, calmly, "For starters, I thought we'd sit down and have us a nice bubble and squeak with some good old fashioned bangers for good measure."

"Is performing sexual acts the only thing you scientific types ever think about? There are far more important things in this world than sex… like basket weaving, for instance! Oh, Professor, don't you understand? I've just got to get back to my own time and to the non-parallel world I belong in!"

"I don't suppose you'd consider staying on as co-pilot of the Thunderbox?" the Professor asked with a feeble smile intended to hide his sadness, but unsuccessful in its objective. "Traveling alone through the corridors of time and space in a souped-up port-a-potty does tend to invest a man with more than his quantum of loneliness."

Turquoise told the Professor that she was very flattered by his proposal; but, nonetheless, her only desire was to return home to Chupacabra. He nodded his head in understanding, and without a single word, he quickly retreated from the room, leaving Turquoise wondering what to make of his sudden departure. A minute later, he returned with a strange-looking device resembling an old-fashioned divers' helmet, but covered with dials and clock-like mechanisms. At the very top of it were a red button and a silver switch.

"What is that contraption?" Turquoise enquired, unsure if she should be curious or frightened by it.

"This is a computer-generated living matter diverter, which I designed and built myself," the Professor replied proudly. "It plugs into the main circuit board of the Thunderbox's computer system and is capable of teleporting any living thing, including you, to whatever physical location, time and/or dimension at which its dials are set... err, theoretically."

Turquoise's mounting optimism suddenly plummeted like a nose-diving pterodactyl. "Theoretically?"

"Well, yes. You see, the living matter diverter has been carefully modulated and calibrated, but it's never actually been tested on any living matter. You'd be the first multi-cellular human organism to undergo multi-dimensional diversion—a guinea pig, if you like. It should work. But, then again, it might not. Either way, try to think of it as your personal contribution to a major scientific achievement; advancement for all humanity; one small step for man and a giant leap for mankind, and all that bollocks. The choice is completely up to you, Turquoise. But as it looks right now, it's your only chance of being un-paralleled and returning home."

"What's the worst case scenario if the diverter doesn't work?"

"Oh, nothing too serious. If the hyper-configurator mechanism should malfunction, or if any of the ultrasonic tissue regenerators overheat and short circuit before intracellular transference is complete, your blood will simply caramelize and then every molecule in your body will explode into a frothy meringue."

After five seconds of profound deliberation, Turquoise responded, "I've thought it over very carefully, weighing all of the pros and cons, and I've made my decision. What the hell... Let's do it!"

"I must warn you, Turquoise. There's no turning back once the actuator is activated. Are you one-hundred percent sure you want to go ahead with this?"

"As sure as the sun rises in the west and sets in the east."

"Very well, then. We shall proceed." The Professor plucked his glass eye from out of its socket and handed it to Turquoise. "Before I send you on your way, I'd like for you to have this ocular prosthesis as a token of my affection, and as an everlasting memento of our carnal interaction."

Turquoise thanked the Professor for all of his help and for the glass eye, and told him she would have it strung on a necklace. "I'll wear it every day and treasure it for as long as I live."

After a long and impassioned kiss, the Professor gently placed the time and space helmet over Turquoise's head and plugged it into the Thunderbox's computer. He bade the braided girl farewell and wished her good luck, and then paused for a moment before depressing the red button and flicking the activation switch on. The device began to hum and whirr, and Turquoise slowly dematerialized before the Professor's eyes.

He popped a Jelly Baby into his mouth. "And Bob's your uncle!"

* * *

Turquoise felt the warm rays of the New Mexico sun dance upon her face as she rematerialized in front of the Squealing Squaw Trading Post, feeling as though she had just awakened from a dream. She pinched herself to ensure that she was, in fact, awake, and with her heart bubbling with joy upon the discovery that she was, she tilted her face up to the azure sky.

"It worked, Professor!" she exulted on the top of her lungs, much to the confusion of a solitary golden eagle soaring high above in the wind currents. "Your computer-generated living matter diverter was a success! Thank you so much!"

Without further ado, she threw open the door and raced inside the teepee-shaped building, goosebumps of excitement springing up on her forearms.

With the exception of its floor stained from the spilled blood of Mason Hawkins and Miss Yvonne, the interior of the shop looked no different than it did before the evil bowl-tergeist had reared its ugly head and chaos erupted like Mount Saint Helens.

Grandmother Loona was standing in her usual spot behind the checkout counter. She looked up from her yellowed, year-old copy of *The Chupacabra Daily Times*.

"Last year's newspaper say drum majorette's emotional support alligator was stolen by microcephalic contortionist claiming to be reincarnation of Allan 'Farina' Hoskins." She shook her head. "What's this world coming to?"

"I don't know," Turquoise replied. "But it sure is good to be back!"

The roar of a flushing toilet heralded Dolores Angry Cloud's emergence from the bathroom. A look of surprise swept across her face as she laid eyes on her cousin.

"Turquoise! Where the hell have you been? We've all been so worried about you! The sheriff has a search party out looking for you. Yesterday, his deputy picked up a girl that he thought was you. She was hitchhiking on the Red Herring Highway near the Mother Trucker all-night truck stop. The really weird thing about it… she was your spitting image, right down to the braids… a real wacko, though. She kept insisting she was from a parallel world! One too many magic mushrooms if you ask me. The last I heard, they took her away in a straightjacket to the State Mental Hospital in Las Vegas."

"Dolores!" cried Turquoise. "I'm not dreaming, am I? Is that really you?"

"What kind of crazy-ass question is that? Of course it's me. Are you okay? What the fuck did those Siamese twin imbeciles do to you? Those goddamn conjoined piss-ants! They didn't touch you down *there*, did they?"

Turquoise shook her head. "No, they didn't do anything like that. But you're not going to believe what happened to me after they kidnapped me and the van crashed. I hardly believe it myself. It's just so incredible! It all started when that comet…"

At that moment, William Cyrus Ballschmieder stumbled into the teepee in an obvious state of intoxication, blathering about his lost straight razor. He spotted Turquoise.

"I had me an X-rated dream about you last night! I was going down on you in one of them portable toilet things, and your coochie was dispensing Jelly Babies like gumballs from a gumball machine."

"You're a thoroughly repugnant pig!" Dolores Angry Cloud yelled in a tone of raging disgust. "Get your drunken, flea-bitten asshole out of this place of business before I give you a Doc Martens colonoscopy!"

"You just want me to ride you like a bull at the rodeo," Ballschmieder taunted. "Go on. Admit it, Dolores! You want me to ride you."

"I'd rather ride a cactus!" the punk rocker shot back.

"I owe you a big kiss, Billy Balls," Turquoise announced, to the unprecedented shock of her cousin and grandmother, whose jaws dropped. "Pucker up and I'll explain later."

Ballschmieder readied his chapped lips for Turquoise's promised kiss, teetered like an axed tree waiting for a cry of 'timber!' and promptly toppled face down onto the floor, sparking a wildfire of laughter from all three women in the teepee.

The front door of the trading post swung open, and to Turquoise's surprise, Grandfather Fukowee trotted in, no longer exhibiting any physical signs of the snapping turtle curse or possession by the evil spirit of Jimmie Yellow Snow.

"Grandfather Fukowee!" Turquoise exclaimed with delight.

"I am not Grandfather Fukowee," the old man replied in Russ Gonzalez's voice. My name is Tania, and I am a revolutionary of the Siamese Liberation Army. Death to the fascist hemorrhoid that festers in the rectum of democracy!"

As Grandmother Loona chased her re-possessed husband out of the teepee, swatting him with her trusty corn broom, Turquoise let out a sigh of contentment and smiled. She stepped over Ballschmieder's unconscious body, stood in the doorway, and watched in amusement as her grandfather scampered down the dusty highway and into the sunset, his irascible wife in close pursuit. Turquoise felt warm and fuzzy all over.

All was right in the world.

THE END

About the Author

Born and raised in the Chicago area, Gerri R. Gray is a novelist, short story writer, and a lifelong aficionado of horror, dark humor, and all things bizarre. She blames her twisted sense of humor on a wayward adolescence influenced by the likes of Monty Python's Flying Circus, Charles Addams, Frank Zappa, and John Waters.

Her debut novel, *The Amnesia Girl* (HellBound Books) was published in October of 2017, followed by *Gray Skies of Dismal Dreams* (a collection of dark poetry and prose), and *The Graveyard Girls* (an all-women anthology of horror.)

Gerri's work has appeared in numerous anthologies and literary journals, including: *Beautiful Tragedies*; *Demons, Devils & Denizens of Hell: Volume Two*; *EconoClash Review: Quality Cheap Thrills: Volume One*; *Deadman's Tome Cthulhu Christmas Special and Other Lovecraftian Yuletide Tales*; *Trump Fiction*; *Jitter;* and *Mixed Bag of Horror*.

She lives in Upstate New York in an historic nineteenth-century house with her husband, a bevy of spirits, and a Siamese cat named Aristede. When she isn't busy creating strange worlds filled with even stranger characters, she can often be found traipsing through old cemeteries with her camera.

For more information, please visit:
The Official Gerri R. Gray website:
http://gerrigray.webs.com/
Follow Gerri on Twitter at:

https://twitter.com/GerriRGray
Facebook:
https://www.facebook.com/AuthorGerriGray/
Amazon author page:
https://www.amazon.com/Gerri-R-Gray/e/B076GTZ8XK
Goodreads:
https://www.goodreads.com/author/show/17311761.Gerri_R_Gray
HellBound Books:
http://hellboundbookspublishing.com/authorpage_gray.html

Other titles from HellBound Books for your delectation...

The Amnesia Girl

Filled with copious amounts of black humor, Gerri R. Gray's first published novel is an offbeat adventure story that could be described as One Flew over the Cuckoo's Nest meets Thelma and Louise.

Flashback to 1974. Farika is a lovely young woman who wakes up one day to find herself a patient in a bizarre New York City psychiatric asylum. She has no idea who she is, and possesses no memories of where she came from nor how she got there.

Fearing for her life after being attacked by a berserk girl with over one hundred personalities and a vicious nurse with sadistic intentions, the frightened amnesiac teams up with an audacious lesbian with a comically unbalanced mind, and together they attempt a daring escape.

But little do they know that a long strange journey into an even more insane world filled with a multitude of perilous predicaments and off-kilter individuals are waiting for them on the outside. Farika's weird reality crumbles when she finally discovers who, and what, she really is!

Gray Skies of Dismal Dreams

Prepare for an excursion into a gloomy world of shadows, where the days are never sunlit and blithe, and where the nights are wrapped in endless nightmares.

No happy endings or silver linings are found in the clouds that fill these gray skies.

But what you will find, gathered in one volume, are the darkest of poems and tales of horror, waiting to take your mind on a journey into realms of the uncheerful and the unholy.

An amazingly surreal collection of short stories and the darkest of poetry, all interspersed with stunning graveyard photographs taken by the multitalented author herself - an absolute must for every bookshelf!

Blood and Blasphemy

If you enjoy your horror dipped in buckets of blood and sprinkled with generous amounts of blasphemy, then you've come to the right place!

Blood and Blasphemy is a collection of over thirty of the most sacrilegious horror stories ever written.

Within these irreverent pages, you will encounter a priest that keeps his deformed spawn chained in a root cellar, a convent where a poisonous species of salamander is worshiped, a demonic altar boy, possessed religious relics that kill, blood-drinking clergymen, a Son of God who feeds on sin, an unsuspecting couple who run afoul of religious lunatics in a small town, the divine (and deadly) turd of Christ, and other terrifying tales guaranteed to make church ladies faint and nuns clutch their rosaries.

Featuring stories by: Aron Beauregard, George Alan Bradley, Cardigan Broadmoor, Scot M. Carpenter, Myna Chang, Clay McLeod Chapman, Nick Dinicola, Jude M. Eriksen, Michael Martin Garrett, Gerri R. Gray, Christopher Hamel, Carlton Herzog, B.T. Joy, A.L. King, Daryl Marcus, Jeremy Megargee, Donna J.W. Munro, Hari Navarro, Trevor Newton, Drew Nicks, C.C. Parker, Wolfgang Potterhouse, J.L. Shioshita, J.J. Smith, Henry Snider, J.B. Toner, Sheldon Woodbury, Ken Goldman, and Shawn Wood.

Graveyard Girls

A delicious collection of horrific tales and darkest poetry from the cream of the crop, all lovingly compiled by the incomparable Gerri R Gray! Nestling between the covers of this formidable tome are twenty-five of the very best lady authors writing on the horror scene today!

These tales of terror are guaranteed to chill your very soul and awaken you in the dead of the night with fear-sweat clinging to your every pore and your heart pounding hard and heavy in your labored breast…

Featuring superlative horror from: Xtina Marie, M. W. Brown, Rebecca Kolodziej, Anya Lee, Barbara Jacobson, Gerri R. Gray, Christina Bergling, Julia Benally, Olga Werby, Kelly Glover, Lee Franklin, Linda M. Crate, Vanessa Hawkins, P. Alanna Roethle, J Snow, Evelyn Eve, Serena Daniels, S. E. Davis, Sam Hill, J. C. Raye, Donna J. W. Munro, R. J. Murray, C. Bailey-Bacchus, Varonica Chaney, Marian Finch (Lady Marian).

**A HellBound Books LLC
Publication**

www.hellboundbookspublishing.com

Printed in the United States of America